FOR DUTY, LOVE & HONOUR

RESIDENTS OF ASHWICK HALL BOOK 3

A REGENCY ROMANCE

JENNY HAMBLY

Copyright © 2025 by Jennifer Hambly
All rights reserved.
No part of this book may be reproduced in any form or by any electronic or mechanical means, including information storage and retrieval systems, without written permission from the author, except for the use of brief quotations in a book review.

The moral right of Jenny Hambly has been asserted.

www.jennyhambly.com

This book is a work of fiction. Names, characters, places and events, other than those clearly in the public domain, are either the product of the author's imagination, or are used fictitiously. Any resemblance to actual people, living or dead, are purely coincidental.

CHAPTER 1

October 1818, Ashwick Hall

Anne regarded her three companions, wondering if they were as content as they appeared. Thanks to Lady Westcliffe they lived a life of comfort, but they also lived a life of seclusion. They had each other for company, of course, and the orphanage provided them with the opportunity to be as much or little occupied as they wished, but it was not the same as being mistress of one's own household, one's own destiny. Her lips tightened. A woman was never truly in charge of her destiny, of course, but she had tried to be within the limits allowed her, and it had led her here, to Ashwick Hall. Her choices had proved themselves to be woefully flawed, and now she had very few available to her.

Her eyes went to Flora whose sharp eyes and managing disposition belied her advanced years. Although none of the genteel residents at Ashwick Hall were officially placed above another, they all deferred to Flora. It was not only the respect due to someone of her age that induced this observance, but the confidence of one sure of her place in the world. It permeated her very being, and Anne felt sure that of them all, it was Flora who had fallen the farthest.

It was possible, Anne supposed, that the respect and company of the other ladies as well as the trust Lady Westcliffe placed in her to oversee the running of the household satisfied her. Her gaze moved on to the new arrival at the hall, a petite young woman of four and twenty who sat beside Flora, busily unravelling a large knot of yarn.

"How did it get in such a tangle?" she said softly. "I am determined that every poor orphan will have a pair of mittens before winter sets in."

"An admirable objective," Flora said dryly. "You might have more chance of succeeding if you remembered to wind the wool carefully before you put it away."

Beth smiled ruefully, Flora's sharp tone not discomposing her at all. "Very true. You have told me several times, yet I somehow forget."

"That is because you spend half of your time woolgathering."

This unintentional but apposite choice of words drew a laugh from the ladies; even Flora's lips twitched.

"I was not being literal as well you know."

"I do know," Beth said. "And I will admit it to be true. It has always been a weakness of mine."

"In our present circumstance, I think it is rather a strength," Anne said gently. "It allows your mind to wander where your feet cannot."

Anne turned her head as the other occupant of

the room sighed. Sukey was a few years older than Anne at two and thirty. She was a quiet, self-contained woman who had never, to Anne's knowledge, bemoaned her circumstances. She smiled ruefully at Anne's surprised regard, pushed her needle into the fire screen she was embroidering, and tucked a strand of dark blonde hair behind her ear. It seemed she, at least, was not quite content with her lot.

"I do not mind the restrictions placed upon us," Beth said quietly. "I have the freedom to think, to be myself, and to do some good." She smiled warmly at Flora. "And I have received more goodwill and advice here than anywhere else."

"Not that you take any notice of it," Flora said brusquely.

Beth chuckled. "If I did so immediately, you would not have the pleasure of telling me again."

Flora's lips twitched once more. "Impertinent chit."

Anne smiled. Although she was a little older, in some ways Beth reminded Anne of Lucy, a young lady who had recently left the hall. Beth was not quite as pretty, shy, or melancholy, but she possessed a similar sweet innocence, although she was beginning to display a burgeoning mischievousness that Anne thought charming. Whatever her circumstances, she was pleased they had not extinguished her spirit. She glanced at the elegant clock on the mantlepiece.

"It is three o'clock. Shall I ring for tea?"

"You should not have to ring for it," Flora grumbled. "We enjoy a cup every day at this hour."

The door to the parlour opened and a tall, elegant lady with raven hair came into the room, a letter clasped in one hand. Excepting Flora, the ladies stood and curtsied to their benefactress. She waved them back down.

"Good afternoon, ladies. I have good news. Lucy is soon to become the wife of Mr Frederick Ashton and is very happily situated in Yorkshire. She sends you her love and best wishes."

"That was quick work," Flora said, her brow puckering. "I do not recall a Mr Ashton. Will he do?"

Lady Westcliffe smiled. "He is a little unusual, but a very pleasant gentleman." She moved into the room and handed the letter to Flora. "Her godmother is satisfied with the match. She added her own letter to Lucy's. It is for you."

Flora opened the missive. "If Honora approves then perhaps all will be well."

Anne's eyes went to the missive. Receiving and sending letters through Lady Westcliffe was a privilege currently only allotted to Flora, and she felt a twinge of envy that was quite nonsensical considering there was no one she wished to correspond with or hear from.

A short laugh escaped Flora, and she sent Beth a sideways glance.

"It seems my advice was not completely lost on Lucy, at least." Her gaze moved to Anne. "Nor yours, my dear. It seems her performance at the pianoforte quite literally brought Mr Ashton to his knees and wrung a proposal of marriage from him."

Although Anne smiled, she also felt that this proposed union was rather sudden. As Lucy had been gone little more than a month, she had had little enough time to really get to know the gentleman, nor to discover his faults. *Stop it. You trust Lady Westcliffe's judgement. If she says Mr Ashton is a very pleasant gentleman, then so he is. And Lucy's combination of innocence, beauty, and talent must invite admiration.*

"He is, it seems, a man of some discernment then."

Flora raised a thin eyebrow, her contrary nature coming to the fore. "Or a sentimental fool."

"I seem to remember that Lucy's playing brought tears even to your eyes, Flora," Anne said. "And yet you are neither sentimental nor a fool."

"Very true, Anne," Lady Westcliffe said, glancing at the fire screen Sukey had been working on. "Your needlework is exquisite, my dear. Embroidering the flowers on a blue background was an excellent idea; they appear so vibrant and colourful." Her eyes moved on to the tangle of wool Beth had not yet finished unravelling. "How is your project coming along, Beth?"

The young woman reached into her basket and withdrew a pair of mittens. "I have completed a dozen pairs thus far."

If Lady Westcliffe noticed that one was larger than the other, she did not comment upon it, merely offering her an approving smile. "I am sure the children will be very pleased with them."

Anne suspected that the gentle encouragement they were given to participate in the life of the orphanage was as much for their benefit as the children's. It was a reminder that there were always those worse off than themselves, and busy hands and minds prevented them from thinking of their circumstances overmuch.

Lady Westcliffe took a seat as a maid entered with the tea tray and a plate of honey cakes. The girl walked slowly to a nearby table, her tongue protruding slightly from one side of her mouth. She set it down a little too firmly, causing the cups to rattle in their saucers. She glanced anxiously at Lady Westcliffe, but she only smiled.

"Thank you, Mary, and thank cook for me; honey cakes are a particular favourite of mine."

The girl offered a graceless curtsy and hurried from the room.

Lady Westcliffe prepared the tea herself as she always did when she joined them in the ladies' parlour.

"Are your knees still paining you, Flora?" she asked as she passed her a cup.

"A little," she admitted. "But as you know, I am not one to complain."

Anne turned her head to hide her smile at this patent untruth.

"I am sorry to hear it," Lady Westcliffe said. "Perhaps it is time I made one of the rooms on this floor a bedchamber for you."

Flora's thin eyebrows rose. "You will do no such thing. I would miss my view of the park."

Lady Westcliffe seemed unperturbed by her sharp tone. "As you wish." She took one of the small cakes and then offered Anne the plate. "I hear you have succeeded in teaching Susan her letters. Well done. Many before you have tried and failed."

Anne felt her heart warm as she thought of the defensive girl who had thought herself too stupid to learn anything. The amazed and delighted smile that had lit up her face when she had succeeded in writing her name had more than compensated for the months it had taken to gain her trust. "It took only patience and an understanding of the barriers that hindered her learning."

"It is like you to make light…"

Lady Westcliffe's hand went to her mouth, her already fair skin turning as white as the porcelain cup she held.

"Lady Westcliffe?" Anne said in some concern. "Is something amiss?"

She dropped her hand and drew in a deep breath. "It is nothing. I suddenly felt a little nauseous. Perhaps the honey cake did not agree with me."

"Nonsense," Flora said brusquely. "As you have already indicated, they are your favourite. You have been trotting too hard. You have had a house full of guests for the last sennight and what must you do but come to us the moment they leave. You should take better care of yourself."

Lady Westcliffe smiled wryly. "Perhaps you are right, Flora. I shall return to Westcliffe Park and rest. Would you offer my apologies to Mrs Primly? I have not yet had the opportunity to meet with her."

"I will, of course. I had intended to speak with her presently as there are several matters that need bringing to her attention."

"Thank you," Lady Westcliffe murmured, rising to her feet. "I beg you to remember, however, that many of the servants currently under her purview are new to learning their trade."

"That is patently clear," Flora said dryly. "You

may be sure, however, that Mrs Primly and I understand each other perfectly."

Again, Anne hid a smile. What Flora meant, of course, was that she would offer several suggestions to the housekeeper which she would irritably adopt, and then in a few weeks' time Flora would change her mind, and Mrs Primly would go back to her usual way of doing things. Judging by Lady Westcliffe's wry smile she understood this perfectly.

"Good day, ladies. I shall call tomorrow when I am a little more rested."

She did not return the following afternoon, however. After waiting for half an hour, Flora rang for tea. Anne glanced up as the maid entered the room. Mary appeared more confident; her tongue was nowhere to be seen. Once she had placed the tray gently on the table, she bobbed a curtsy and came to Anne, holding out a letter.

"This came for you, miss."

Anne stared at the maid's outstretched hand, her breath hitching in her throat.

"Stop regarding it as if it is a snake about to strike," Flora said dryly.

That was precisely what Anne feared. She took the missive gingerly.

Sukey sighed. "You have been granted the privilege of receiving letters. How envious I am."

Anne stared blankly at her friend for a moment and then shook her head. "But I have been granted no such privilege."

"Where have your wits gone begging?" Flora's tone was brusque but not unkind. "If Lady Westcliffe has forbidden you to receive correspondence, then it must be she herself who writes."

The faint buzzing in Anne's head receded as the logic of these words sank in. Turning the paper over, she glanced at the name scribed in a neat hand. Dizzying relief swept over her, and she closed her eyes, a soft chuckle escaping her.

"Of course, how foolish of me not to realise it immediately."

"Our fears often make us foolish," Sukey said gently.

Anne acknowledged her words with a small smile before breaking the seal and opening the letter.

Dear Anne,

As I am unable just at present to leave Westcliffe Park, I invite you to come to me. I have been waiting for just the right moment to discuss your future, and I believe that moment has arrived.

Do not be alarmed, if you do not like my proposal you are under no obligation to accept it and are welcome to remain at Ashfield Hall for as long as you wish. I do suggest, however, that you pack all your things, for if my proposal appeals to you, there will be no time for you to return.

My carriage awaits your convenience.

Lady W

"Anne?" Sukey said gently. "You look a little stunned. I hope it is not bad news."

Anne put a hand to her forehead, trying to gather her thoughts. "No, at least, I do not think so. I am invited to Westcliffe Park and there is a possibility I may not return."

"I shall miss you, of course," Sukey said, a little

wistfully. "But I am happy that Lady Westcliffe has found a way to help you."

"I cannot imagine how," Anne said.

"You will find out soon enough," Flora said. "And I hope you will follow the advice you are given. Lady Westcliffe rarely puts a foot wrong where her ladies are concerned. Now, you had best go and pack."

"Good luck," Beth said, her brow furrowing as she picked up a dropped stitch.

There seemed no more to say. Anne went swiftly to her room and packed her trunk. She had barely finished when Jack, a footman in training, appeared at her door.

"Ah, you have come for my trunk."

"Yes, ma'am. The carriage is waiting."

Anne did not like to be rushed. She would not go without saying goodbye to Susan. "You may inform the coachman that I will be down in a moment."

The orphaned girls had practical lessons in the afternoon. She found Susan hunched over a large piece of white linen, her face pinched with concentration as she attempted to sew the seam of a shift. Anne exchanged a smile with Miss Long, the first school mistress, and approached Susan. The girl did not look up until Anne complimented her on the neatness of her work.

The girl grinned. "Thank you, miss. It's like with me letters; I can suddenly see how things go together."

Anne sat down. "I am pleased to hear it, Susan. It was not a lack of ability that held you back, but fear and a lack of faith in yourself."

Susan nodded. "I'd been told so often that I was

useless before I came here, and the others seemed so much better than me at everything that I believed it."

"Well, now you know it is not true."

"Thanks to you, miss. Somehow you made me see things differently. I can't ever thank you enough."

Anne smiled. "I was able to afford you a little more time than Miss Long, who has many children under her care, that is all. You may thank me by continuing with your progress whether I am here or not."

The girl's expression darkened. "What do you mean, miss?"

"Lady Westcliffe may have found me a position. If I deem it suitable, I must leave straight away. I hope you will be pleased for me, for it is what I have been hoping for."

Susan's lips trembled. "Why can't you stay here and help Miss Long?"

"My stay here was always going to be temporary; I believe I told you that at the start of our lessons. Although I have enjoyed teaching you, it is not quite what I am used to. I believe Lady Westcliffe supposes I would enjoy a position which might challenge me a little more."

Susan regarded her steadily. "I'm sure I've been challenge enough. You mean you should be teaching those as are better than us."

Anne laid a hand gently on the child's arm. "We all have our differing places in the world, Susan, but we are all equal in the eyes of God. I shall not forget you. If things work out well for me, I shall ask Lady Westcliffe to forward the letter I hope very much you will write to me when you are able."

Susan brushed her hand across her eyes. "It might

be a while before I can do that, but I'll keep trying until I manage it."

Anne rose to her feet, relieved that Susan had taken her news so well. "I shall look forward to it. Goodbye, my dear."

Susan mumbled a response, dipped her head, and picked up her needle.

Anne found Sukey waiting for her in the entrance hall.

"I am so glad I have not missed you," she said. "I wished to give you a parting gift."

She held out a reticule decorated with exquisite embroidery. Silken silver and gold thread wound over the dark blue velvet creating an intricate pattern of stems and leaves interrupted at intervals by vibrant flowers depicted in two shades of pink.

"It is beautiful," Anne breathed, "and it is very kind of you to offer me it, but I cannot imagine that I will have the opportunity to use such a splendid gift."

"You need not use it," Sukey said. "Beautiful things should be admired for their own merit, not because they impress others. Take it out now and then and think of me."

Anne took Sukey's hands in hers. "Thank you, I will." She hesitated a moment, for they were not supposed to enquire too closely into each other's circumstances. "I sensed earlier that you are beginning to find your stay a little wearing, but be patient, Sukey. When the time is right, Lady Westcliffe will find a way forwards for you."

"Yes, I know it," she said, smiling wryly. "And I am really very grateful for this opportunity to regroup somewhere that I feel neither judged nor need fear… fear being homeless and friendless."

Anne embraced her. "I understand completely." Stepping back, she added, "Would you grant me a favour, Sukey?"

The woman smiled. "Of course."

"Would you mind keeping an eye on Susan? She has been making such good progress and I fear that my leaving might impede it somewhat."

"I shall certainly try to encourage her in her endeavours," she said, "but I fear I do not possess your skill of drawing the children out."

"Nonsense," Anne said. "Pheobe hardly leaves your side whenever you are with the children."

A soft smile lit Sukey's face. "Pheobe is a special case." She sighed. "You possess a serenity I can only envy."

Anne laughed softly. "I could say the same of you, my dear. You hide your feelings very well."

Her friend shook her head. "I have learned to cloak them, but I am not like you, Anne. I cannot imagine you becoming ruffled in any situation."

"That has been said of me before," Anne admitted. "I lack sensibility and am a most unnatural female."

"I do not believe either of those things to be true," Sukey said softly, leaning forward and kissing Anne's cheek. "Good luck."

CHAPTER 2

Edward sighed, pushing away his reluctance and mounting the stairs to the nursery wing. He had not seen the children for several days; it was too hard. He had not expected it to be, and he was amazed by his own cowardice. He was a man who had fought for his country, his position in the world, and his very existence. He had been driven by the belief that a man should forge his own destiny and should be judged on his ability alone. A belief his father had instilled in him.

The Royal Navy had given him that opportunity and he had taken it, fighting illness, enemies, and privilege along the way. He had been one of the few commoners who had risen from ship's boy to midshipman. It had seemed he was destined to go no higher, for although he had passed the lieutenant's examination with ease, there had always been someone with friends in higher places when positions became available. He had been fortunate enough to be present at Trafalgar, however, and after acquitting himself well, had achieved the desired promotion. Again, he had watched others rise through the ranks before him, year after year, but he had eventually risen to the rank of commander. It had all been achieved by toil, aptitude, and grim determination.

He paused outside the nursery door, a wry smile touching his lips. And yet he found himself reluctant to face two small children. Gathering his resolve, he pushed open the door. A scene of chaos greeted him. Toys were strewn across the floor, many of them broken. The children sat in the midst of the mess. They regarded him steadily, defiance and fear strangely intermingled in their eyes. His heart twisted; he had seen that same expression in their father's eyes moments before he died.

"It appears you did not like the toys I acquired for you," he said quietly.

Emily, the eldest sister, scowled. "We don't want no toys; we want our ma."

"That, alas, is a wish that is outside of my power to grant."

A young woman with tight lips and despairing eyes sat looking defeated in the corner. She stood, her hands tightly clasped and resignation etched on her face.

"I'll pack my things, shall I, sir?"

His heart sank. The governesses had come and gone, but Nora had stood firm. Until now. She had been the one constant in the orphans' lives since he had brought them here, and he felt sure that their behaviour was aimed at him not her.

"I shall be sorry to see you go, Nora. You have proved yourself to be both patient and resilient, but I quite understand that you have been pushed to your limits."

The nursery maid suddenly burst into tears. "I've tried my best, sir, I really have. I don't want to go, but I can do nothing with them. I don't know what will become of me. I shall probably end up back in the workhouse as I can hardly expect a reference."

His gaze returned to the girls to see how these words affected them. He had found them in a workhouse in Manchester, separated from their mother who had been lying on her death bed in the women's wing. He had liberated Nora from the same workhouse when he had been assured she had some experience of caring for children.

The girls glanced at each other, a look of uncertainty creeping into their eyes.

"It appears Nora would prefer the workhouse than the task of supervising you both. Does that please you?"

Barbara, the youngest of the sisters, shook her head. "I don't want Nora to go to the workhouse. It's a bad place."

Her elder sister, Emily, frowned. "But we don't want her acting like our ma, neither."

Edward began to see a way forward. "I doubt very much that Nora has any desire to replace your mother." He paused, sighing. "And who could blame her?"

The girls glanced a little guiltily at the maid who offered them a wan smile.

Edward sat on an upturned box. "I cannot remember my mother; she died when I was barely breeched, but I remember my father and how much I missed him when he died. I was your age, Emily, and so I understand your feelings. No one could replace him in my affections."

The girl's eyes widened a fraction, but then they narrowed, a hard look in their brown depths.

"We lost our father too, and it was your fault!"

His chest tightened and he stood abruptly. "Your father would not agree. I held him in my arms as he died, and with his last breath he begged me to look after you and your mother. I was too late to do anything for Mrs Proctor, but I gave my word and I'll be damned if I break it."

A little respect crept into Emily's eyes at his use of a curse word.

"That does not mean, however," he continued, "that I will allow either the wanton destruction of property or my servants being treated in such a way. You have a choice; either apologise to Nora and mend what you have broken, or I will find you another maid and you will have no toys."

Emily looked mutinous, but Barbara crawled over to Nora and leant her head against the maid's knee. "Sorry, Nora. Stay, please."

The maid stroked her hair, her gaze resting on Emily. The child lowered her head, mumbling something that might have been an apology.

Edward did not push her further. He was tempted to leave things there, but he had learned that the girls did not like surprises.

"I am holding interviews for the new governess in a few days."

Emily dropped the headless doll she had been clutching. "We don't want no governess. They all think we're stupid and they look down their long noses at us."

Barbara whimpered. "I don't like standing in the corner facing the wall until my legs hurt, or having my hands struck for fidgeting."

Edward briefly closed his eyes, guilt worming through him. All three governesses he had hired had presented very well at interview, but the first two had lasted no more than a few weeks, complaining that the girls were undisciplined, wild, and unruly. They had insisted that they were both unwilling and unable to learn anything of use and claimed that their competence and reputations would be called into question if it should be discovered that they had tried and failed to instil even a modicum of propriety or knowledge in the sisters. The third had been made of sterner stuff and had been determined to succeed by any method she thought necessary. He had been shocked to discover Barbara cowering in a corner and Emily sitting stony-eyed at the table with a gag about her mouth.

"I will admit that you have some cause to dislike the notion of a governess," he said gently, "but you must be educated."

"We can sew a little, and set a fire and wash pots," Emily said mutinously.

"All very practical accomplishments," he acknowledged. "But we have maids to set fires and wash pots, and if you wish never to face the prospect of the workhouse again, you must become educated so that you might find husbands who can keep you in comfort when you are of an age to wed."

"We could just stay here," Emily argued. "You have plenty of brass."

"And you will always be welcome here, but I would like to marry one day," he said, "and have children of my own. How do you think they will regard you if you cannot read, write, or conduct yourself in a ladylike manner?"

"They'll hate us like the governesses," Barbara said on a sob.

"They certainly would not respect you. I shall endeavour to find you a governess who will neither look down her nose nor physically punish you. Indeed, I shall make it clear that I will not tolerate such behaviour, and I shall insist that Nora be present while you take your lessons. She will report to me each day as to both your and the governess's behaviour."

Barbara looked up at Nora, offering her a tentative smile. "That would be—"

"It won't make no difference," Emily said flatly. "They might not show it, but they will still despise us."

An idea popped into Edward's head. He was tempted to dismiss it out of hand, but the faintest wobble of Emily's chin affected him far more than her belligerence.

"What if I permitted you to help me choose your next governess?"

Both girls regarded him, surprise in Barbara's eyes and mistrust in Emily's. She crossed her arms.

"You won't listen to us."

He flinched inwardly. Apart from feeding and clothing them, he had given the girls little reason to trust him. Their father had died whilst under his command, he had been too late to save their mother, and he had removed them from everything that they knew and understood. He had expended little effort getting to know them. What did he know of young girls, after all? He had, however, overseen boys only a little older than Emily, and he had learned that a strict but fair hand was the best approach. Perhaps it would work with the girls if he proved himself honest and consistent in his approach.

"I may not agree with you, but I give you my word that I will listen to and consider what you have to say."

Emily lifted her chin, displaying a sceptical expression that had no place on such a young child's face. Her next words revealed the sharpness of her mind and trampled into dust the governess's suggestion that she was stupid.

"What use is your promise? You will pretend to listen to us and do what you want anyway."

Frustration began to rise within him. He was not used to being challenged by his subordinates. *They are not your subordinates but your wards, you fool.* He drew in a slow breath.

"I would ask you to remember that the only reason you are no longer in the workhouse is that I am a man of my word. Do you accept that?"

Emily's chin lowered a fraction, and she gave a brief nod.

"And are you, Emily, a girl of your word? Can you keep your promises?"

Another brief nod.

"Then I shall make you another. I will not choose a lady you have taken in dislike; it would be better that we agreed on the most suitable candidate. You, however, must give all the applicants a fair chance and refrain from goading them. Can you do that?"

"I'll try," she muttered.

He glanced at Barbara.

"Yes," she murmured.

"Very well. You may accompany me." He cast a look around the room. "In the meantime, you have work to do. I expect the new governess to find everything in order when she arrives."

He retreated to the library, a handsome room with well-stocked shelves. He had never had the luxury of reading for pleasure, nor the inclination if truth be told. Anything that was not pertinent to his craft had been discarded as frivolous. His lips twitched into a bitter little smile. And yet here he was, aping the life of an indolent class he had reason to despise. He sighed, his eyes roaming over the several paintings depicting ships that adorned the walls. Would he ever become accustomed to this landlocked life? Even now his legs were braced against the wooden floor as if he expected it to suddenly tilt and sway.

Passing over the volumes of poetry, Greek philosophy, and histories, his fingers twitched as they passed a book on astronomy, a subject he knew something about. Reluctantly, he reached for a weighty tome that claimed to be the complete guide to farming. Grimacing, he sank into a chair and opened it. He must learn something about the acres he now owned.

Admiral Richard Tewk, his mentor and benefactor, had died some three years earlier. No one had been more surprised than Edward when he had discovered he had left him the estate. The letter informing him of the inheritance had taken some six months to reach him, however, and by then he had been fully invested in his mission to enforce the prohibition of the trade in slaves along the West African coast. He had requested that a minimal staff be maintained and then given the estate little more thought. Only when his hand had been forced had Edward returned to England and taken up residence at Hayshott Hall.

Although the house had been kept in reasonable order, as his health had declined, the admiral had become a poor landlord, neglecting his land and the needs of his tenants who had one by one abandoned the farms belonging to the estate when rents had remained high but crop prices had fallen. It was time he found new ones. The problem was, he had no idea where to begin.

He was not sorry when an hour later, he was disturbed by his housekeeper. His head was full of wheat, barley, turnips and clover, the problems of a variety of soils, the differing merits of the use of chalk, lime, or seaweed to dress them, and the importance of adequate drainage. Although he could grasp the concepts, he had no practical framework in which to place them. He did not know what type of soil prevailed in this part of the country, which crops prospered here, or the value to be had from them.

Mrs Thirsk bobbed a curtsy and handed him a card. "You have a visitor, Captain Turner."

He frowned. In the three months he had been in residence, there had been very few visitors to Hayshott Hall. The vicar and his wife had called, and Sir Godfrey Webster of Battle Abbey, who had been as self-interested as the majority of his class and had only wished to assure himself of his new neighbour's vote in the upcoming elections. He had not gained it, for however much he claimed to be a proponent of electoral reform, Edward had discovered that his family's fortunes were closely connected to the slave trade. His lip curled at the thought.

Mrs Thirsk cleared her throat, reminding him of the card in his hand. He glanced at it. *Mr Thomas Townsend, Lavington House, Sussex*. He had heard of Mr Townsend, who was his closest neighbour. The vicar had informed him that he was an amateur antiquarian and preferred battered old coins and indecent statuary to his fellow man.

"He wanders about the country in search of new finds and when he is here, rarely remembers to attend church."

Edward could hardly blame him. Mr Adams' sermons were far from inspiring and his manner severe. He was a fire and brimstone preacher who tried to rule his congregation by fear, assuring them that their current hardships were nothing compared to what would follow if they did not repent their wickedness. He seemed largely preoccupied with wickedness. It coloured his judgement. Rather than applauding Edward for taking in two orphans, he had decided to put the basest interpretation upon his actions, clearly believing that Emily and Barbara were his by-blows. When Mr Adams' daughters had tried to approach them after church, his wife had shooed them away from the girls as if they were plague ridden.

For their sake, he should try and dispel such unsavoury rumours. He had thought to have a word with Sir Anthony Fairbrass, whose family had granted the parson the living, but he had not yet had the pleasure of making his acquaintance.

Judging by the parson's remarks on his neighbour, it seemed unlikely that Mr Thomas Townsend would be able to aid him in the matter, but it could not hurt to make his acquaintance.

"Show him in, Mrs Thirsk."

Mr Townsend was not quite what he had expected. He had no acquaintances who were antiquarians, but had assumed, apparently quite erroneously, they would be studious looking, perhaps bespectacled, and of a certain age. The man who strode into his library bore no resemblance to the image he had conjured. He could have few more years than his own six and thirty, and his eyes, rather than vague and bespectacled, were of a rather piercing blue and possessed a latent twinkle, not unlike the deep blue sea on a sunny day. His skin was tanned, suggesting that he spent at least as much time outdoors as he did hunched over musty books. This gentleman did not offer him the distant bow bestowed upon him by Sir Godfrey Webster but strode forward with his hand outstretched and a rueful smile on his lips.

"Thank you for receiving me, Captain Turner. You must think me extremely rude not to have called on you before."

He shook the proffered hand firmly. "Think nothing of it, Mr Townsend. The vicar informed me that you are often called away by your interests."

His visitor laughed. "But not in those terms, I feel certain."

Edward smiled wryly. "No, but comfort yourself

with the knowledge that I almost certainly rank lower than you in his esteem."

"Oh, now you interest me greatly, Captain Turner. Tell me what it is you have done to earn his disapprobation. Was one sermon enough for you? Have you transferred your allegiance to the church in Midhurst? I would not blame you; I often go there myself."

"I will admit that one sermon was plenty, but I have committed a greater crime than going to another church; I have not gone at all since."

Before Mr Townsend could answer, a knock fell upon the door. Nora entered the room, the girls following close behind. The nursery maid's face fell as she saw he had a visitor.

"Forgive me, sir," she said quickly. "I did not know you were occupied. We will come back later."

Barbara and Emily, who stood holding hands, shuffled backwards through the door.

"Come in, girls," he said. "I would like to introduce you to our nearest neighbour."

The girls huddled behind Nora, Emily peeping around one side of her skirts and Barbara the other. Nora bent and whispered something in their ears, and they stepped forward offering something approaching a curtsy.

Mr Townsend bowed, the twinkle in his eyes becoming more pronounced. "Who have we here?"

"Mr Townsend, the children are my wards, Miss Proctor and Miss Barbara."

Emily frowned, her nose wrinkling. "Why am I Miss Proctor and not Miss Emily?"

It was clear she suspected a slight. Edward had mistakenly thought that treating her as an adult rather than a child would please her. He was beginning to wonder if the girl would challenge everything he said or did.

"You are the eldest," Mr Townsend said, "and so the distinction of being called Miss Proctor is yours. Think how confusing it would be if you and your sister were both called Miss Proctor when in the same room."

The child regarded him seriously. "I am the eldest, but I would rather be called Emily, then you could not be confused, could you?"

"I could not, but if we are to dispense with formalities," he said gravely, "you must call me Thomas."

For the first time in the months he had known her, Emily's lips stretched into a grin. It transformed her thin, rather hard face, making it almost pretty.

"I used to have a friend called Tommy. Can I call you Tommy?"

Mr Townsend laughed. "No, imp."

Edward envied his neighbour's easy manner. He had always been reserved, observant, and incisive; attributes that had served him well in his career and earned him his men's respect, but had not endeared him to his colleagues, nor it seemed, his wards.

Nora cleared her throat. "The girls have something they would like to say to you."

He was aware of a feeling of disappointment when they regarded him warily. "Well?"

Emily cast a mulish look at Nora. Clearly, she was a reluctant participant in this interview. He was surprised when Barbara stepped forward; she generally seemed content to remain in her sister's shadow.

"W-we're sorry, Captain Turner. We should not have broken your gifts."

Her voice wobbled and her large brown eyes were anxious. The thought that she might be afraid of him appalled him. He went down on one knee and gave her what he hoped was a reassuring smile. A tentative response hovered on her lips for an instant, but it disintegrated when Emily turned on her heel and marched from the room.

"She don't mean it," Barbara whispered, before racing after her.

He rose to his feet, and seeing Nora's mortified expression, said gently, "Your intentions were good, but perhaps it was a little premature to expect such a capitulation."

The maid nodded, bobbed a curtsy, and went in search of her charges.

"Ah," Mr Townsend said, "I think I perceive why Mr Adams disapproves of you."

Edward stiffened. His visitor seemed to perceive it, for he gave a disarming smile.

"He has a habit of jumping to conclusions. I, do not, I assure you. Although I may sometimes have to make an intuitive leap, my conclusions are generally based on facts and evidence. As the only evidence I have is that you have two wards, one of which refers to you as Captain Turner rather than Papa, I have made no leap intuitive or otherwise. I will admit to a certain curiosity, but I do not expect you to satisfy it. Let us rather change the subject. I noticed you have repaired the roof of the house at Westfield Farm. Do I take it you have found new tenants?"

Edward relaxed. "Not yet. I have spent more years

at sea than I have on the land and will admit I am a little lost as how to proceed. Perhaps you could advise me?"

Mr Townsend grinned. "Not I, but I know a man who can."

Edward gestured him to a seat and went to a sideboard bearing two decanters and glasses. "Wine or brandy?"

"A small glass of wine. I have some notes to write up about the excavation of a long barrow in Wiltshire."

"A long barrow?"

The visitor laughed softly. "Forgive me. It presents as a long oval mound of grass but generally hides an ancient burial site built of stone or wood."

Edward handed him his glass and sat down. "Did you find anything interesting?"

Mr Townsend sighed. "Only a few pottery fragments, arrow heads, and bones. Although these things and the structure of such chambers are in themselves interesting, I always hope to find something as yet undiscovered or so well preserved that it must shed new light on the era it portrays." He shook his head. "It is not always wise to ask me about my antiquarian interests, Captain Turner. I can ramble on for hours never noticing that the eyes of my unfortunate listener have quite glazed over."

"Very well," Edward said. "I will admit that my immediate concerns are of the present not the past. Who is this man who might offer me some advice?"

A fond smile touched his guest's lips. "My brother, Rufus. My father was a keen historian with a particular interest in the Roman Empire. He admired

Lucius Verginius Rufus, a senator who refused the office of emperor on more than one occasion, claiming he wished to serve his country rather than himself."

"He sounds like a good fellow," Edward allowed. "Do I take it that your brother embodies such virtue?"

Mr Townsend laughed. "It would be more accurate to say that he serves *the* country rather than *his* country. He is as passionate about land management as I am ancient artefacts, and I am glad of it. He is but two and twenty, but having grown up following our steward about, he has knowledge beyond his years. He has spent the last few months with Coke of Holkham, who is a leader in agricultural matters, you know." He grinned. "Of course you wouldn't. The thing is, it may be that we might be able to do each other a good turn."

Edward nodded. "Go on."

"Rufus is a trifle unusual. When I say he is interested in the land and everything related to it, be it crops, livestock breeding, or inventing machines that might make sowing, ploughing, or harvesting a much more efficient business, I mean he is exclusively interested in them. He is very comfortable talking of these things but is a fish out of water with regard to anything else. He is socially inept, can rarely look another in the eye, and becomes frustrated easily if someone is not quick to take his meaning. He has come back from Holkham with ambitions to manage a far larger estate than my own, but I fear that his uniqueness may lead him to be disappointed."

"I imagine he might have trouble at an interview,

never mind dealing with a tenantry who were unused to him," Edward acknowledged.

Mr Townsend sighed. "Precisely. However, if he were given the opportunity to manage both our lands, perhaps he would be satisfied. I admit, I would prefer to keep him at home. There, everyone is so accustomed to him that I am not even sure he is aware of his... his...."

"Uniqueness," Edward finished for him.

Mr Townsend nodded. "Precisely. I have had charge of him since he was twelve, and did not send him to school. He became quite agitated at the thought of leaving Lavington, and I was surprised when he started a correspondence with Coke, and astounded when he accepted his invitation to visit. It seems that Coke was pleased with him. In fact, I know he was, for he wrote to me. He said that he would have been happy to employ him if he had a position available, but he is such an enthusiast of agriculture that it is only natural he might overlook Rufus's odd habits."

Edward glanced at the clock. It wanted only ten minutes to six. "I believe a man should be judged on his merits rather than his social graces but let us discuss this more over dinner." He raised a questioning eyebrow. "Unless your brother will be alarmed by your absence?"

Mr Townsend smiled. "Certainly, I shall stay. Rufus is quite used to my comings and goings, although I never made any extended trips until recent years."

CHAPTER 3

It took only half an hour to reach the gates of Westcliffe Park, and another five minutes to reach the large Palladian mansion.

Anne followed the very correct butler who greeted her, outwardly serene but her heart beat a little faster. Weeks had passed since Lady Westcliffe had first mentioned that she had a proposition she thought Anne might find interesting, and she had waited with both anticipation and dread to hear what it might be. She would not be welcomed into the strata of society she was used to, that was certain, and surely that left only some menial position. She straightened her shoulders and reminded herself that her choices had brought her to this pass.

The butler led her to a modest but comfortably appointed parlour that overlooked the terrace at the back of the house. Lady Westcliffe rose from her chair by the fire.

"Come in and warm yourself, my dear. It seems

the mild weather is finally at an end and I expect you became quite chilled in the carriage."

Anne handed her pelisse and hat to the butler and moved to the chair indicated. "Not at all. I was provided with a blanket and a hot brick. I hope you are recovered from your nausea?"

"I am much better, thank you. I am only glad that Westcliffe departed with our guests to attend to a matter of business in Town, for he would insist the doctor attend me, and I cannot abide being fussed over and cosseted for a trifling indisposition."

They exchanged a few more pleasantries, but Anne was pleased when her hostess soon came to the point of her visit.

"I can see that you are not quite comfortable and so I shall keep you in suspense no longer." She passed her a newspaper clipping. It was an advertisement that had been placed in a London newspaper.

Wanted. A respectable and educated woman who can teach all the subjects necessary to two young girls of six and ten. In addition to the former requirements, the successful applicant must possess patience, compassion, and a cheerful disposition. Interviews will be held at The Golden Cross, Charing Cross, on the 15th of October. They will commence at 9:00 and finish at 3.00. All applicants must send a reference in advance to said establishment directed to Captain E Turner.

Anne looked from the newspaper to Lady Westcliffe several times trying to gather her thoughts.

"A governess? Surely, I am the last person to apply for such a post."

Lady Westcliffe smiled. "You are more than qualified to fulfil the position if you can find it in yourself to step so far down in the world."

"Step down? The position of governess is more than I can hope for, but you know it is impossible. My ability to teach the girls is not in question, but I cannot give them the one thing that is more essential than any number of accomplishments."

Lady Westcliffe poured out two glasses of ratafia and brought one to Anne. She sat in the chair opposite her and sipped delicately at the beverage. "Ordinarily, I would agree with you, my dear, but there is nothing ordinary about this position, and I believe you to be uniquely qualified."

Anne's brow furrowed. "What can you mean?"

Lady Westcliffe put down her glass and leant forward a little. "Do you remember me telling you that your talents were quite wasted at Ashfield Hall because we raise our girls to enter the working world?"

Anne gave a brief nod.

"I cannot deny, however, your success in teaching some of our more difficult pupils the rudiments of reading and writing. You have succeeded where others have failed, and that is what makes you particularly suited for the post advertised."

A bemused expression crossed Anne's face. "But how can there be any parity between the orphans I have attempted to aid here and the children of a distinguished family?"

Lady Westcliffe smiled. "Take another look at the advertisement, my dear." She waited until Anne had had time to do so before saying, "Is there any mention of a distinguished family?"

"No," Anne conceded, once more scanning the lines before her. "If you mean to imply that the family is or has been engaged in trade, however, it can make little difference. My circumstances still make me ineligible for such a position."

"Why do you not let Captain Turner be the judge of that?" Lady Westcliffe said gently. "He is a most unusual gentleman who has never moved in the first ranks of society, and I believe he has little desire to. In the last few months, he has run through three governesses. I imagine he is beginning to feel a little desperate."

This piqued Anne's interest. "In what way is he unusual? Does the problem lie with the children or with him?"

Lady Westcliffe laughed softly. "As usual you go straight to the heart of the matter. I would not be surprised if the children played a part in their governess's departure. Captain Turner has taken two orphans from a workhouse in Manchester under his wing. He has recently resigned his commission in the navy, and I believe they are the children of a man who died under his command."

"That was very kind of him," Anne said, wondering how Lady Westcliffe knew so much about the man.

Lady Westcliffe smiled wryly. "It speaks of a good heart or a guilty conscience."

"Are the two opposed?" Anne said. "Would not a good captain regret the loss of any of his men?"

"Indeed, he might," Lady Westcliffe concurred. "It is most unusual for a captain to take a subordinate's children under his wing, however."

Anne frowned. Could it be that Lady Westcliffe did not approve of the lower orders being raised up in society? She would not be alone in such a view.

"I would have thought you would have applauded his philanthropy."

"And so I do," she said. "It is why I wish you to take the position. It will not be easy to turn the girls into young ladies. The departure of so many governesses suggests that they are not easy pupils."

Anne glanced again at the advertisement. *The successful applicant must possess patience, compassion, and a cheerful disposition.* Something else struck her as odd. She had seen such advertisements before, but generally they listed the particular subjects required, and it was the lady of the house who conducted the business.

"Is Captain Turner a widower?"

"No. He has never married."

Anne drew in a breath. She was not sure how she felt about residing in the house of a single gentleman. And yet his actions suggested he was an honourable man.

Lady Westcliffe gave her an understanding smile. "You need have no qualms in accepting the post, my dear. I have heard nothing to suggest any improper behaviour on Captain Turner's part. At least not where his private affairs are concerned."

Anne raised her eyebrows. "Am I to infer from that comment that you have heard something prejudicial against him in his public affairs?"

"Only that he had little choice but to resign his commission. He had distinguished himself on many occasions, both at Trafalgar and several other engagements. He was fortunate after the end of the French wars not to suffer the fate of many who were forced to become half pay officers, but was sent to the West

African Squadron to help enforce our ban on the slave trade."

An unwelcome voice echoed in Anne's mind. *Do not worry, my dear, our fortunes are unlikely to wane. There are far too many people with vested interests for this extreme measure to work. Not all countries are bound by this embargo, and it is easy enough to raise a false flag.* Anne repressed a shiver.

"I have heard of the fleet, and certain rumours that there have been strong inducements for them to turn a blind eye or for certain traders to adopt a different flag in the hope of being left unmolested. Do you mean to imply that Captain Turner was of their ilk?"

Lady Westcliffe shook her head. "No, I do not mean to tell you that. He was accused of the crime, by a man of superior rank and breeding, Captain Turner being one of the few men of humble origins to rise to the position of commander. There was very little corroborating evidence, however."

Anne knew to her cost that it was not beneath the dignity of some gentlemen to resort to dishonourable tactics if it served their purpose.

"Is it within the realms of possibility that the person who brought the charges against him had a motive other than patriotic duty?"

Lady Westcliffe rose and poured them another glass of ratafia. "I thought you might be quick to grasp the fundamentals of the situation. As I do not wish to besmirch the reputation of an individual whom nothing has yet been proven against, I will say only this. At first, the squadron was only of a very small contingency, and its lack of success might easily be explained. However, its efficiency grew exponentially after the arrival of Captain Turner. He was awarded several prizes for his capture of slave ships and the liberation of their cargo."

Anne winced at slaves being referred to in such terms but felt a burst of compassion for the unknown Captain Turner. "Then it seems highly unlikely to me, as I'm sure it must to anyone of intelligence, that he could be guilty of committing any act that would ensure slaves remained destined for captivity."

Lady Westcliffe sipped the amber liquid in her glass. "It is why I do not accuse him of it. Perhaps things might not have become so serious if he had not held a superior officer at sword point and then locked him in his cabin or become so zealous that he boarded a French vessel where he had no authority to act. That nation has agreed on principle to discontinue trading in slaves from Africa, but they have not conceded authority to the British to search their vessels." She smiled ruefully. "To go directly against orders, to imprison a higher ranked officer, and to potentially cause a political breach, especially with a country with whom we are so recently at peace, are all grounds for dismissal. He would, of course, have lost his prize money and his reputation. His previous exceptional service and acts of bravery, plus the suspicion that this final charge laid against him was untrue, saved him from that fate." She placed her glass down carefully. "He has offered faithful service to his country, but he would not be the first to turn against it when his dreams, and everything he has fought so hard to achieve has been taken from him."

Anne was beginning to realise that Lady Westcliffe's desire for her to accept the position was prompted by more than her wish to provide two orphaned girls with a governess. She was aware that Lord Westcliffe was a person of some influence with ties to the government, although his exact role was unclear to her.

"What is it precisely that you accuse Captain Turner of?"

"I do not accuse him of anything, but he has been brought to my husband's attention as a person of interest. I do not know if you are aware of the rumbles of discontent in the north?"

Anne shook her head.

"Over the past several years there have been various groups who have met and discussed the possibility of parliamentary reform. Some of these meetings have been harmless enough, being led by intellectuals with a peaceable bent. Others, however, have been led by radicals quite prepared to encourage their followers to take up arms and march to London. After the murder of Perceval, and the unfortunate rejoicing in some quarters by those that considered his murderer's actions just, these groups grew in number. Several conspiracies have been uncovered and foiled by agents who act for the Home Office."

"And one of these agents, or should I say spies, has laid information against Captain Turner?"

"Only in so far as he was seen at a meeting in Manchester, where certain troublemakers we are aware of were stoking the fires of discontent. He did not overtly participate, and it may be that he was at the inn by chance. This agent followed him to Sussex where he has inherited a modest estate. It has been reported that he entertained Sir Godfrey Webster, who is a member of parliament known to hold radical views."

"And on this flimsy evidence, Captain Turner becomes a person of interest to the government?"

Lady Westcliffe smiled at the hint of indignation in her voice. "One can never be too careful in these matters. Sussex generally gives the government trouble with relation to smuggling, and its efforts to curb it have been difficult enough. Hopefully, the recently formed Coast Blockade will contain that irritation. However, the agricultural depression that followed the war has hit the rural community hard, and as the navy has so reduced its numbers, the shipbuilding businesses in the county have also suffered. Hardship provides fertile ground for radical seeds to be sown, but prevention is always better than cure, and it is in the interests of the government to ensure that ground remains fallow. It may well be that Captain Turner is no threat and the agent involved overzealous; either way, it is better that we know which it is."

Anne's heart sank. "I owe both you and Lord Westcliffe a debt of gratitude, but I would not feel comfortable spying on my new employer if that is what you require of me."

Lady Westcliffe laughed softly. "Nothing so dramatic, my dear. I would ask only that you keep your wits about you whilst carrying out your duties. You might notice, for example, who comes and goes, or perhaps strangers lurking where they have no right to be."

CHAPTER 4

It did not take Edward long to realise that the wording of his advertisement had not had the desired effect. His intention had been to attract only those of an acceptable disposition; what he had failed to consider, however, was that any lady worth her salt must have been able to read between the lines and assume that his charges were not the ideal pupils. He scoffed at his own naivety.

He could divide the applicants he had thus far interviewed into two camps. Those clearly so desperate for a situation they were prepared to entertain any sort of behaviour in exchange for a roof over their heads and a reasonable wage, and those who were convinced that the girls must be merely overindulged and were confident in their ability to show them the error of their ways.

The first contingent, he had discovered, were desperate for a reason. They were frankly not up to the task, their education being rudimentary and their gentility questionable. Their references, he felt sure, had been written by some acquaintance for whom they had never acted in the role of governess. They had appeared not at all dismayed by the girls' ignorance; how should they be when the girls could not reveal their own? Perhaps they had seen his previous advertisements and concluded that he must be so desperate he would be prepared to overlook these deficiencies.

The second contingent had learning enough but had not endeared themselves to his wards or to him. On hearing the girls speak, two ladies had looked at him coldly, and informed him that they only worked for respectable families. He could not help reflecting that they would probably enjoy Mr Adams' sermons. The current prospect, Miss Masterson, had almost managed to mask her surprise, but had proceeded to ask the girls a series of questions she must have known they would be unable to answer.

Emily grew more resentful with each question, and when she was finally asked one she did know the answer to — *who is the present king?* — she answered with relish.

"Mad George."

Miss Masterson's eyes narrowed, although her lips still bore the trace of a smile.

"Very good, although it would be remiss of me not to mention that it is unfitting to refer to our monarch in such terms, however ill he may be. Which George is he?"

Her smile grew a little as Emily looked bemused.

"What do you mean?"

"I mean that he is not the first George to take the throne. So which one is he? The second, third, fourth, fifth?"

Emily's cheeks reddened, and after casting a worried glance at her, Barbara hazarded a guess.

"The fifth."

Miss Masterson sighed. "I see we have a lot of work to do,"

"What's the king got to do with us?" Emily said crossly.

The would-be governess raised her brows. "Very little, I imagine. You are his subjects, however, and as such should at least do him the courtesy of knowing his position and those of the other kings that went before him and helped make our country great." She pushed a slate towards the child. "But we need not worry about such things yet. Let us start with something simpler. Perhaps you would write your name for me."

It had to be said, that Edward was just a shocked as Miss Masterson when Emily, her tongue protruding from her lips, painstakingly formed a cross. He had known the family to be poor, but so had his own been, and yet he had learned to read and write, as well as do basic arithmetic at Sunday school. His aptitude had been noticed by the vicar, who had been far more benevolent than Mr Adams, and had taken it upon himself to give him private tuition when he had soon streaked ahead of his classmates. It seemed the girls had not attended such a school or perhaps girls were taught other things.

These thoughts moved rapidly through his mind in no more than a few seconds, and it seemed something similar had passed through Miss Masterson's. Her lips had tightened, deepening the fine lines that encircled her mouth. She rose to her feet.

"Captain Turner, I am neither a nursemaid nor a charity school teacher. I am afraid it would be beneath my dignity to accept this post."

Angry that she had said as much in front of the children, he replied briskly. "Then it is as well I have not offered it you. Indeed, I do not comprehend why you applied for the post when you are clearly lacking the patience and good temper I requested. Good day, Miss Masterson."

He strode to the door and held it open, closing it firmly behind her as soon as she had stalked from the room.

"You didn't like her neither," Emily said gleefully.

Edward sighed. "No, I did not."

Emily picked up the chalk and slowly but accurately scratched her name on the slate. She then passed it to her sister and nodded. Barbara, with much squeaking of chalk, wrote her name beneath her sister's.

A chuckle escaped Edward before he could prevent it, and suddenly they were all laughing. It relieved the tension of a singularly unproductive and frustrating day.

"I am pleased to see that your previous governesses, however unsatisfactory, at least taught you something."

It was the wrong thing to say. Emily frowned and her face slipped into the sullen expression he was accustomed to.

"It was Ma who showed us how to write our names."

Edward was sorry that their rare moment of accord was over and attempted to rectify his blunder. "Did she indeed? Then I am sure she would be very proud that you have not forgotten. Can you write anything else?"

Emily shook her head, tears welling in her eyes. "She was always working and didn't have no time."

"She sounds like a remarkable woman," he said gently. "And I quite understand that you might not like anyone taking her place, but think how proud she would be if you learned all your letters."

Emily's brow furrowed as she considered this, but it was Barbara who spoke.

"Was your pa proud of you when you learned to write?"

"Very," he said, leaning forward and adding in hushed tones, "if you can keep a secret, I shall tell you why. Can you?"

She nodded, her eyes large in her thin face.

"My father was a sailmaker, and he could set a stitch as quickly and neatly as any you will see, but he could not write. He worked aboard a ship until his leg was blown off."

The girls gasped, their hands lifting to cover their mouths. He berated himself for a fool. He was a private man, unused to talking of himself in such a way, but he had sensed the girls needed something from him and he thought that the knowledge that he too had once been poor might give them some common ground. To put such an image in their minds, however, was unforgivable.

"Forgive me, "he said quickly, "I need not have told you that."

The initial shock having worn off, Emily shrugged. "We've seen injured soldiers often enough on the streets of Manchester, it's only that he was your father that made it seem worse. Is that how he died?"

Edward shook his head. "No, he survived, came home, and found employment ashore. He used to talk to me of his life at sea and made it sound so wonderful and exciting that I wished for such a life too. I wanted to become a sailmaker and follow in his footsteps, but he always said I should strive for more. I went to sea soon after I was orphaned."

The door opened and Nora, who had been greeting the candidates and providing them with refreshment, came in.

"That one looked like she'd swallowed sour milk."

Edward sighed. "Let us hope that the next is a better prospect."

"Are there many more?" Emily said, stifling a yawn.

"There's only one lady still waiting."

Edward glanced at the clock on the mantle. As it was almost half past two, she surely must be the last candidate, although there were still two recommendations before him. Perhaps the other lady had changed her mind. He opened them both and scanned their contents.

"What is the lady's name?"

"Miss Burdock."

He sighed. He had hoped that it might be Mrs Huxley, for she had not turned her nose up at teaching at an orphanage and so might possess the compassion and skills needed to teach the girls. He prayed that Miss Burdock was suitable, or they would have to go through this whole rigmarole again. He glanced again at her reference which had been written by a Mrs Lychfield of Broom House, Derbyshire.

Miss Burdock is amiable, does not put herself forward, and is quite capable, I feel sure, of teaching young girls who are not overly spirited.

His heart sank. It was hardly a glowing encomium. For a moment, he was tempted to send Nora back with a message that the position had already been filled, but only for a moment. He would not offer her such a discourtesy when she had given up her time and for all he knew spent a sum she could ill afford to travel to London.

"Send her in, Nora."

A small, white-haired woman, who must have been somewhere between fifty and sixty came into the room with slightly unsteady steps. Whether that was because of the large, carpet bag she carried or some infirmity was difficult to tell. Faded blue eyes could be seen behind the spectacles that kept slipping down her nose.

Edward rose to his feet. "Good afternoon, Miss Burdock." He held out a hand. "Please, let me take your bag. It looks heavy."

"Thank you, so kind," she murmured, clutching it to her chest as if it contained the crown jewels. "But that is unnecessary."

"Then please, take a seat."

They sat at a large, round table. Most of the applicants had seated themselves midway between him and his wards, but Miss Burdock placed herself between

Emily and Barbara. Ignoring him, she smiled at each of them.

"What pretty names," she said gently, rummaging in the carpet bag. She pulled from it two cloth dolls clothed in dresses made from scraps of silk, their heads topped by miniature bonnets from which woollen ringlets peeped, and laid them on the table.

The girl stared at them in some surprise and perhaps mistaking their expressions for disapprobation, she added, "I made them myself but did not think to have the pleasure of giving them to you in person." She reached out a hand towards them. "However, I quite understand that my poor efforts might not excite your admiration."

Privately, Edward thought them very well made and a testament to her sewing skills, at least. As the girls seemed to take any gifts he gave them as a personal affront, he was surprised when Emily snatched up the doll before Miss Burdock could reclaim it.

"Ma made a doll for each of us, although they weren't as fine as this." She held it out to her sister. "You must have this one because it has blonde hair like you."

As Barbara inspected it, Emily picked up the other one. "This one has brown hair like me." She looked at Miss Burdock. "Thank you." She sent an uncertain glance at Edward, before saying, "but we will give you them back if you do not get the position."

Miss Burdock smiled sweetly. "Oh no, they are yours to keep. I had intended to request that Captain Turner pass them on to you whatever the outcome of this interview."

Barbara tilted her head. "Did you know that George the third is the king of England?"

"And that he is mad?" Emily added.

Miss Burdock sighed. "Oh yes, and it is such a shame for I saw him once when he was younger. He was quite handsome and had a lovely smile. But perhaps it is for the best for his son, the Prince Regent, who was also once quite handsome, has gone off sadly. He is really excessively fat and sadly expensive."

Emily giggled. "Mad George and fat George."

Miss Burdock seemed to find nothing amiss with her disrespectful words. "Yes, indeed. I wonder if it was wise to call them George, for I once had a cousin so named and although he was not mad, at least, I do not think he was – but then I didn't know him very well – he was certainly fat."

Both girls giggled this time. Miss Burdock shook her head sadly. "We should not make light of it however, for poor Queen Charlotte has had much to bear; it is no wonder she is unwell. And as for her other sons…" She suddenly seemed to recall her audience and cast Edward a look of confusion.

There was something about the gentle lady that made it difficult to dislike her. But although the gift of the dolls had been kind and she was the first candidate the girls had warmed to, he hardly thought an intimate knowledge of court gossip qualified her for the position.

"How are you with figures, Miss Burdock?" he said.

She peered at him over the rim of the glasses which had once more slipped down her nose. "I used to keep the household accounts for my brother," she said and then sighed. "It was a very trying experience."

"Trying in the sense that you found it difficult?" Edward asked.

The lady's eyes grew distant as if she were recalling a memory. "Indeed, I found it very difficult. I could never balance the books, you see."

"Then perhaps you might find it difficult to teach another how to do so," Edward said gently, not wishing to discompose her.

"Oh, there was nothing wrong with my calculations. I could not balance them because however much I practised economy, I could not bring my brother to do so." She shook her head sadly. "We had to sell the house in the end, and Marcus bought a commission in the army with the little money that remained. Unfortunately, he died within the year."

There was no resentment in her voice, only sadness.

Edward was fast running out of reasons to reject Miss Burdock. She was as unassuming as her previous employer had suggested. He was fully aware, however, that for the most part, the girls had been on their best behaviour. There was no guarantee that they would continue in the same vein. There was also the problem of her advanced years.

On the one hand, that might prevent the girls making unfavourable comparisons between her and their mother, but on the other, they were likely to run circles around her if they so chose. And then there was the question of her infirmity. He firmly believed that all children, whether male or female, should spend at least some time outdoors.

"Thank you, Miss Burdock. If you will step outside, my wards and I will discuss the matter of your employment."

She rose to her feet, and he thought he saw a spark of hope in her eyes. The door had barely closed behind her when Barbara said, "I like her. She is nice."

"But will she be able to play games with you or take you for walks?" He gave them a mock severe look, "Or be able to control your more destructive impulses?"

Emily looked a little shamefaced. "That was me, not Barbara. And it won't happen again."

"Nora can take us for walks," Barbara said hopefully.

Edward was forced to acknowledge that he was running out of options. He had no desire to go through this again anytime soon. There was every likelihood, of course, that he would need to hire another governess in the future, but perhaps by then the girls would be so much improved that it would not be so difficult a feat. He was about to concede and offer the position to Miss Burdock when Nora came into the room.

"A Mrs Huxley has arrived."

For a moment, his hopes were raised but then he registered the rather dubious look in her eyes.

"Is something amiss with Mrs Huxley?"

"I can't rightly say, sir," she said. "She's a veil pulled over her face."

His brows rose. Her references praised her to the skies and Lady Westcliffe claimed she was a sensible woman. Had she inflated her good qualities, perhaps to compensate for some disfigurement? Such an unfortunate circumstance would not weigh with him; he had seen enough injuries to last him a lifetime and carried a fair few scars of his own, but however many soldiers they had seen on the streets of Manchester, he could not imagine the girls would be so unaffected.

"We want Miss Burdock," Emily said. "And I'm tired. We don't need to see her."

"Perhaps not," he said, "but as Mrs Huxley has arrived within the stated time, it would be very rude of us not to give her an opportunity."

Emily screwed up her face. "Old Mrs Madley used to wear a veil because she only had one eye, a huge hooked nose, and open sores on her face."

"The unfortunate woman," he said. "Did you not feel sorry for her?"

"No," Barbara said in a hushed voice, her eyes wide. "'Cos she used to spit and cackle and say she'd grind our bones to make her bread."

"I wasn't afraid of her," Emily said.

"Yes, you were," Barbara said. "You used to take my hand and run away."

Emily looked scornful. "That was because you were scared, stupid. You don't make bread with bones. You should know that; we watched Mam make it often enough."

Edward cleared his throat, judging it time to call a halt to the brewing argument. He suspected the poor woman had contracted some dreadful disease and run quite mad.

"We shall still see Mrs Huxley, however. And if she should be disfigured in any way, you must not be afraid or show any sign that you have noticed. You would not like to hurt her feelings."

The girls did not look convinced.

He felt a moment's pity for Mrs Huxley; she was not going to have an easy time of it.

"Remember, you promised that you would give everyone a fair chance."

CHAPTER 5

Despite her reservations, a feeling of anticipation gripped Anne as her carriage reached the outskirts of London. Her new life was about to begin, or at least it would if she could but make a good impression on her prospective employer. Now that she understood Captain Turner did not move in the first circles, nor apparently had any desire to, her initial fears and concerns had abated. Lord Westcliffe's desire to know if he was a troublemaker was understandable, but however much Captain Turner had been disappointed, she doubted that a man whose every action had been driven by honour or compassion, who had witnessed the death of so many men fighting for their country, would wish to set them against each other. He also had two wards to consider. There would be very little point in rescuing them from a life of poverty only to get himself arrested for encouraging rebellion at best or treason at worst.

She had often been accused of a lack of sensibility, and if such were true, she was glad of it, for she could meet Captain Turner, she believed, without alarm or prejudice. The only thing that troubled her a little, was that whilst she was armed with a great deal of information about him, he knew very little of her and nor must he. This lack of openness did not sit well with her, but she eased her conscience with the thought that if she were so fortunate as to be offered the position of governess, she would carry out her duties with all the diligence he could hope for.

As she stepped out of the carriage in front of The Golden Cross, she pulled forward the veil attached to her bonnet. It was a busy coaching inn and although she thought the risk slight, she would not risk being recognised.

She had purposefully arrived only twenty minutes before the time stated for the interviews to end. Not only was it safer, but she hoped it would give her a strategic advantage. When Captain Turner came to make his decision, surely it would be the latter candidates who remained uppermost in his mind. Of course, this plan carried some risk. It was entirely possible that he might already have appointed one of the applicants for the post, but she put her faith in the notion that an officer of the Royal Navy would consider all possibilities before coming to a decision. It was true, she imagined, that he must have been forced to make snap decisions in the heat of battle, but surely they would have been based on all the knowledge he had at his disposal.

When she entered the inn and asked a passing maid the whereabouts of Captain Turner, that young lady cast her a curious glance.

"Good luck, ma'am. There's been a stream of

ladies coming and going all day, but most of them have left in high dudgeon looking like they've been sucking on lemons."

Behind her veil, a smile of satisfaction curved Anne's lips. When she entered the parlour that she indicated, a young woman, a servant of some sort judging by her plain clothes, rose to meet her.

"Have you come for the position, ma'am?"

"I have," she said. "I am Mrs Huxley."

A white-haired lady came into the room. She took a seat and smiled at Anne.

"You have been protecting your complexion from the sun, I see. Very wise."

Anne would have raised her veil to greet the woman, but something about her seemed familiar, although she could not place her.

"Yes, indeed, ma'am."

"I think you will be perfectly safe in here, however, for the window is small and the day quite overcast."

She looked up and saw the maid regarding her with a peculiar stare. How awkward this was.

"I'll just go and tell Captain Turner you're here," the woman said.

"Thank you," she murmured.

"Of course," the older lady continued as if they had not been interrupted, "you must do whatever makes you comfortable." She sighed, the exhalation of air containing regret mingled with longing.

Anne was left with the impression that the lady in front of her was not used to her comfort being considered at all. Her open, gentle expression suggested that Anne's caution was unnecessary, yet rather than receding, the notion that she had met the woman somewhere before was growing, although where and when remained tantalisingly out of reach.

"I will admit that I am more comfortable with the veil, although I find myself unable to explain why."

Miss Burdock gave an understanding smile. "Ah, I think I understand. Circumstances have forced you down in the world, and you would rather not risk some tittle-tattle recognising you, expressing sympathy to your face and then spreading the tale of your misfortune amongst his or her acquaintances. It is very unlikely I would recognise you, however, for I have been living in a very out of the way place for some time, and I can assure you that I would never do you such a disservice if by some strange chance I did."

Anne sat down abruptly by the woman and impulsively took her hands. "I do not think so ill of you, ma'am. Indeed, I find myself regretting that I might stand between you and this position."

Miss Burdock patted her hand. "The position should go to the best candidate and, if I am honest, my dear, I am not at all sure Captain Turner is convinced of my suitability for it. I cannot blame him for that, for I am not as young or fit as I once was."

Before Anne could reply, the young woman reappeared. "Come this way, Mrs Huxley."

Anne thanked her, following her into the corridor and entering a door opposite. She shut it behind her and raised her veil, pinning a smile on her face as she turned. It became a little fixed as she saw the curious looks turned her way. She had not expected the children to be present, even less had she expected them to stare at her as if she had grown two heads.

"Is something amiss?" she said.

"Not at all, Mrs Huxley. Please come in and take a seat."

Her eyes swivelled to Captain Turner, who stood and inclined his head. He was tall and slim, the simple cut of his fawn coat revealing the breadth of his shoulders. His dark hair was cut unfashionably short, and a small frown hovered between his grey eyes. He looked rather forbidding, and she turned her attention to the children.

Like Miss Burdock before her, she sat between the girls. They did not return her friendly smile; on the contrary, the one she judged to be the eldest scowled and the other regarded her with some suspicion. She regarded Captain Turner and raised her eyebrows.

"I had not expected to meet your wards, sir, although I think it an eminently good idea. Would you mind introducing them to me?"

The lines between his eyes deepened. "I do not believe I mentioned in my advertisements that they were my wards. They could very well be my daughters."

It was a clumsy blunder, but Anne was far too level-headed to let it throw her.

"That is true, sir. But if you will forgive me for saying so, your advertisement gave very little information apart from the girls' ages. It gave me the impression that you did not really know what it is they needed apart from compassion and understanding, of course." She sent the girls an apologetic glance. "That could have meant that they had recently lost their mother, and you were a widower. However, they have not the look of you, and I expect you would have mentioned your situation in your advertisement if you were a widower. As you did not, I assumed they were your wards."

"Our mother *is* dead," Emily said, her voice hard. "And we don't want another."

"No, of course not," Anne said gently. "Why should you?"

"Why was you wearing a veil?" Barbara asked. "You ain't got no scars or warts or crossed eyes."

"That is very true," Anne agreed. "For which circumstance I must hold myself fortunate."

She got the impression that this lack of disfigurement had somehow disappointed the girls.

"Why cover your face unless you're ugly or hiding?" Emily asked with disastrous insight.

Anne glanced at Captain Turner, hoping that he might perhaps reprimand the girls for their inquisitiveness, but realised he was looking at her, Emily's question reflected in his eyes. They had darkened like the sky before a storm and were uncomfortably penetrating.

"Jim Taylor hid his face, 'cos the constable were after him," the younger girl said.

Anne looked suitably interested. "Indeed? Was he a friend of yours?"

Barbara shook her head. "No, he was a bad lot my ma said."

"Oh dear. Then it is as well you had nothing to do with him. What had he done?"

"He prigged someone's snuff box," Emily said.

Anne returned her attention to the girl. "Prigged? That is a new word to me. How delightful. I do like to learn new things. Am I correct in assuming it means to steal?"

Emily was not to be sidetracked. She seemed determined to hold Anne in suspicion.

"It does. How do we know you ain't prigged something and want to become a governess so you ain't caught?"

Anne chuckled. "What a fertile imagination you have. I am no more a thief then I am disfigured. How could I be when I have been at an orphanage and been recommended for this position by a great lady?"

"You act as if you was a great lady," Emily continued, her eyes narrowing. "You speak finer than the vicar's wife. Why would someone like you be working at an orphanage?"

Anne had expected to face some difficult questions from her prospective employer, not to be interrogated by a ten-year-old child. She did not glance at Captain Turner, although she could feel his eyes upon her. She decided it would be best to stick as close to the truth as possible.

"Very well, I see you have found me out and so I will admit I was hiding."

She had the satisfaction of seeing Emily's eyes widen, and Barbara gasped.

"Is it so surprising?" she said. "Have you never hidden from anyone before?"

"We have," Barbara admitted. "We used to hide from Mrs Madely. She wore a veil 'cos she looked like a witch."

The children's obsession with her veil began to make sense.

"But we're only children." Emily said. "Why do you need to hide?"

"Yes," Captain Turner said, leaning forward,

planting his elbows on the table, and resting his chin on his hands. "Why do you need to hide, Mrs Huxley?"

She met his keen grey eyes calmly. "I have come down in the world, Captain Turner, and this is a very busy coaching inn."

A rather bleak smile touched his lips. "You would save yourself the humiliation of being looked down upon by those who would consider themselves better than you?"

"I would, sir."

Something that she could not identify flickered behind his eyes.

"And yet, if I should offer you the post of governess, it is something you must become accustomed to. What is more, if you consider the position beneath you, I cannot think that your heart will be in your work."

"What does he mean?" Barbara hissed to her sister.

"It means that she thinks she's too good for us," Emily said sourly.

"Then I want Miss Burdock," Barbara said. "I like her."

"I can hardly blame you for that," Anne said. "I like her myself. I do not think myself too good for you, at all, but I was afraid that I might meet an old acquaintance here and thought to save us both the embarrassment of acknowledging my lowered position in the world."

There was an uncomfortably long pause whilst Captain Turner stared at her unblinking. She forced herself to hold his gaze and raised her eyebrows questioningly.

"You mentioned, Mrs Huxley, that I did not appear to really understand what it is the girls needed to learn. I would be interested to hear what you think on the subject."

"That depends on what they already know." Her eyes alighted on the slates. "You have spelled your names correctly, well done, but I think, perhaps, we might work on making your hand just a little neater."

"That's all we can write," Emily blurted, a challenge in her eyes.

Mrs Huxley nodded. "Well, you are already acquainted with eight letters, and that is a very good start."

Barbara pulled both slates towards her and moved her fingers along the letters as if silently counting them.

"Eight?" she said, looking puzzled. "I make it twelve."

"Your counting is excellent," Mrs Huxley said gently, "but if you look a little closer, I think you will find three of them are the same. Can you find them?"

Barbara looked again, drew a line under each a, and said her name slowly. "But they sound different."

"So they do," she said. "When certain letters are put together, the sounds of letters can change. Let me show you."

She pulled the slate towards her, swiftly and deftly drew a rather comical fat cat, and wrote the word beneath it. She then drew a jar, wrote the word beneath it, and asked Barbara to say it. "Do you see how the sound has changed?"

"Why do we need to read anyway?" Emily said sulkily.

"I do not suppose you really need to if you don't mind being unable to read all the wonderful stories that exist, nor wish to one day be able to write letters to your friends."

Emily folded her arms. "We don't have no friends, not no more."

Anne heard the unhappiness beneath the girl's words, and her heart ached for her. "But you will perhaps one day. And when you are older and you and Barbara no longer live together, you may wish to write to each other. You might marry and it would be very difficult to run a house if you could not read the butcher's or the dress maker's bill. Why, they might charge you for something you had not ordered if they knew you could not read or add up the amounts next to each item."

That seemed to strike a chord with Emily. "I wouldn't let no cheating swindler get the better of me."

Anne nodded. "I am sure you would not if you were aware they were doing it. And then, there will be those who will look down their noses at you and think you are stupid which would be very unpleasant, but that is the way of the world I am afraid."

"It sounds like hard work," Barbara said anxiously.

Anne chuckled. "Perhaps, at first. But hard work can be fun especially if we make a game of it. Understanding how letters and numbers work is like a secret code and once you get the way of it and see the patterns it becomes much simpler. And there are many other things you must learn which are great fun, such as learning to play the pianoforte and sing and dance. And you need not spend all day in a stuffy schoolroom you know; many things can be learned on a long walk."

Emily began to look a little interested but then a rather sly expression entered her eyes. She held up her doll. "Miss Burdock gave us a gift."

Anne smiled, noticing that Barbara was gently stroking the silk gown of another doll. "That was very kind of her, and they are lovely. I believe, however, that rewards should be earned. For example, when you have achieved a small task set for you, that is the time to be given a treat. In my experience, a gift of any kind is valued far more highly if you have had to strive to deserve it."

She glanced up as she heard the scrape of a chair. "Thank you, Mrs Huxley. If you would take a seat in the parlour, my wards and I shall discuss our options."

She thought she saw a measure of approval in Captain Turner's eyes and was not unhopeful of a successful outcome. This had become more important to her as the interview, if you could call it that, had progressed. Emily and Barbara were in desperate need of a firm but kind hand, and the suspicion, confusion, and anxiousness she had seen in their eyes tugged at her heartstrings.

When she entered the parlour, she was surprised to see that Miss Burdock was no longer there. She cast an enquiring look in Nora's direction.

The maid shrugged. "She said there was no point in her staying as she was sure you'd get the position, and she said something else that was curious."

"Indeed?" Anne said, a faint feeling of guilt settling in her stomach. "And what was that?"

"She said she had a feeling you needed this job more than her, ma'am."

Her expression suggested she was sceptical of this assertion, and in truth, so was Anne.

"I'd best go and tell Captain Turner."

~

"Well?" Edward said as the door closed behind Mrs Huxley.

The girls looked at each other.

"I would like to learn how to dance," Barbara said. She picked up her doll and held it to her chest. "But Miss Burdock was a nice lady and perhaps she could teach us."

Edward was surprised when Emily did not immediately agree that Miss Burdock was the better choice. He had by now a fair idea of how acute the girl was and felt reasonably sure that she had already weighed up who would be the harder taskmaster.

"Mrs Huxley explains things very well. Perhaps learning would not be so difficult if she is to teach us."

Edward rested his chin on steepled fingers and considered the women. Neither lady had been at all shocked by the girls' manner of speaking or their lack of knowledge. Mrs Huxley, however, seemed to have clear, and in his mind, sensible ideas about the girls' education. Her experience with orphans was certainly an asset, and he felt reasonably sure she would use her wits rather than the rod to get her way.

On the other hand, his instincts told him she had

not been completely honest when she had explained the reason for her veil, and he had learned to trust his instincts. She had a quiet assurance that he admired, however, and had been highly recommended. He made his decision and was about to inform the girls when Nora came back into the room.

"I thought you'd want to know that Miss Burdock has gone."

"Where has she gone?" he said, surprised, and in truth, a little relieved.

"That I couldn't tell you, sir. She seemed to think Mrs Huxley would get the position, so I expect she's gone wherever she came from."

He glanced at the girls, glad that the decision appeared to have been made for them. There would at least be no tears or tantrums.

"Very well, ask Mrs Huxley to come in." Barbara sniffed, and he said gently, "The decision has been taken from us and we must make the best of it."

The girl's eyes shone with unshed tears. "Miss Burdock reminded me of our grammy. She used to look after us when Ma was at work." Large tears began to fall on her thin cheeks. "But she died of the influenza, just like Ma. Everybody dies."

Her grief touched him, but he did not know how to assuage it and was relieved when out of the corner of his eye he saw Mrs Huxley had entered the room. It seemed she had heard Barbara's words for she went to her at once and put an arm around her.

"It might seem that way to you, and indeed, you have been very unfortunate, but not everybody dies, and you are not alone. I am sure Captain Turner will take very good care of you."

"I shall do my best with your help, I hope, Mrs Huxley."

She glanced at him. "You may be sure of it, sir."

A half smile touched his lips. "You are rash to agree before we have discussed your wage."

She glanced at the girls. "I think we may discuss that later, sir."

She was right. The children should not hear what price he put upon their education and indeed any figure he mentioned must seem enormous to them. They were so unpredictable that he could not foresee how they would react. It was entirely possible that they would resent their new governess; they did not yet understand the importance of the things she would teach them, and their mother had earned a pittance, although from all accounts she had worked long hours leaving Emily to look after her young sister after their grandmother had died.

"When can you start?"

She smiled. "Why, immediately. Lady Westcliffe suggested I bring my things in case you should be in need of immediate assistance."

CHAPTER 6

Whilst waiting for her things to be transferred to his carriage, Captain Turner suggested that Nora take the girls outside for a breath of air. Anne's heart beat a little faster when they were left alone, although she remained outwardly calm. How that had infuriated… no, she would not give *him* a name. It had become repugnant to her. She stilled an inward sigh. At first, her hard fought for seeming equanimity had been assumed to protect herself. She had been afraid that *his* volatility would only become worse if she provoked him by a show of displeasure. Later, when she had no longer cared what he thought of her, it had come quite naturally. She could hardly have known the lengths he would go to to punish her indifference.

"Mrs Huxley? Are you well? You have become quite pale?"

Forcing the unwelcome thoughts from her mind, she smiled. "I am quite well, thank you, just a little tired."

His keen, grey eyes held hers for a silent moment.

They were far too penetrating for her liking, and she hoped very much that he was not about to ask her any questions she would find difficult to answer.

"Very well. I propose a wage of eighty pounds per annum to be paid quarterly, if that is acceptable to you?"

It was more than she had hoped for, and she agreed to it readily.

"I suggest a trial period of three months. If I decide to terminate your employment at that point, you will, of course, be paid the twenty pounds owing to you. And I should warn you that my wards' nurse, Nora, will be a constant presence in the schoolroom, at least at first, and will report back to me. If I hear of any cruelty on your part, I reserve the right to dismiss you immediately."

His voice remained even, but she could not miss the iron implacability beneath his words.

"That is understandable. Fate appears to have dealt Emily and Barbara cruel blows enough."

He nodded, looking at her searchingly. "Have you any questions you would like to ask me about my wards?"

"Am I to assume from these precautions that one or more of the girls' previous governesses have treated them ill?"

He dropped his eyes but not before a flicker of guilt passed through them. "I am afraid so. The girls have little reason to trust me, or you I am afraid."

"Then we must give them reason to do so. I assume you wish them to have a traditional lady's education?"

His lips twisted. "You are quite correct in your

assumption, Mrs Huxley. I have very little idea what that entails. I would certainly like them to be able to move comfortably in genteel society when the time comes. I do not look for a splendid match, certainly not an aristocratic husband, but a sensible man who has the means to support them."

She nodded. "I am glad your ambitions are so realistic."

"Is there anything else you wish to know about my wards?"

"Not at the present moment."

He raised an eyebrow. "You must have deduced from their demeanour and speech that they are of humble origin. Are you not wondering why I have made two such children my wards?"

"No," she said. "Your motivations are your own, sir. My only interest is the children."

He gave a rather bitter laugh. "How refreshing. I suppose I should inform you that there is a rumour circulating that they are my illegitimate children."

She met his gaze squarely. "If they are, then I can only praise you for owning them and ensuring they are provided for, if they are not, then your philanthropy is to be admired."

He rose to his feet. "Your luggage should have been stowed by now." He held the door open, murmuring as she passed, "Although I appreciate your disinterest, Mrs Huxley, they are not my children, but those of a very good and honourable man who served under my command. If you have any opportunity to counter the rumours, I should be very grateful. A lie unchecked becomes the truth."

She glanced up at him. He was uncomfortably

close, perhaps that is why prickles ran up and down her spine. "If the opportunity arises, I shall certainly do so."

As they stepped into the corridor, their attention was caught by a commotion towards the front of the inn. People crowded around the entrance and shouting could be heard outside. Their eyes met, startled, and then he ran, pushing people out of his way. Anne followed as best she could.

She did not know what she expected to find, but it was not the scene that greeted her. The shouts turned into laughter, and a boy, who could not be much older than Emily lay sprawled on the ground some fifty yards from the inn. Emily and Barbara perched upon his back, and beside them a carpet bag lay on the ground. Nora was comforting Miss Burdock who appeared a trifle discomposed. Edward paused halfway across the street, as if trying to comprehend the scene before him.

"Emily! Barbara! Get off that boy!"

Emily lifted her hand revealing a netted purse. "He prigged this from Miss Burdock. If we get off him, he'll scarper."

"You may be sure he won't," he said, striding up to them.

They scrambled off the thief, and Edward bent down, grabbed him by his ear, and hauled him to his feet.

A voice came from the dispersing crowd behind him. "Hand him over to the constable."

"Don't turn me in," the boy pleaded, his eyes wide in an ashen face. "I wouldn't have done it, but me and my sisters are starving."

His ragged and skinny appearance gave some credence to his words, but Emily appeared to feel no mercy.

"Miss Burdock took out her purse to give him a penny, but he swiped the lot," she said indignantly. "We were poor too, but we never stole nothing."

"You never stole anything," Miss Burdock said absently.

Edward glanced at her. "Did he hurt you, ma'am?"

"Oh, no," she said. "Let the poor thing go, I beg of you. I quite see now that by taking out my purse, I put temptation in his path. He can hardly be blamed for not resisting it." She smiled at Emily. "Although I am very grateful for your prompt action, my dear, and thank you for it. All the money I possess is in that purse."

"If we let him go," Edward said, "he will do it again."

The boy looked afraid. "I won't, sir. If you hand me over, what will happen to my sisters?"

"Have you no parents?" Anne said.

The boy looked at her, the hunted expression in his eyes confirming her suspicion. "What you wanna know about them for?"

"How old are your sisters?"

"Five and six," he said sullenly. He turned anguished eyes on Edward, and then scrubbed at his eyes with a dirty sleeve. When his arms dropped, tears had left trails through the road dust that covered his face. "They'll end up in the workhouse, and it's a bad place. I saw bodies laid out in the yard 'cos there's pox in there."

Emily tugged at Edward's sleeve. "P'raps we should let him go."

Barbara nodded mutely.

"I have a better idea," Anne said. "I have recently come from an orphanage in the countryside. The children are very well cared for and taught a trade. You and your sisters would be well fed and benefit from the fresh air."

He looked at her suspiciously. "Would we be separated?"

She knelt before him. "You would be housed separately, but you would be near them and allowed to see them." She glanced up at Edward. "What he did was wrong, Captain Turner, but it should not blight his whole life. Do you not agree this would be the better solution?"

He nodded.

She smiled at the boy. "The kind lady who oversees the orphanage sent me here in her own carriage, and I am sure she will not object if I send you back in it. Have you ever ridden in a fine carriage?"

He shook his head, and she turned to Captain Turner once more.

"Would you mind waiting for me whilst I go with…" She smiled at the boy. "What is your name?"

"Paul," he said.

"With Paul to fetch his sisters?"

He frowned. "I will go. I doubt it will be safe for you."

She stood up and shook out her skirts. "Very well. I will write a letter to Lady Westcliffe and arrange for her carriage to wait until you return." She smiled at the girls. "Come, we will go inside."

At that moment, Lady Westcliffe's carriage swept through the archway and into the street, followed closely by Edward's.

"I have a better idea," he said. "You go with the children now; that way you will arrive at the inn I have booked for the return journey in time for them to have supper and go to bed. Paul and I will go in Lady Westcliffe's carriage and collect his sisters." He frowned. "But surely such young children should not go unattended."

Anne smiled. "They will not be. Lady Westcliffe sent a very capable maid with me; she will be able to look after the girls." She glanced at the liveried footman who sat next to the coachman. "And Finn will take Paul in hand."

Edward glanced at the man whose muscles bulged through his tight-fitting coat. "I expect he will."

"If you give me a moment, I will explain everything to Finn, that way I will not have to delay you. Goodness knows what squalor Paul's sisters are living in."

"It ain't that bad," Paul mumbled.

Finn did not turn a hair but climbed down from his perch and held the door open for Captain Turner and the boy. As the carriage trundled off, Barbara took Miss Burdock's hand.

"What about Miss Burdock?"

"Well, perhaps we should first return her purse to her so she may return home." She held out her hand and Emily dropped the purse in it. The drawstring had come open and a sovereign, a sixpence, and a few pennies rolled into her palm. She opened the purse further and could not help noticing as she tipped them back in that it was empty of any other coins or notes. She frowned. "Miss Burdock, you said that the purse contained all the money you possessed. This is not enough to keep you for more than a few days."

"That is true," the woman said with false cheer. "But I daresay something will come up."

Anne knew that to be extremely unlikely, especially for a woman over fifty. "Have you no relatives who might take you in?"

Miss Burdock sighed. "None at all."

Guilt smote Anne's conscience. If she had not applied for the position, it was Miss Burdock who would have been appointed governess, she felt sure.

"She will end up in the workhouse," Barbara said anxiously.

"No, that she will not," Anne said decisively.

If she had realised the dire nature of Miss Burdock's circumstances, she might have been tempted to send her with Paul and his sisters. But the coach had left, and she did not know where it had gone. What is more, she knew that Lady Westcliffe had only a limited number of places and liked to choose which ladies she aided herself. As she could not help every impoverished lady, she generally chose those who were in particularly delicate and unusual circumstances, and whose safety often depended on their whereabouts remaining a secret.

She felt a tug on her sleeve, and glancing down saw Emily regarding her. "Why can we not have two governesses?"

A small smile touched Anne's lips. She could already see several advantages to this arrangement and with very little extra cost to Captain Turner. It was not in her interests to suggest the wage he had proposed be divided between her and Miss Burdock, but forty pounds was still a reasonable income for a governess.

"Why not indeed," she murmured.

Nora's brow furrowed. "I'm not sure Captain Turner will like it, and it's not as if the girls need three of us to look after them."

Anne touched her arm. "Your position is safe, Nora. A nursery maid's duties are very different, whereas I am sure Miss Burdock's talents will complement mine."

Miss Burdock looked a little flustered. "Oh, but Mrs Huxley, surely Captain Turner must be consulted before—"

"Leave him to me," she said firmly. "He seems a sensible man, and I am sure I can show him all the advantages of such an arrangement."

Barbara began to pull Miss Burdock towards the carriage. The little lady suddenly laughed. "Wait, I must pick up my bag."

"I will do that," Anne said.

It was heavy, presumably because it contained everything that poor Miss Burdock owned. She marvelled that the lady had been able to carry it at all.

⁂

Edward nodded at the maid and introduced himself. "I am sorry to inconvenience you in this way, ma'am."

"'Tis no inconvenience if a trifle irregular," she said. "But if Mrs Huxley thinks it the right thing to do, then so it must be." She looked at the unkempt urchin who sat pale and silent beside him, saying sternly, "There's no need to look as if you're on your way to the gallows, but you'd do well to remember that you might well have been if not for Mrs Huxley's kindly intervention. You may repay her by mending your ways and setting your sisters a good example."

The boy nodded, rubbing at his reddened ear.

"You think highly of Mrs Huxley, I see," Edward said.

"I should think I do. She's as fine a lady as ever you'll meet, and yet she's no airs or graces, and not above helping those as everyone else has all but given up on."

It struck Edward that he knew very little about Mrs Huxley. Although there was nothing objectionable in her manner, she possessed a reserve that did not invite intrusive questions. He did not hold that against her; he was reserved himself. He knew the urge to press the maid for more information about Mrs Huxley's circumstances but controlled the impulse.

That she was a lady, Edward had no doubt; her manner, bearing, and quiet confidence all attested to it. That and the competence she had shown in handling the children, is why he had offered so high a salary. He assumed she was a widow, perhaps one who had not benefited from a generous jointure and had no relatives willing to take her in. Or perhaps she preferred to earn her living rather than be beholden to them. Either way, as long as she tamed his wards, he would be satisfied.

He glanced out of the window, realising they had entered a less salubrious part of town. The carriage trundled down narrow streets, and an unpleasant odour permeated the closed windows of the carriage. He had no idea where he was and it struck him as odd that Lady Westcliffe's footman had seemed to find the way with no difficulty, especially as Paul had given him but brief instructions which Edward had found incomprehensible. The carriage came to a halt by the last house in the street. The windows were boarded up and the brickwork crumbling. As he descended from the carriage a rat ran across his boot. He grimaced as the odour of human waste assailed his nostrils. He looked around, sensing unseen eyes peering from behind dark, dirty windows then glanced at the ragged urchin beside him.

"Lead on, Paul. The sooner we remove your sisters from this pestilent place, the better." He glanced up at Finn. "Have you a pistol to defend yourself if need be?"

The man grinned. "There's no need for you to worry about me, sir. There's no one hereabouts who will molest me, you may be sure."

Edward nodded, thinking that Lady Westcliffe kept some very odd servants. "Very well."

The boy led him through an overgrown patch of wasteland that ran along the side of the house. A rickety fence, partially concealed by scrubby plants and long grass marked the boundary of the back yard. Paul pushed aside a shrub revealing a gate hanging from its hinges. Beyond it a small, cobbled yard gave access to the back of the house. The back door had planks nailed across it.

"This way," Paul said, walking towards two barrels that rested against the wall. He laid one down and rolled it out of the way. Edward followed suit with the other, revealing a trap door. He frowned. "Do you mean to tell me you have left your young sisters alone in a dark damp cellar."

Paul shrugged. "It was the only safe place, at least it was before you rolled up in your fancy carriage."

Edward recognised the futility of pointing out that it was not his carriage, or that he could think of few less safe places to hide with his sisters. His scepticism must have shown on his face for Paul gave him a sly smile.

"No one will touch this house because it belongs to Ned Granger. He's a fearsome brute what everyone's afraid of, but he's in hiding 'cos the runners are after him."

Edward raised an eyebrow. "Were you not afraid he'd return and find you here?"

The boy shrugged. "He had a soft spot for me ma, so I reckon we'd have been safe enough."

"And would, no doubt, have had your feet set more firmly on the criminal path you somewhat inexpertly ventured onto this morning," Edward said dryly, leaning down and pulling open the door.

There came the sound of scurrying feet, and two faces peered up, the whites of their eyes standing out against the gloom. For a moment, Edward saw many more orbs, all regarding him with a mixture of resignation and despair. He squeezed his eyes shut and shook his head.

When he opened them, the girls had retreated into the darkness.

"Do not be afraid," he said quickly. "Paul is with me, and you are to go with him to a safe place where you will have enough food and a soft bed to sleep in."

They shuffled back towards the light. As there appeared to be no steps, he knelt and held out his hands. "Come."

When the younger girl whimpered, Paul knelt beside him. "It's alright, he could have handed me over to the constable, but he didn't, and there's a basket of food in the carriage."

These words had the desired effect, and the girls climbed onto a box and held up their arms. As he pulled them into the light, Edward saw their matted hair and emaciated frames. Good God! He had seen stray dogs who were better fed. Edward could only be glad that Mrs Huxley had taken matters into her own hands, for if he had handed the boy over, the girls would surely have starved. Both she and Miss Burdock had shown the compassion he had been looking for, and that he perhaps lacked. Young, unruly boys needed disciplining, but now he saw Paul's sisters, he could not blame him for his actions. They clung to their brother, shivering in rags that might once have been dresses.

"Come along," he said, leading the way out of the yard.

CHAPTER 7

Emily and Barbara were quiet in the carriage, the excitement of the day catching up with them. They slumped against Nora and soon fell asleep. Miss Burdock pulled some knitting from her bag and began to ply her needles. No one would guess that only a short while ago she had faced being poverty stricken and quite alone in the world.

"Miss Burdock," Anne said, "why did you leave before Captain Turner had made his decision when it appears you had nowhere to go?"

The woman looked up, a slight smile on her lips. "I knew you would get the position, my dear, and thought to save Captain Turner the unpleasant task of turning me down."

Miss Burdock had shown no sign of recognising her, but there was still something vaguely familiar about her face. It was entirely possible, of course, that she merely resembled someone Anne had briefly met. She glanced at Nora and seeing she had also closed her eyes, bent her head, and asked the question uppermost in her mind. "You told Nora that you suspected I needed the position more than you, but why would you say such a thing when you were in such desperate straits?"

Miss Burdock began once more to ply her needles. "You are, it would appear, also friendless as you have been reduced to accepting a post as governess. Thus far we are equally unfortunate." She glanced towards the sleeping children. "Not that having the opportunity of teaching Barbara and Emily is an unfortunate circumstance, of course. I am sure it will be rewarding, but it is not the path either of us would have taken in an ideal world. You were the better candidate for many reasons, not least because you still have time to improve your circumstances whereas I am considered past the age of being useful. I only secured my previous position because I was willing to accept little more than board and lodging. If one of us should be forced to the workhouse, it is better it should be me." She put down her knitting and placed a hand on Anne's arm. "I have always put my faith in the Lord, however, and he has never let me down. Something always turns up when I most need it, as happened today. How fortunate that poor boy tried to rob me."

Anne relaxed. It seemed that Miss Burdock's comment had nothing to do with Anne's particular circumstances. She laughed softly. "What a peculiar thing to say."

Miss Burdock smiled. "Do you think so? I meant only that his misguided actions revealed both his plight and mine, and now it would appear we are both saved, largely thanks to you, my dear."

Anne only hoped her words proved true. As the

journey wore on, her confidence in being able to convince Captain Turner of the merits of employing two governesses dwindled. She comforted herself with the thought that at the very least he might give Miss Burdock shelter until she could send a letter to Lady Westcliffe.

After the children had retired to bed with Nora in attendance, she left Miss Burdock in the bedchamber they were sharing, and returned to the private parlour Captain Turner had hired to await his arrival. She had not expected him to be more than an hour behind them and hoped that no ill had befallen him. She put another log on the fire, recalling his stern countenance. He looked like a man who could take care of himself, and besides, he had Finn to assist him.

Her breath hitched as she heard a firm tread in the corridor. She rose to her feet as it paused outside the door, her eyes darting to the mirror to check her hair was tidy. A waft of cooler air announced someone's entrance, and she turned. Captain Turner paused on the threshold. He looked weary, his frown marked. Her heart sank. This did not seem a propitious time to plead on Miss Burdock's behalf.

"Mrs Huxley? I did not expect you to still be up. I hope nothing is amiss?"

His words were clipped, edged with irritation and perhaps anxiety.

"The girls are well and abed, sir," she said, pleased that her voice held no quaver of uncertainty. "Please, come in and sit by the fire. I am sure you must be chilled."

He moved to the table and poured himself a glass of wine but remained standing.

"Did everything go well?" she asked. "You are later than I expected."

"Paul's sisters were retrieved without incident." He sighed. "They were in a worse case than Emily and Barbara when I found them. Thank you, Mrs Huxley, for providing a solution for them all." He rubbed his eyes. "Is there anything else?"

He was dismissing her, and for a moment she was tempted to allow him to. He might find it more difficult to refuse her proposal if Miss Burdock and the girls were present, but she could not bring herself to use such underhand tactics.

She folded her hands composedly before her, saying quietly, "I am afraid there is, Captain Turner. After you left, we discovered that poor Miss Burdock was both penniless and homeless."

He raised an eyebrow. "If that is the case, why on earth did she leave before I had informed her of my decision?"

She grasped the opportunity to sing Miss Burdock's praises. "She is an extraordinarily kind woman. She felt sure you would not offer her the position and wished to save you the unpleasant task of telling her so."

His frown deepened. "Well, she was correct, and unfortunate as her circumstances are, I am not at all clear as to why you felt you should stay up to inform me of them."

Anne swallowed. "Emily had an idea I thought had merit."

He laughed dryly. "Go on."

"She asked why she and Barbara could not have two governesses."

Her clasped fingers tightened as a hard glint entered his eyes. She had rushed her fence and braced herself for the consequences.

"Do you mean to tell me, Mrs Huxley, that in my absence, you decided to adopt my ward's idea? That Miss Burdock is here? That you have raised false hope in her breast, and forced me into the intolerable position of disappointing both her and my wards for a second time?"

When put like that, her actions did seem high-handed. "Must you disappoint them?"

He tossed off his drink and placed his glass on the table with such precision that she could tell he was carefully controlling his emotions.

"Perhaps not," he said, his voice dangerously soft. "She was their first choice, after all, and if you are so easily influenced by Emily, then I may as well employ Miss Burdock for the position. It seems, Mrs Huxley, that you have shot yourself in the foot. I employed you to manage the children, not me."

Something told her that this was her real offence. "Sir, I have no desire to manage you, but you were not there to consult, and I would have been heartless to abandon Miss Burdock when she had nowhere to go. If my actions have so prejudiced you against me that you wish to retract your offer of employment, then I will accept your decision. However, I took you for a man of reason, and I would ask that you hear why I thought Emily's idea had some merit."

His shoulders sagged, he refilled his glass, and walked towards her. "Very well. Please sit, Mrs Huxley. My curricle suffered a damaged wheel, hence my delay, and I will admit to being both cold and tired. I must warn you, however, that although I am comfortably situated, I am not fabulously wealthy, and there is much work to be done on my estate. However much Miss Burdock has my sympathy, hiring two governesses is an extravagance I really cannot justify."

She perched on the edge of a chair. "I think the children need more than education, Captain Turner. We spoke earlier of gaining their trust, something which Miss Burdock seems to have done easily."

"It is true they took to her immediately," he said wearily. "Her age precludes her from being in competition with the memory of their recently departed mother. For some reason, Barbara was not averse to Miss Burdock reminding her of her grandmother."

Anne nodded. "Perhaps because that loss is not quite so raw. I think the girls would benefit from such a figure in their lives. They need affection, and I believe Miss Burdock perfectly placed to offer it. She is also, of course, quite capable of teaching them; I am sure you noticed how fine her needlework is. I do believe, however, that she might struggle to provide the firm hand the children require." She gave a small smile. "I believe that we would complement each other very well, and I am quite happy for you to divide the wage you proposed equally between us. Thus, you and the children will benefit for very little extra cost to you." She cast her eyes down. "And although I do not mean to impugn your honour in any way, Captain Turner, I admit I would feel more comfortable with another lady of similar standing in the house."

There was an uncomfortably long silence, and she winced as Captain Turner stood abruptly. "I will consider your proposal, Mrs Huxley, and speak with you again in the morning. Goodnight."

He strode from the room on the words, leaving her to sink back into her chair, her legs not quite steady. She had angered him again. He had, however, said he would consider her proposal. That was something, at least.

~

Edward went to his room, kicking the door behind him and tugging irritably at his cravat. He flung it aside with a carelessness at variance with his character. He did not like to be manipulated; he had suffered enough devious machinations in his life and had hoped he had put an end to such tactics by becoming master of his own estate. Not only had it been borne upon him that he must, at least at first, rely on others to guide him in an enterprise that was completely alien to him, but now Mrs Huxley, had taken it upon herself to undermine his authority by all but hiring Miss Burdock. The audacity of the woman!

After striding about his room like a caged lion for several minutes, he threw himself in a chair and called upon the calm that had seen him through many dangerous engagements. A wry laugh escaped him. Whatever precarious situations he had found himself in, he had maintained a cool head and controlled the variables as best he could. His men had understood the risks a life at sea entailed, but even so, he had never forgotten, once in command, that he was in large measure responsible for them.

That said, he had never imagined when he had

promised his master's mate, Michael Proctor, that he would take care of his family, his daughters would become his wards. He owed his life to the man, and it had seemed the least he could do to give him peace as the light faded from his eyes. He had seen a younger version of himself in Proctor, and had hoped to help advance him in his career, as he had been helped. Together, they had completed the required papers to ensure that Mrs Proctor received a share of the man's wages each month, and he had not expected to find his family in such dire poverty, or that the girls were soon to be orphaned.

He lay his head back against the chair and sighed. He had noticed Mrs Huxley had flinched when he had stood so abruptly and was sorry for it. He was tired and irritable, and although he felt his annoyance at her interference in his affairs was warranted, he should have controlled himself better. That was at the heart of the problem, he realised. He did not feel in control. He was stumbling about like a blind man, and he did not like the sensation.

He had never been above listening to advice, however, and he had to admit her arguments had made sense. The girls would benefit from the kindness Miss Burdock seemed to possess in abundance, and considering the rumours that already swirled about him, her presence would also offer the much younger Mrs Huxley a measure of respectability. She had all but forced his hand, but her reasons were sound.

Rising, he crossed the room and bent to pick up his discarded neckcloth. He glanced at the ruined garment ruefully before folding it and placing it neatly in his valise. It seemed, like his, Mrs Huxley's life had taken an unexpected turn, but where he chafed against his new restraints, she accepted hers with calm and grace and appeared determined to make the best of it.

Well, so would he. He was captain of a different ship now and must learn to navigate uncharted waters, and he would do so with the determination that had seen him succeed in his former career. The dream of reaching the pinnacle of that career and attaining the rank of admiral had been taken from him, but he could still make a difference in the smaller world he was stepping into, and there would be some satisfaction in seeing his neglected estate prosper once more.

He slept surprisingly well. He habitually woke early, well before sunrise at this time of year, but the grey light filtering through his eyelids warned him that he had overslept. Not that it mattered. There was no night watch to relieve, no course to check, no logs to peruse, and no orders to be given.

His eyes snapped open as he recalled where he was and the small party under his protection, and automatically swivelled towards the window to gauge the weather. A blanket of pearlescent cloud stretched across the sky, too light to threaten rain, and no breath of wind sighed against his windowpanes. Good. He had no desire to drive his curricle through a quagmire of mud, nor be buffeted by a gale.

A wry smile touched his lips. He was getting soft. He had stood on his quarterdeck in all weathers, using the conditions to his advantage whenever possible, feeling great satisfaction when his ship had responded as if she were a living being eager to please. A dry laugh escaped him. Driving a curricle harnessed to actual living creatures was an entirely different proposition. He had not been bred to it, and they seemed to have minds of their own. Hence, his accident. He knew that the fault was his own, however. He should never have been so ambitious, but he had baulked at the thought of being shut up in a closed carriage with his wards for two days, the memory of their journey from Manchester still fresh in his mind. He sprang from the bed. It was just as well. There would be no room for him now.

He paused in the doorway of the parlour, pretending not to notice the anxious eyes cast his way, merely offering a brief bow and a greeting before taking his place at the table. Whether he was supposed to bow to the women he did not know, but it felt like the right thing to do. Whatever his present circumstances, the ladies were of better birth than him.

He felt rather awkward; he had not shared a meal with his wards since he had brought them into Sussex, and neither was he used to breaking his bread with refined ladies. He concentrated on his food, aware of the growing tension in the room. Out of the corner of his eye, he saw Barbara squirm and raised his eyes.

"Is there something you wish to say, Barbara?"

As the girl opened her mouth, Emily nudged her, hissing, "Remember what Miss Burdock said."

His eyes skimmed over Mrs Huxley, who appeared calm but had eaten very little, and moved on to Miss Burdock. She held a cake, and her eyes were closed as she savoured it, a small smile edging her lips. Of them all, she appeared the most unconcerned. "As it has reduced my charges to silence, I would be very interested to hear what it is you said, ma'am."

She gave a little start, her eyes opened, and she returned her cake to her plate. "Oh, just that, in my experience, gentlemen are often not at their best before breakfast, and it would be unwise of them to speak unless directly addressed."

His eyes returned to Barbara. Her large brown eyes held a mixture of anxiety and hope.

"Miss Burdock was quite correct, but as I have now addressed you, Barbara, you may speak."

Her words came out in a rush. "Can Miss Burdock be our governess too?"

"As she seems to be a good influence, I am prepared to hire her for a—"

He broke off as Barbara pushed back her chair, ran around the table, and threw her arms around as much of him as she could reach.

"Thank you, thank you, thank you."

Shock held him still for a moment, then he awkwardly patted her on the back, his eyes flying to Mrs Huxley for rescue. Hers had softened and seemed more blue than grey. Was that a hint of amusement he saw in them?

"We are all grateful that Captain Turner has made so favourable a decision," she said. "And although you thanked him very prettily, I do not believe gentlemen like being hugged at the breakfast table any more than they like being spoken to."

Barbara stepped back, her eyes clouding. "You won't change your mind?"

"No," he said, embarrassment making his voice harder than he had intended. He glanced at Emily, who was biting her lower lip, although whether she was attempting not to laugh or prevent herself from berating her sister for embracing the enemy he could not tell. "But I had not finished. Both Mrs Huxley and Miss Burdock will have three months to convince me of the suitability of this arrangement. That will, in part, depend on whether I see an improvement in the manners and education of you both."

CHAPTER 8

October was not perhaps the best time to view a garden; the summer blooms were long gone and unless it was very carefully managed, it could look untidy and reflect the dullness of the sky above. The grounds at Hayshott Hall appeared to have suffered a sad want of management. Whilst a more natural landscape was often embraced, and even an artificial wilderness sometimes incorporated into the overall scheme of a park, here nature had been allowed to reign supreme. The tangle of overgrown shrubs and neglected flowerbeds that occasionally peeped between the overlong grass were somewhat ameliorated by the fiery colour of the turning leaves of the many trees that bordered the drive and were scattered over the park.

Perhaps it was not fair to blame Captain Turner, who had only been in residence a bare few months and was more used to a seascape than a landscape. She was surprised he had not imposed more order on his surroundings, however. As they approached the house, Anne could see that some effort had been made to clear the area in front of it, at least.

Hayshott Hall was built of a pleasant dark honey coloured stone that was obscured in several places by ivy. Judging by its erratic appearance, Anne suspected this was by accident rather than design. It did not possess the symmetry that graced the elegant mansions of Mayfair or Lady Westcliffe's abode, but its rambling aspect had its own charm. She suspected it may have once been a farmhouse that had been added to over the years. There was no turning circle, and the carriage pulled up beside the house, next to a door which boasted a portico which seemed rather too grand for the building. To her left, an overgrown carriageway stretched away, disappearing into woodland. Presumably, at one time, that must have been the main approach to the house. A blur of movement in the fringe of trees caught her eye, and she saw a man raking the carriageway. She could not imagine why he should not start nearer the house and work backwards.

As they descended from the carriage, the door opened, and a rather sharp-faced woman appeared. Her features softened as Barbara jumped down from the carriage and raced towards her, Emily following more slowly.

"Mrs Thirsk, Mrs Thirsk," Barbara said, "we're back."

"We've been expecting you," the woman said. "Cook has just taken a batch of biscuits from the oven, and if you have been good, I am sure she will send some up to the nursery."

"We have been very good," Barbara said. "So good that we have two governesses."

Descending from the carriage behind Nora, Anne observed the woman's face register surprise, and if she was not mistaken, some perturbation. She turned to help Miss Burdock from the carriage.

As Nora disappeared into the house with the children, Mrs Thirsk came forwards.

"I am Mrs Thirsk, the housekeeper. I did not expect one, never mind two governesses to arrive today, and so I have no rooms ready."

Anne smiled. "I am sure that is something that can be easily remedied, Mrs Thirsk."

A curricle pulled up next to the carriage and Captain Turner jumped down and strode towards them, the gravel crunching to the rhythmic tread of his long stride.

"I apologise I was not here to make the introductions," he said. "I was delayed by a cart hogging the centre of the road."

Anne remembered the cart; they had passed it with ease a mile or so before they had reached the gates of Hayshott Hall. It appeared Captain Turner was not a confident driver, and considering his accident of the previous evening, perhaps not a competent whip either.

"I am sure we did not expect any such observance," Miss Burdock said with a kind smile. "However, you are just in time, sir, for we were about to introduce ourselves."

Captain Turner performed the office briskly. "As the yellow and green rooms have a sitting room between them, Mrs Thirsk, I think they would be the most suitable."

"As you wish," she said woodenly. "I'll show the

ladies to the schoolroom while their rooms are prepared, and I'll have some tea sent up with the biscuits."

"Very good," Captain Turner said. "I'll leave you to settle in, ladies. I have an appointment this afternoon."

With a brief bow, he strode away in the direction his groom had driven the curricle. They followed the housekeeper into a large, square entrance hall. Several doors led from it, one of which opened onto a long, narrow, inner hall, from which a staircase rose. A window halfway up allowed enough light for them to see the way and revealed a small courtyard, around which other wings had been built.

The schoolroom was at the back of the house. It was a large, pleasant room, with far-reaching views of rolling countryside dipping into a wooded valley. Anne's eyes scanned the shelves, noting the toys ranged there, and the few books. She frowned. They were far too advanced for the girls.

"Don't worry, my dear," Miss Burdock said, coming up beside her. "I brought several books with me that will be far more suitable."

"Ah," Anne said. "That is why your bag was so heavy."

A door at the far end of the room opened, and the girls, now relieved of their coats and bonnets, came in with Nora.

Anne smiled. "While we wait for the biscuits, why don't you show me your favourite toy?"

Barbara went to the doll's house and opened the front. "We mended most of the things as Captain Turner told us to."

"Shh," Emily hissed.

Anne glanced into the house, an eyebrow rising. It was an expensive gift, and the furniture exquisitely produced. The repairs were obvious and not entirely successful. As the girls had been asked to make them, and Emily appeared embarrassed, she could only assume that the damage had been done intentionally. She suspected Emily was the main culprit, and glancing sideways, she saw the girl's arms were crossed and her chin jutted stubbornly forward, but beneath the defiance in her eyes, there was a flicker of wariness. She clearly expected to be reprimanded.

Straightening, she said, "Well, accidents do happen, and perhaps we might acquire some glue from the estate carpenter to make the repairs a little more enduring."

At that moment, a maid appeared carrying a tray, and the pleasant smell of freshly made biscuits wafted across the room. A restraint that had been absent in the carriage seemed to possess the girls, and instead of running over to the table, they glanced at Anne uncertainly. It seemed unpleasant memories still lingered in the schoolroom.

"Let us sit and enjoy cook's offering before the biscuits go cold, shall we?"

Nora hung back, but Miss Burdock beckoned to her. "Come, Nora. There are enough for us all."

The nurse looked uncertain. "It's not fitting. None of the other governesses offered me such courtesy."

"We are not the other governesses," Anne said gently, looking from her to the children. "And as I believe you are to be present at our lessons, at least at first, it would be better that you take part in whatever we are doing rather than merely being an observer."

"Oh, yes," Miss Burdock agreed. "How very dull it would be to sit there like a statue."

Barbara giggled.

"I've my own duties to attend to," Nora said, startled. "The girls' clothes to keep in order."

Anne sensed that she was reluctant to display the limitations of her knowledge.

"Then you must, of course, bring your sewing with you. We will not begin any formal learning today, however. Once we have settled in, perhaps we might go for a walk. I am sure Emily and Barbara would like to stretch their legs after being confined in a carriage for several hours."

Mrs Thirsk came into the room. "If you would like to come this way, Mrs Huxley, Miss Burdock, I will show you to your rooms."

They rose from the table.

"We will be back in half an hour for that walk," Anne said.

She was surprised to discover their rooms were some way from the nursery in an adjacent wing, and though only of modest proportions, very comfortably appointed with fires burning in the grates. The sitting room between them was very cosy, with sofas set either side of a fire, a table under the window, and bookshelves set into two alcoves.

"But surely these are guest rooms," she said.

Mrs Thirsk nodded.

Anne sensed that the housekeeper did not fully approve, or perhaps she was concerned about the extra work they had brought her. It seemed Captain

Turner lived quite simply, for not only did there appear to be no butler or footman, she had seen very few maids since her arrival.

"I am impressed that the house does not reflect the neglect of the park, Mrs Thirsk, and I assume it is due to your good management."

"Indeed," Miss Burdock agreed. "Everything is as it should be, and how comfortable we shall be here."

If Mrs Thirsk did not preen at this praise of her housewifely accomplishments, her expression certainly softened, and she stood a little taller. "I've been housekeeper here for ten years and was left as caretaker of the house when the admiral died. I've done my best to ensure that each wing of the house was aired and cleaned regularly."

Anne further secured her good opinion by alleviating what was most likely her chief concern. She suspected that they were some distance from the kitchen, and without a full complement of staff, it would be troublesome to deliver meals to three separate areas of the house.

"As Emily and Barbara need to learn how to go on in company, if Miss Burdock agrees, I think we should eat in the nursery with the children for the time being."

"Oh, yes. That is a very good idea," Miss Burdock said. "How are the poor things to know how to go on if they have no example to follow?"

The housekeeper's mouth relaxed. "Very well. They eat at five o'clock."

"As we wish to take them for a walk, we had better unpack immediately," Anne said. "But perhaps tomorrow, you or a maid might show us the rest of the house, that way we will be in no danger of accidentally intruding into Captain Turner's domain and disturbing him."

As the housekeeper left the room, Miss Burdock said, "Would you mind very much if I did not accompany you on the walk, my dear? I am a little tired."

"Of course not," Anne said. "Perhaps you should lie down."

"Oh, no. I am not that tired, I assure you. I will unpack my things and then organise the schoolroom a little."

When she asked the children to show her their favourite spot in the garden, Nora said, "I am afraid we have not explored very far. The park is so overgrown, and when I took the girls in the woods, they got lost."

"How?"

"We were playing hide and seek," Nora said, not quite meeting Anne's eyes. "And after that, we played only in the courtyard."

Anne believed that the children had hidden and that Nora had sought them, but she suspected from their sudden interest in their boots, that the girls had run off without permission.

"Well, we shall keep the house in sight today so that none of us get lost. The view from the schoolroom window was very pretty, and I thought I saw a walled garden. Let us walk in that direction."

"Why have you brought a basket?" Barbara asked.

Anne smiled. "You never know what interesting things you might find on a walk; at the very least we may find some interesting things to draw."

As they rounded the house, the child saw a rabbit

and gave chase as it bounded away, Nora hurrying after her. Emily kept step with Anne, who was aware of her sideways glances, but kept her eyes on the view ahead. She sensed that the child wished to say something and thought it might be easier without her direct scrutiny.

"You know I broke the things in the doll's house, and you know we hid from Nora. Why did you pretend you didn't?" Emily suddenly blurted.

Anne was not surprised by the girl's insight. Twenty-four hours in her company had alerted her to her watchful, observant nature.

"These things happened before Miss Burdock and I arrived, and I am sure have already been dealt with. How unjust it would be to rake you over the coals a second time. We have all done things we regret, Emily, and that were not perhaps wise—"

"I didn't say I regret 'em," the girl said, kicking at a blade of grass.

"No, you did not. You have had a difficult time, and it is only natural that you might be angry sometimes, but I think you know what you did was wrong and do not need me to tell you so. No one can replace your mother or your father—"

"I hardly knew him," the girl muttered.

"That is a shame. Perhaps you should talk to Captain Turner about him. I am sure he would have many stories to tell."

"He don't want to talk to us. He never took any notice of us, not until I broke his gifts."

"Is that why you did it? Did you want Captain Turner to notice you?"

Emily shrugged. "Even our pa didn't want us, so why should he?"

Anne gently touched the child's shoulder. "I am sure you are mistaken. Your papa would not have asked him to take care of you if he had not worried about you."

The girl's lips trembled. "He abandoned us, Ma said so. He promised to send money, but we didn't get a penny after the last time he was home, and he promised to write to her, and no letters came. Ma once said he could burn in hell for all she cared, and maybe that's why he thought of us in the end, 'cos he was afeared."

Anne's heart ached for her. This intelligent child carried so much pain, had so many unanswered questions, and probably feared being abandoned again. She did not yet trust this change in her and her sister's fortunes.

"Whatever the case with your papa, Captain Turner cannot be blamed for his actions, you know," she said gently. "He is not, perhaps, the most approachable of men, but—"

The girl gave an unladylike snort. "I almost bust a gut when Barbara hugged him. He looked as if a cockroach had crawled up his arm."

Whilst Anne did not quite agree with the girl's perception of the event, she remembered the pleading look Captain Turner had sent her and her lips twitched. "This is all new to him, Emily. He has spent his life with men and boys and on the sea rather than the land. He has much to learn and is perhaps a little overwhelmed by all his new responsibilities. I think it was very sensible of him to allow you some say in who your new governess would be. You must at least give him credit for that."

"Barbara wanted Miss Burdock," Emily muttered. "But I wanted you."

Anne felt both touched and surprised by this revelation. "Then you both have what you wanted. Thank you, Emily, for your vote of confidence. I will remind you of it whenever you are displeased with me."

Her tone was grave, but perceptive Emily did not miss the twinkle in her eyes and offered her a small smile.

"I didn't want to learn with the others, and Barbara was too afraid, but I think it will be different now."

Anne held out her hand and after a moment, Emily took it. "Yes, I think it will. Come, let us catch up with the others."

The walled garden housed an untended orchard, and they spent a pleasant twenty minutes filling Anne's basket from the latest windfall.

"We shall take them to cook," Anne said. "I am sure she will be very pleased and most likely make several desserts with them. But I shall keep a few for us to draw."

"What's the point in drawing apples?" Emily asked. "Anyone can do that."

"Most people might be able to draw something resembling an apple," Anne allowed. "But could they capture the texture of the skin or the light illuminating a particular spot. Could they bring the picture so much to life that one could almost imagine taking a bite out of the fruit?"

"I still don't see the use," Emily grumbled.

"Apart from drawing and painting being considered ladylike accomplishments," Anne said with a smile, "I think you will find the practise will hone your observations skills even further, and that it is an enjoyable and relaxing occupation in itself."

"Ugh!" Barbara spat out a mouthful of apple. "It's horrid."

Anne laughed. "That is because that one is for cooking not eating."

As they left the orchard, a rhythmic pounding of hooves could be heard as two men approached on horseback.

Emily took a step closer to Anne, but Barbara caught sight of another rabbit and gave chase. Nora gave a shriek of alarm and ran after her as the child crossed the approaching riders' path. A young man with dark hair and piercing blue eyes pulled his horse sharply to the left, and an older man with a marked similarity, no doubt his older brother, pulled his to the right. Barbara gave a howl as she tripped and fell. The younger gentleman sprang from his horse and bent over her.

"Sir!" Nora protested as he began examining her leg.

He ignored her, and after a moment straightened, addressing his brother. "There's no broken bones that I can tell."

The older gentleman swung down from his horse, saying, "That is a relief indeed. Come, Miss Barbara, do not cry, you will frighten the rabbits that are hiding in the warren beneath us." He knelt and parted the long grass. "Look, you no doubt stepped in this rabbit hole."

As Barbara bit her lip and peered at it, he rose to his feet and bowed in Emily and Anne's direction.

"Good afternoon, Miss Emily. Would you do me the honour of introducing me to your companion?"

The girl smiled. "This is my governess, Mrs Huxley."

He lifted his hat. "I am pleased to make your acquaintance, Mrs Huxley. I am Mr Thomas Townsend, and this is my brother, Mr Rufus Townsend. We are neighbours of Captain Turner. Make your bow, Rufus."

The young man's eyes were fixed on Barbara, who was inspecting the rabbit hole closely, but he gave an absent bow.

"We have another governess called Miss Burdock," Barbara said, reaching her arm into the hole against her nurse's advice.

"What? Two governesses?" Mr Thomas Townsend said in mock horror. "I do not know if you are to be congratulated or pitied."

Emily grinned, and his words had so much playful lightness in them that Anne also smiled.

"Only time will tell, Mr Townsend." Her gaze shifted to Barbara. "Remove your arm from the hole, Barbara. Not only are you dirtying your dress, but you will not like it if your fingers are bitten."

"The rabbits are unlikely to bite her," Rufus said unhelpfully. "They are timid creatures."

"There is something in here," the child said, twisting onto her side to lengthen her reach.

"Barbara," Anne repeated more firmly. "I expect you to do what you are told."

"I've got it," the child said, pulling her arm out.

She opened her hand, revealing a clod of earth. "It's in here."

"Thomas, we will be late," Rufus said, a small frown furrowing his brow.

"You go on," his brother said. "I know you hate to be late. I will follow in a moment when I have discovered what treasure Miss Barbara has discovered."

Rufus shuffled from foot to foot. "But you are to make the introduction."

"Very well, I will be but a moment."

The child, still kneeling by the hole, began to roughly crumble the soil. Mr Townsend bent over her, a sudden gleam in his eye as a rounded edge began to emerge. He took her hand, saying gently, "You must be careful not to damage whatever you have found. Let me help you."

He very gently brushed the soil with his finger until the object was revealed. A delighted smile curved his lips. "It is a Roman coin." He rubbed his finger over it. "A silver denarius. Wait, there is another." He repeated the process, uncovering a second coin. "You have indeed found treasure, Barbara. And what is this?" As he gently brushed at the remaining earth in her hand, he picked out what looked like a small brown stone, roughly square in shape, although its edges were not quite straight. This seemed to excite him most of all. "It is a mosaic tile," he breathed. "And where there is one, there will be more."

"What is a mosaic tile?" Emily asked, coming forward to regard the object. 'It doesn't look like much."

Mr Townsend glanced at Anne, his lips quirking into a rueful grin. "You are in an enviable position, ma'am. Your history lessons must take precedence, I feel. But I will leave you to explain the significance of this find to your charges. We are late for an appointment, and I must see Captain Turner immediately. I wish for permission to dig up his park." He put his hand in his pocket and pulled out a gleaming, shiny sovereign. "Would you exchange your treasure for this, Miss Barbara?"

The girl looked doubtful, but her sister, her eyes growing round at the offered bounty, nudged her. "Take it."

Reluctantly she did, and Mr Townsend turned on his heel, went to his horse, and bid them goodbye. Barbara gave the coin to her sister and bent once more to the rabbit hole.

"Perhaps I can find some more, and Mr Townsend will give us another gold coin."

Anne bent, and taking the girl's arm, gently pulled her to her feet. Barbara staggered and let out an anguished cry.

Anne put an arm about her. "You may not have broken any bone, but it appears you have sprained your ankle, my dear." She glanced at the disappearing horses. "It is a pity we did not realise it earlier, for Mr Townsend might have taken you up on his horse."

"I can carry her, ma'am," Nora said, lifting the girl into her arms.

"We shall take it in turns," Anne said. "I think you will find even a burden as slight as Barbara will soon grow heavy."

CHAPTER 9

Edward glanced at the clock, a slight frown between his brows. He liked punctuality, and his visitors were already ten minutes late. He strolled to the window, his shoulders relaxing as he saw two horsemen heading towards the stables. His lips twisted wryly. The rules of the countryside were no doubt vastly different from those at sea. The state of watchful alertness that would warn of an enemy ship on the horizon, the mixed anxiety and excitement of a possible prize that had necessitated each and every one of his crew being precisely where they needed to be in good time, had no place here. A dozen things may have delayed the Townsend brothers. Perhaps they had stopped to pass the time of day with an acquaintance or paused to survey a delightful prospect.

He winced, his eyes moving over the meadow that by rights should be his lawn. It would take an army of gardeners to impose any sort of order on his land, an expense he was unwilling to commit to until he knew what income he might expect once his farms and cottages were tenanted and productive once more. He had searched in vain for the account books that might shed some light on the situation. He should have looked into it before now, should not have spent his first weeks licking his wounds, railing futilely against an unjust world. He had single handedly repaired the farmhouses, it was true, the physical labour helping his resentful mind to quieten, but he was still guilty of gross inefficiency.

His frown grew deeper and he squinted, a small group of figures catching his attention. Strolling back to his desk, he grabbed his eyeglass and returned to the window. It was the children with their nurse and Mrs Huxley. For some reason, Nora was carrying Barbara. As he watched, Mrs Huxley bent forward and received the child on her back, tucking her arms under the girl's legs as Barbara wrapped hers about her neck. Putting his eyeglass down on the window seat, he turned and walked swiftly from the room, calling for the housekeeper. He was almost at the front door when she appeared, and barely hesitating, called over his shoulder as he opened it.

"I fear there may have been some accident, Mrs Thirsk. Mr Thomas Townsend and his brother Mr Rufus Townsend will be with us momentarily. Please see to the comfort of my visitors whilst I see what is amiss."

Anxiety gnawed in his gut. His responsibility for the two girls weighed heavily on him. It became clearer every day that he could not merely provide them with shelter, leave them in the hands of females and be done with them. The benevolence he had had for their father had led him into a philanthropic action, and he had not thought much beyond that. He had certainly not expected them to be such infernal nuisances, rebelling against his generosity and somehow persuading him to negotiate with them. But in doing so, something had shifted between them. Not only had they forced him to acknowledge they possessed a vulnerability that demanded a greater care than he had fathomed, that he had added to their pain, however unintentionally, rather than diminished it, but they had somehow touched him in the process.

He was not a sentimental man; he had never had the luxury. The mistrust and defiance of Emily struck a chord, for he recognised those traits in his younger self. In his present self too if he were honest. Barbara was younger and less hardened than her sister, and when she had hurled herself at him in gratitude, completely throwing him off guard, beneath his embarrassment he had been aware of a feeling he could not quite name. It had felt like weakness, but that did not adequately describe it either.

He was aware of the same feeling now. He did not like to think of her in distress, and the feeling only grew when he saw the dried streak of tears that had left a trail down her muddy right cheek.

"Well, Mrs Huxley," he said sternly, as he came up to them. "Can it be that on your first day at Hayshott, you have allowed my ward to become injured?"

He knew his words were unjust, but they were out of his mouth before he could stop them. She regarded him coolly.

"It is indeed an unfortunate circumstance, Captain Turner. Barbara stepped in a rabbit hole; an event neither of us could have foreseen as it was quite hidden by the overlong grass." She regarded him steadily for a moment before turning her head and addressing Nora. "Perhaps you would take the apples to cook and bring some cold water and bandages to the schoolroom. I believe it is only a sprain, or Barbara would be in much more pain."

It struck Edward that she spoke with the surety of someone who was used to commanding a household. Well, she would not command his beyond the schoolroom.

"Don't be cross," Barbara said, opening her palm to reveal a gold sovereign. "I found treasure and Mr Townsend gave me this for it."

He frowned. "Treasure?"

"Some coins that Mrs Huxley says are very old and were left here by the Romans," Emily elucidated. "And a funny little stone that came from a mosaic, which she says was no doubt pretty." Her tone suggested she was not convinced by this. "And it is not fair that you should blame Mrs Huxley. My sister saw a rabbit and chased after it. As we've only seen them hanging up outside the butcher's shop, you can't blame her neither."

"Thank you, Emily, but the word you are looking for is either," Anne said, "and you should not talk to Captain Turner in that manner." Her admonition was lightly delivered, her words lacking any sting. "Now, if you would excuse us, sir, I will see to Barbara's ankle. I would like to remove her boot before any swelling occurs."

He saw a bead of sweat on her brow and stepped behind her. "I will take the child."

He cradled Barbara in his arms and spoke quite kindly to her. "Mr Townsend has brought his brother to see me so that we may talk about him managing my estate, but until the long grass has been cut, I would ask that you do not run through it."

The child nodded.

"Good." He smiled. "I imagine Mr Townsend was quite delighted with your finds."

"He wants to dig up your park," Emily said, a mischievous grin on her lips.

He grimaced. "Then he will be disappointed. The last thing we need is more chaos."

As they entered the schoolroom, Miss Burdock rose from a sofa by the window.

"Oh, here you are at last. I saw that there had been some accident. Lay her down here, if you please, Captain Turner. How very kind it was of you to carry poor Barbara upstairs. Yes, very kind indeed, although I am sure she was light as a feather to such a strong man as you. That's the way, very nicely done. Now, if you would step aside, I shall see what is amiss. I believe you have some visitors, so you must not feel as if you should stay. I am sure it is only a trifle."

However politely and inoffensively delivered, he felt as if he had been dismissed.

"I hurt my ankle, Miss Burdock," Barbara said.

"Did you, my dear? It is so easy to turn an ankle, is it not? So tiresome for you but I have just the thing to make you feel better." She held up a jar. "As soon as I saw Mrs Huxley was carrying you, I fetched some of my special salve from my room, which is guaranteed to soothe any hurt. I will take your boots off at once and make you more comfortable."

Feeling awkward and out of place, he turned to leave so abruptly he brushed against Mrs Huxley. She stepped quickly out of his way, her expression blank but her shoulders rigid. He suddenly felt ashamed of his prior churlishness.

"Forgive me, Mrs Huxley, if I appeared to apportion blame for what was no doubt an unavoidable accident."

She inclined her head. "Think nothing of it, sir. You were no doubt worried about your ward."

Her tone was colourless, offering him no inkling of her true feelings. He suddenly found her aloofness as irritating as Miss Burdock's gentle twittering.

"If you find Barbara's injury worse than you suspect, please do not hesitate to inform me of it, and I will send for the doctor."

He glanced up as Nora came into the room followed closely by Mr Townsend. He somehow seemed to fill it.

"Thomas! He won't let you dig up the lawn."

Emily uttered this in a tone that suggested a great injustice. The man barely missed a step, but smiled, bowed, and greeted Edward before turning to the girl. "Miss Emily, you are clearly not acquainted with my powers of persuasion." He made a sweeping gesture with his arm. "I must offer my humble apologies to you all. If I had understood that Miss Barbara was injured, I would have taken her up on my horse." He strolled over to her. "Can you forgive me?"

She giggled and nodded; even Mrs Huxley smiled.

"You are magnanimous indeed, young lady." He cocked his head and regarded Miss Burdock. "Ah, you must be the infamous second governess."

She blinked up at him. "I have never been infamous in my life, sir. Not that I can claim any great virtue in that circumstance as in truth I have never been given the opportunity to be." She sighed, adding on a note of regret. "And now it is too late."

"Never!" he protested. "It is never too late for anything, Miss Burdock."

"What does infamous mean?" Emily asked, regarding him with interest.

He laughed in his easy way. "While I admire your enquiring mind, imp, you are far too young to be offered an explanation."

Having had enough of this errant nonsense, Edward said brusquely, "I would never employ a governess who was infamous, Mr Townsend. Now, come. Let us leave the ladies to their duties."

∽

Anne followed them to the door and closed it behind them, her heart beating uncomfortably fast. Whether from the strange jolt she had experienced as Captain Turner had brushed against her, his parting comment, or his sorry excuse for an apology, she was unsure. Appeared to apportion blame, indeed, the words delivered with the awkward abruptness she was coming to expect from her employer. She nibbled her bottom lip. *I would never employ a governess who was infamous.* Would he consider her to be if he discovered her true circumstances? Should she go to him later and lay them before him? Lady Westcliffe had advised her against it.

Wait, at least until you have proven yourself in your new

position and hopefully become an invaluable member of his household. As he has proven such a loyal friend to a member of his crew, it is entirely possible he may reward your good work by overlooking your unfortunate situation. He has a history of supporting the underdog, after all. It is another reason I thought this might be the very post for you.

Whilst she could see the good sense inherent in Lady Westcliffe's words, her deception weighed on her conscience. He had not questioned her directly on her circumstances and so she could not be accused of lying to him directly, but that was mere semantics, especially now he had made his feelings clear. She glanced down as she felt a gentle tug on her sleeve and met the two enquiring brown eyes trained on her.

"Will you tell me what infamous means, Mrs Huxley?"

"Perhaps, one day," she said, hoping that day would be far in the future. "But only when it is necessary for you to know. There are many other words you must learn to read and write first."

Emily frowned but then nodded. "Will we start learning them tomorrow?"

"Indeed, we will. And perhaps I will be able to find a history book about the Romans in Captain Turner's library so that I may show you an illustration of a mosaic. Then you might understand why Mr Townsend is so excited about the prospect of discovering one."

"I like him," Emily said. "He said I might call him Thomas, his eyes smile, and I think he is kind. I wish he was our guardian, then I could help him dig up the lawn."

Anne smiled. "Perhaps Captain Turner will give

him permission, after all, in which case, he might allow you to watch, at least."

Emily's expression conveyed her scepticism at this likelihood.

"A lady should never roll her eyes, my dear, and you should know that kindness comes in many forms. Although Captain Turner may not have the ease of manner of Mr Townsend, his actions speak for him. He has been very generous to you and your sister. Also, I wish you will consider this. As Mr Townsend has no responsibility for you, he has the luxury of indulging you in a way that Captain Turner does not. He must bear the stricter role, for others will judge not only you but also him by how well or ill you behave. Do you understand?"

"I think so," the child said slowly. "Ma used to box my ears if I didn't do my chores 'cos she said what would people think if they found us living in a pigsty." Her shoulders slumped. "But only Mr Rogers called to collect the rent. He smiled with his mouth but not his eyes, and then he threw us out when Ma became too ill to work."

"And Captain Turner took you in, and if you learn to behave like a lady and learn your lessons well, he will not regret his decision. He will help ensure you and your sister have a far better future than your mama could ever have imagined. I think that would have made her very happy, don't you?"

Emily nodded but then scowled, and uttered words she had no doubt heard her mother say. "I don't want a good for nothing, feckless husband though."

"Certainly, you do not," Anne agreed wholeheartedly.

The girl's expression lightened. "P'raps I could become a governess like you."

"Perhaps, if you apply yourself to your lessons, you might," she agreed.

"Come, Miss Emily," Nora said. "You must wash before dinner."

As the girl slipped away, Anne's brow furrowed. Perhaps she would follow Lady Westcliffe's advice. Emily appeared to be responding to her already, and there really was very little likelihood of him discovering her circumstances by chance.

CHAPTER 10

Edward watched the brothers ride away, a perplexed expression in his eyes. How on earth had Townsend managed to turn all his arguments against his proposed excavation on their head? He had listened patiently, nodding as if he was in complete agreement, then leant forward in his chair, his eyes alight with enthusiasm and launched into an impassioned speech.

"Yes, yes, of course it would be a little chaotic, at first, but if it is to be done at all, it may as well be before you have put everything in order. It will cost you little, for I will bring some of my own men for the rough work and I will carry out the close work. If, of course, we find anything. It may be that there is nothing else to discover, in which case, everything will be returned to a better state than we found it."

Edward had looked at his brother. "Surely you cannot think it a good idea?"

The young man had shrugged, saying bluntly, "Your land is in such disarray that a small section of the park being dug up can make little difference. It will also encourage the rabbits to move elsewhere, although what you really need to do is cull them. If you do not wish to employ a gamekeeper just yet, you could set aside a week, perhaps, and let it be known that anyone may shoot them for that time. They need not come into the park; there are plenty in the woods. It would certainly raise your stock in the neighbourhood as there are many families in need of food."

And so he had capitulated, and then agreed to ride over the estate the following day with Rufus so that he might explain what needed to be done to the farmland to make it ready for incoming tenants. Tenants, he had assured him, he could find.

"There's plenty of smallholders hereabouts with sons who have been born and bred to the work but need their own farms. If you are willing to take them on for less than the going rate whilst they get up and running, they will no doubt help with the fencing, clearing the ditches, and so forth."

He had then asked Edward a series of basic questions he had been unable to answer. The young man had stared at him in blank astonishment for a few moments, and Edward had been grateful when his brother intervened to relieve his embarrassment.

"You can't expect a navy man who was not raised on the land to know aught about it, Rufus. Why else would Captain Turner need you?"

"But surely you would like to learn?" he had said. "Even Thomas knows a thing or two about the land, although he leaves it all to me."

In his defence, Edward had picked up the heavy tome on farming that lay on his desk. "I would, but I must admit I do not understand much of what is written in here."

The boy had waved a dismissive hand. "I wouldn't waste your time. That book is out of date. Have you read Mr Tilbury's ledgers?"

"Mr Tilbury?" he had asked.

It appeared that Mr Tilbury had lived in the nearby village of Hayshott and had been the admiral's bailiff.

"He lived in Rose Cottage, but it has been locked up since the old curmudgeon died not long after the admiral. It is in a sorry state of repair; the thatch all green and rotting in places, but if you have not discovered them, perhaps the ledgers are there. We will visit it in the morning."

"Rose Cottage? I have not heard of it."

"I don't know how that may be, but it is certainly part of the estate."

This had been news to him. The deeds to the cottage had certainly not been amongst the other documents he had perused.

All in all, he was feeling woefully inadequate, but he could not deny that he felt a stirring of excitement. He was not by nature an idle man, and the prospect of finally getting to grips with his inheritance and being engaged in meaningful work pleased him. He had known intimately and understood every job on his ship, and he was determined that he would come to learn those required for the smooth running of his estate if it took him years.

Glancing at the clock, he realised it was time to change for dinner. It seemed a pointless exercise when he would dine alone, but his clothes still bore the traces of dust kicked up by his curricle and now he had leisure to be, he was fastidious in his appearance. He sighed. Whilst never a gregarious man, he had enjoyed inviting one of his lieutenants or the ship's surgeon to dinner to discuss various matters and stay abreast of the morale of his crew or any problems brewing. His own company was beginning to pall on him.

Suddenly restless, he took the stairs two at a time but paused at their head. On impulse, he turned his steps towards the nursery wing. Mrs Huxley had not requested that the doctor be sent for, but then she might be one of those managing women who liked to think she knew everything. He would satisfy himself that Barbara was more comfortable before commencing his evening.

The door to the schoolroom was open, and he paused on the threshold as he saw the domestic scene before him. Barbara sat on a sofa, her foot now bandaged and raised up on a cushion whilst Miss Burdock fed her. A small frown tugged at his brow as he realised Nora was nowhere in sight.

His eyes turned to the table where Mrs Huxley dined with Emily. As he watched, she turned to the child.

"A lady does not shovel her food in her mouth as if it might be her last meal, Emily. She takes a small morsel on her fork like this."

She spoke in her usual calm manner, no hint of disapprobation in her words, and smiled encouragingly as Emily watched her keenly, nodded, and copied her.

"Very good," she said, and then chuckled as Emily

bent her head low as if she feared the slice of chicken would fall from the implement before it reached her mouth. He liked the sound. It was low and rich.

"Let us try again," she said, "but this time you must raise your fork to your mouth like this, all the while keeping your back straight and your elbows off the table."

The girl did her best, but just before her fork reached her mouth her fears were realised, and the chicken fell onto her lap. She scowled and the fork clattered onto her plate as she dropped it.

"It's too hard," she said sulkily, picking up the errant morsel with her fingers and bringing it to her mouth, her defiant eyes fixed on the governess.

"I am sure it feels strange," Mrs Huxley said gently. "But as you have a napkin to protect your dress, it is of no importance."

When Emily made no move to pick up her fork, Mrs Huxley laid down her own.

"I did not think you the girl to give up so easily, Emily, merely because something is a little difficult. I thought you more resilient."

The child tilted her head, her natural curiosity overcoming her sulks. "What does that mean?"

"It means to be strong and brave even when things are difficult. To not allow your misfortune to make you give up. You have shown such fortitude after losing your mama, and I am sure attempted to protect your sister as far as you were able."

"I have always looked out for Barbara," she mumbled.

"And you are to be admired for that, but if you wish to continue to protect Barbara from future ridicule, you must set her a good example. If she sees you are unwilling to at least try and improve yourself, you will put her in a very difficult position. She will wish to please both Miss Burdock and me, I suspect, for it is her nature, but she will not like to displease you. I am sure that the last thing you wish to do is make her unhappy."

The girl sighed and reached for her fork.

Mrs Huxley nodded encouragingly. "Very good, let us try again. Like this."

With a frown of concentration, Emily tried again, this time succeeding.

Edward could only admire Mrs Huxley's deft way of handling his truculent ward. She neither tried to browbeat her nor make her feel stupid, but spoke to her reasonably, in terms she could understand, making her see the utility of her request. Unwilling to undermine her efforts, he decided to withdraw quietly before they became aware of his presence, but Barbara spotted him before he could do so.

"Captain Turner! I am much better now."

For some reason, his eyes darted towards Mrs Huxley. She had lifted one eyebrow, and he thought he saw surprise in her eyes. He felt a spurt of irritation. He had every right to be there. No one had a better.

"I am pleased to hear it, Barbara. I wished to reassure myself of it before I dined."

"How very kind of you," Miss Burdock said. "She will need to keep her weight off her foot for a day or two, and you may be sure I will ensure she does."

"Thank you," he said, his embarrassment at being caught hovering in the doorway making him brusque. "I did not expect you and Mrs Huxley to dine with the children; it is why I gave you a sitting room. You are entitled to some time of your own. Nora is quite capable of supervising them."

"But surely Nora is also entitled to some time of her own," Mrs Huxley said. "And whilst you insist she be present at lessons, she will have very little of it. Besides, with so little help, we would not give Mrs Thirsk the extra work of carrying meals all over the house, nor cause you the extra expense of hiring more servants than you can easily afford."

He felt again the sting of his inadequacy. He had not even thought of the inconvenience he might have caused the housekeeper by his arrangements.

Although there was no overt criticism in her words, her cool tone grated, and he thought he saw a glimmer of reproach in her eyes. She dropped them so swiftly, her hands settling in her lap, that he could not be certain of it, however. Both Emily's gaze and words left him in no doubt of her feelings.

"Why shouldn't Miss Burdock and Mrs Huxley eat with us?" she muttered. "We ate with our ma at home."

As he had eaten with his father. But it was different in the homes of the gentry, wasn't it? He stiffened at the thought. Although both his status as a commander and his inheriting a landed estate raised him to that level, he had no intention of adopting the superior stance those born into privilege often adopted. Some of those born into privilege, he corrected himself. Townsend's easy manner with both him and the children illustrated he could not allow his experience of such men to cloud his judgement and reminded him that he must judge each individual on their merits, including those before him now.

His knowledge of genteel women and young girls was barely more extensive than his understanding of land management, and there was only one way to remedy it. He must get to know them. His shoulders tensed at the thought, but he was forced to admit it might be as beneficial to him as to anyone else. Unless he wished to live as if he were cast away on an island, he must eventually begin to mingle with other families in the neighbourhood beyond the Townsends, and his society manners were rough and unpolished.

He had excused himself from as many social engagements when in port as his ingenuity had allowed. When it had failed and he had been forced to attend an event, he had found it an excruciating experience. Word of his exploits at sea had often preceded him, but the interested sparkle in the flashing eyes of both single and married ladies had quickly turned to disappointment, pity, or derision when they discovered he possessed neither clever repartee nor the talent of having words of flattery trip from his tongue as many of the other officers did. Of course, these imperfections might have been overlooked if he had come from a family of standing, or if the rife rumours about the fortune he had acquired through prizes had not been wildly exaggerated. *Sophia*. He ruthlessly banished the name, unwilling to open a wound that still stung.

"And Mrs Huxley is teaching me table manners," Emily continued defiantly.

He gave an abrupt nod. The family he had adopted had no better pedigree than he had, but he was as stubborn as Emily and determined he would raise them up.

"I am pleased to hear it. When you have mastered them sufficiently, you shall all eat with me." His eyes turned to Mrs Huxley, whose grey-blue eyes held neither the surprise nor approval he had hoped for, but the blank expression that increasingly irked him. "That way, Mrs Thirsk will be put to even less trouble, and I may monitor your progress."

He turned abruptly but had barely put a foot outside the door when Barbara's voice drifted to him.

"Captain Turner. May I look for more treasure when I am well? If Thomas will pay me for it, I can give you money for our keep."

His heart stuttered for a moment and the feeling of weakness came over him again.

"No," he almost barked.

He winced as the sound of a stifled sob reached his ears. He deserved to be flogged. Turning, he forced a cough and pretended not to see the gentle reproach in Miss Burdock's eyes.

"Forgive me, Barbara, I did not mean to sound so harsh. There was something caught in my throat. It was kind of you to think of such a thing, but you must keep your sovereign. Mr Townsend will be finding his own treasure from now on, but I am sure he will show you his finds, if, indeed, there are any to be found."

∼

"Close your mouth, Emily," Anne said mildly. "It is only natural that you are surprised, but that is not the way a lady shows it."

"How should she show it, then?"

A faint smile twitched at Anne's lips. "If she must show it at all, perhaps she might allow her hand to flutter to her chest and say, 'oh, my,' or 'goodness me' in fainting tones, like this."

Emily and Barbara giggled at her demonstration, and then both copied her before falling into squeals of laughter.

"Just so," Anne said. "Your mimicry was excellent, and so we shall make being a lady a game. You must pretend you are acting, and then one day, you will find it will come quite naturally." She rose from the table. "It has been a long day, and I shall leave you to the care of Nora. Get a good night's sleep, both of you, for tomorrow you shall start your lessons." She glanced at Miss Burdock and raised an eyebrow.

That lady pointed to the shelves, which now bore several more books. "I will be along presently, my dear. I thought I might read the children a bedtime story. I think *The History of Little Goody Two-Shoes* might be appropriate."

Anne chuckled. "How true, but do not be too long, Miss Burdock, for you too need your rest."

In truth, she was glad of a few minutes alone. She had been as surprised as Emily at Mr Turner's parting comments. Whatever she had said to the contrary, she really had not expected him to allow Mr Townsend to have his way, but it appeared that gentleman was as persuasive as he had boasted. As for inviting them all to dine at his table, that had truly startled her.

She had just begun to think that she and Miss Burdock might be truly content at Hayshott Hall, had envisioned them being left very much to their own devices, but that comfortable vision had already begun to fray. *That way, Mrs Thirsk will be put to even less trouble, and I may monitor your progress.* He had been speaking to Emily, but she felt sure his words had been directed at her as if she was the one who required monitoring. Did he mistrust her? Had she revealed by some word or gesture her alarm at his earlier words? *I would never employ a governess who was infamous, Mr Townsend.*

She entered her sitting room and went to sit by the fire, willing her disquiet to abate. She was surely imagining things. She had become very adept at hiding her feelings, and Mr Turner did not strike her as the most sensitive of men. He unsettled her, however, although she could not find an adequate reason for her unease. She nibbled at her lower lip. Perhaps it was because when those stormy grey eyes settled upon her, she felt almost transparent, and she much preferred to feel invisible.

She glanced up as the housekeeper came in with a tea tray.

"Oh, Mrs Thirsk, I would not have put you to so much trouble. When I am better acquainted with the house, I will come to the kitchen and fetch it myself."

The housekeeper set the tray down on a convenient table. "You will do no such thing, Mrs Huxley. Nora has told me how the children are already beginning to mind you and Miss Burdock and how you achieve it without ever raising your voice or being unkind, and I am heartily glad of it. Those girls have been left to the mercy of tartars who should never have been allowed within a hairsbreadth of a child." She straightened and set her hands on her narrow hips. "I'm not saying they're angels for I know they are not, but what do you expect when they have been plucked from the only life they knew, however unfortunate, and plonked down amongst a parcel of strangers? After losing their mother too, poor lambs."

"What, indeed, Mrs Thirsk?" Anne said, reflecting that most of the housekeepers she had been acquainted with would have turned up their noses at such undistinguished infants.

As Mrs Thirsk bustled out, Anne frowned at the closing door. What was she about thinking only of herself? Mr Turner was still very much a stranger to the children, and he must not remain so. He had shown some consideration for their feelings when he had allowed them some say in their governess – although he may have been motivated as much by desperation as any regard for their opinion – but she knew only too well how that was unlikely to continue if he remained a distant figure and they existed only as another of his responsibilities. No, it was far better that he develop some affection for them.

She suspected that he was already a little susceptible to Barbara's innocent charm, but Emily also needed to be seen, to be understood, and perhaps above all, to find some answers about her father. Absently, she stirred the tea in the pot. She would do everything in her power to foster their relationship, and if that meant she must be more frequently in his presence than was comfortable to her, so be it.

CHAPTER 11

Mrs Thirsk dutifully showed Anne and Miss Burdock over the house early the following morning.

"You've no need to worry about disturbing Captain Turner," she said. "He had an early breakfast and has already gone out with Master Rufus to look over the estate."

None of the wings of the house were overly large, and neither were they particularly grand. They lacked a feminine touch, perhaps, but on the whole, it was an unpretentious, rather pleasing residence that could comfortably house half a dozen visitors even with herself and Miss Burdock having been given two of the guest chambers.

The main rooms on the ground floor were larger, and the drawing room very pretty although the wallpaper was a little faded, probably due to the large windows facing south. Mrs Thirsk observed the direction of Anne's gaze.

"The admiral wouldn't have the shutters closed," she said, a little defensively. "He remodelled the drawing room and library. He had this room decorated to his wife's taste, and after she died, he said he could still feel her presence in here, and that she loved the sun flooding the room. I closed them up after he died, and it wasn't until Mr Turner came that I opened them once more."

"It is a very pleasant room," Miss Burdock said. "Is that a pianoforte I see in the corner?"

"Mrs Tewk used to love playing," she said. "It is why the admiral had his library close by, so that he could leave the door ajar and hear her play."

Miss Burdock sighed. "He must have loved her very much."

"That he did," she said. "She wasn't a beauty and was a poverty-stricken spinster when he met her. But she was an intelligent, lively woman who loved entertaining, and Admiral Tewk liked nothing more than to see her happy. She dearly wanted a child; they both did, but it never happened, and I suspect that filling the house with people distracted her from the lack." She shook her head. "It was a tragedy, for she was much younger than him, barely three and thirty when the influenza carried her off, and he was never the same. He went into a slow but steady decline, although he lingered for three years before the good Lord took him." She sighed. "He barely glanced out of a window or left the house, nor would he have visitors. It was as if he wanted to shut himself up with the memories of his lady. The only glimpse he had of the world outside was through the newspapers. He insisted the house be kept in order mind and everything be kept just as it was before she died."

"It is a very affecting tale," Anne said, although she could not help but feel the story a little mawkish. "Although it is a shame that his lands and tenants suffered from his despair."

Miss Burdock put a handkerchief to her eyes, clearly possessing enough sensibility for them both.

"Oh, but Mrs Huxley, you must make allowances. True love is such a rare thing that one cannot underestimate the wound the heart must suffer when it is so abruptly lost."

It seemed Mrs Thirsk leant more towards Anne's view. "Well, I do not deny that his wound was deep, but to leave everything to Mr Tilbury was a mistake. He was a good enough man in his way when directed by the admiral, but he made a sad mull of things when left to his own devices. Very unpopular he became too. He'd been dead a month before anyone thought to check on him, and barely a soul attended his funeral."

Miss Burdock's hand fluttered to her chest. "Oh, whatever his mistakes, I pity him. To die alone and quite forgotten is a terrible thing."

Anne heard the honest anguish in her voice and suspected that for all her seeming acceptance of what life threw at her, Miss Burdock had perhaps envisaged such an end for herself. She put a hand on her arm.

"You, at least, will never be forgotten, Miss Burdock, for you will have left an impression on every child you have taught. Now, if Mrs Thirsk allows, shall we see how well the pianoforte sounds? We have half an hour before we need start lessons, after all."

The housekeeper smiled. "By all means. It will be good to hear music in the house once more."

～

Rufus Townsend may have lacked the charm of his elder brother, wasting no time on pleasantries, his bluntness and occasional irritation at Edward's ignorance verging on rudeness, but he shared one trait. His eyes shone with enthusiasm when he spoke of his passion. He may have gone too far and too fast for Edward to always follow him, but he gleaned enough to know that his land would be in safe hands if managed by him. The sorry state of it seemed to inspire rather than dismay Rufus.

"It is almost like having a blank canvas to work with. And it will have done no harm to allow the fields to lie fallow for a few years. We must sit down and discuss the funds you have at your disposal, then we may prioritise the work to be done and the animals you may wish to purchase for the home farm. Of course, we will have to make forecasts, so it is of the utmost importance that we retrieve the account books."

With this aim in mind, they rode into the village of Hayshott. It was rather quaint, with mellow stone cottages straggling along either side of the road and an inn set on one side of a green, the church and parsonage on the other.

"Many of the houses belong to the Fairbrass estate," he said. "Although a few were sold off in my grandfather's time. I believe that is when your estate acquired Rose Cottage. It is this way."

They turned onto a narrow lane with grass springing up in the middle and after a few hundred yards came to a cottage set back from the road. Edward was surprised to discover it was larger than any house in the village he had seen save the parsonage, boasting two windows either side of a door from which blue paint hung in peeling strips. The thatched roof was as Rufus had previously described; green and rotting, and Edward wondered how much it would cost him to turn this liability into an asset. The garden gate screeched its protest as they entered. Closing it behind them, they left the horses to wander into the overgrown garden. Edward pulled two keys he had found in his desk from his pocket.

"As Mrs Thirsk had no knowledge of the whereabouts of the key, I hope it will be one of these."

After glancing at the lock, he chose the larger one. It slotted in easily enough but refused to turn. He stepped back.

"It appears we will have to break in."

"Perhaps," Rufus said, grasping the knocker and giving it a shove.

The door swung open, revealing a tiled hallway with stairs rising to the first floor.

Edward's eyebrow shot up. "Good God! Do not tell me it has been unlocked all these years."

Rufus shrugged. "They are honest enough folk hereabouts, and a stranger is unlikely to stumble upon it."

As he stepped inside, the smell of damp hit him. The parlour and dining room were not in as bad a state as he had feared, although spots of mould peppered the walls near the ceiling. Only that and the thick layer of dust gave the clue that they had been unused for some time for everything was very tidy, nothing out of place.

"It is rather a fine house for a bailiff, is it not?" Edward said. "Especially one who lived alone. Surely one of the estate cottages would have been more appropriate?"

"There was a family living here; the Mortimers. When they left, the cottage stood empty for a year, and when Tilbury grew too old to manage his farm, he moved in to be caretaker until a tenant could be found." He frowned. "Tilbury always collected the rents, but he should never have been given the running of things. After Mrs Tewk died, the admiral cared for nothing. I don't understand it."

"Neither do I. He always ran a tight ship. But then love does strange things to people."

Edward's heart thudded heavily in his chest for a beat or two, a fleeting aberration, a mere echo of the despair a pair of flashing dark eyes had caused him. He had cared for little for some time afterwards, and it had only been his responsibility to his men that had saved him from becoming even more reckless than he had been.

Rufus looked bewildered. "I love my brother, but I would never abandon the land if he died."

Edward's lips twisted. "Romantic love is another thing altogether."

Rufus's fingers tapped against his leg as they had several times that day when he was trying to contain his impatience. "Then I hope I never experience it. Let us find the study."

Here were signs of habitation. Piles of papers

littered every surface, many mildewed and curling at the edges, and by the empty grate, an old leather wingchair stood, a pipe on the table beside it. In the far corner a narrow truckle bed was made up. It seemed that Tilbury had lived in this room.

It was Edward's turn to feel a surge of impatience. "Why on earth did not the solicitors sift through all this?"

Rufus shrugged and strode to the shelves filled with bound books set above the bed. "If the deed was not amongst the admiral's papers up at the house, perhaps they never knew it was part of the estate."

Edward ran a hand through his hair. "It will take days if not weeks to sort through all this."

Rufus did not reply but flicked through one book after another. Edward strolled to the desk and pulled open a drawer. It was crammed with more papers, as were the others.

Rufus glanced up. "These are in Admiral Tewk's hand. There is none more recent than six years ago, but they will give us an idea of what might be achieved in time."

Edward snapped a drawer shut. "They will have to do. I think it is too much to hope that Tilbury kept organised records. I will return later to collect these papers. Now, let us go upstairs and see the worst of the damage."

Edward returned to Hayshott Hall in a pensive mood. Repairing the farmhouses and the gardener's cottage had already cost him a pretty penny, and there were two other cottages on the estate in need of work besides Rose Cottage. The roof would need to be rethatched, the bedrooms stripped of furniture, and the whole house repapered. There was no doubt it would make a lovely home for someone once it was done, but who could say if he would be more successful in finding a tenant than the admiral? Who would wish to live in such an out of the way place?

He sighed. The admiral had apparently not taken Edward's route and invested in the funds. He had left him the estate but little money, and at this moment it felt more of a burden than a boon. His income of one thousand a year had seemed more than ample to support himself, the girls, and their governess, and he had saved a reasonable amount, but it would be swallowed up by his obligations if he was not very careful.

Rufus had stuffed his saddle bags with the ledgers, remembering at the last minute that his brother had asked him to invite Edward for dinner that evening.

Edward strode into the library and went straight to the brandy decanter. His hand paused, his glass halfway to his lips, as a trill of music drifted through the open door. He stiffened and tossed off the drink. Sophia had been an accomplished musician, and her playing had helped make his attendance at a soiree bearable, at least until she had humiliated him. The present player was no more than competent, and the sound grated on him. He strode swiftly from the room, intending to object to the din.

The door to the drawing room was ajar. He took the handle and was about to throw it open when girlish laughter drifted towards him. Putting his eye to the crack, he saw Barbara sitting next to Nora on a window seat, her face alight with pleasure, her uncritical ears clearly delighted by Miss Burdock's performance.

Suddenly, Mrs Huxley and Emily came into view. She held Emily's hand above her head and twirled her around, then, as the music came to an end, the governess stepped back and bowed whilst Emily dipped into a curtsy, her brow furrowed in concentration. As Mrs Huxley's face relaxed into a warm smile, he retreated, the sound of applause following him, and he was surprised to feel his own lips tilting up, his former ill humour fleeing as swiftly as it had come.

He went to his desk and pulled a sheet of paper towards him, filled with a renewed sense of purpose. He would make his own list and compare it against Rufus's. However competent the young man appeared to be, he intended to keep his hand on the tiller. He had covered no more than half a page when he heard light, quick footsteps in the hall. The door opened and Mrs Huxley, a pleasant smile still fixed on her lips, came briskly into the room.

The desk was set in an alcove towards the back of the room, and she did not immediately see him, but went straight to the wall lined with bookshelves. He was about to address her when she began to hum, her long, slender fingers skipping across the spines. He set down his pen, content to observe her. She moved with unconscious grace, the stiff posture she so often exhibited in his presence entirely absent.

"There you are," she said, as if greeting an old friend.

Going up on tiptoes, she reached for a book on a shelf some way above her.

He rose to his feet and walked towards her. "Allow me."

She swung about, a gasp on her lips, the animation

leaching from her face as her habitual mask of impassivity fell into place. Irritation and disappointment warred within him. It appeared her smiles were reserved for anyone but him. It was as if she wished to hide her true self, and he did not like it. It seemed as dishonest in its way as Sophia bestowing her smiles on him and pretending an admiration she did not truly feel.

"I apologise, Mr Turner," she said woodenly. "I had not realised you had returned and did not mean to disturb you."

He reached for the book, his tone matching hers as he said, "Think nothing of it, Mrs Huxley."

It was a tome dedicated to the Romans. He stiffened, remembering the small smile Townsend had won from her, and the thought that she might wish to ingratiate herself with him crossed his mind. A gentleman born and bred would, of course, be more to her taste than a rough mannered nobody.

"Is this not a little advanced for my wards?"

A hint of colour warmed her cheeks, and she took a half step backwards. Goaded by the apparent confirmation of his suspicions, he spoke his thoughts aloud.

"Or is it that you wish to impress Mr Townsend with your knowledge?"

His accusatory tone brought her chin up and her eyes flashed with anger. If he had not been observing her closely, he would have missed it, for they quickly dulled from blue to grey like clouds covering the sun. Her sandy lashes swept over them as she dropped her gaze to the floor, clasping her hands in front of her in a humble attitude, and he suddenly felt like a crass fool.

What was he about? He was her employer not a prospective suitor, and yet here he was behaving like a jealous idiot. What did her smiles matter to him? However far above him she had once been, she must be painfully aware of her position now, and her reserve towards him was only natural. Besides, she was not to his taste. Sophia had been an exotic creature with glossy, ebony hair, and dark eyes that danced with laughter and mischief. Mrs Huxley's hair was a mixture of blonde and red, resulting in a colour that lacked the vibrancy of either shade in its natural state, her blue-grey eyes pale, and her lashes sandy. She verged on plain unless animated, when she became only passably pretty.

"Forgive me," he said abruptly. "I do not know what I was thinking. I have much on my mind, but it was inexcusable of me to throw rash accusations at you."

She, at last, raised her eyes. "Let me put your mind at rest, Captain. If you are afraid that I have only accepted this position in the hope that I may catch a husband, you are much mistaken. Matrimony no longer holds any attraction for me, and my only interest is in furthering the girls' education. I was hoping there might be some illustrations of mosaics in the book that I may show Emily. It would be remiss of me not to use the artefacts found in the park as a learning opportunity."

He held it out to her. "Your logic, Mrs Huxley, is unimpeachable, and I am in complete agreement with you. I expect Emily, in particular, will flourish more easily if her learning has a tangible purpose, some connection to the present."

Was that surprise he saw in her eyes? Did she think him completely insensible to the needs of his wards?

"You are correct, sir. Her life thus far has been governed by need, and she has had little opportunity to enjoy pursuits for their inherent pleasure alone."

"I understand that, Mrs Huxley, but as I believe you gave her a dancing lesson this morning, I am sure she will soon learn the art of enjoyment for enjoyment's sake."

A rueful smile touched her lips. "Perhaps, in time, but at present it is only her desire to set a good example for her sister and to please you that motivates her."

He was uncertain whether it was the smile or her words that surprised him most.

"Please me? Surely you are mistaken? I am the villain who is responsible for the death of her father in her mind."

"If she has said as much, I am sure she does not mean it. She is angry with her father, as her mother was, for abandoning them. As he is not here to vent her spleen on, I am afraid you became the target."

His brows snapped together. "He did not abandon them. He requested that half of his wage be sent to Mrs Proctor. I helped him fill out the forms myself, but there seems to have been some mix up for she never received it. I made enquiries but got no satisfactory answers."

"However, it was," she said. "I think Emily would benefit from knowing that."

"You may tell her, Mrs Huxley, for I have much to do."

She hesitated a moment before nodding her head and offering him a curtsy.

"Very well, sir. Now, if you will excuse me, I must get back to the children."

He executed a half bow. "Certainly, Mrs Huxley. Please feel free to avail yourself of the library at any time."

CHAPTER 12

Anne left the room prey to several emotions. Captain Turner possessed a mercurial nature she could not admire, but just when he had succeeded in setting up her back, he would say or do something to disarm her. His apologies were abrupt and unexpected but sincere. She could not imagine why he had suspected she might have an interest in Mr Townsend. She was certain she had given him no cause. She could well imagine his temper might be exacerbated by the thought he might lose yet another governess, but there was nothing of the siren about her, indeed; she knew very well that she was not a beauty. Had something happened in his past to make him suspicious of all females?

She shivered. She had spoken honestly when she had informed him that she no longer had any interest in matrimony. She clasped the book to her chest, frowning as she remembered him reaching above her to retrieve it. He had stood so close that she had been able to smell his cologne, and his nearness had discomfited her. The thought that he had intended to intimidate her flitted across her mind, but she swiftly dismissed it. She had known bullies, and for all his idiosyncrasies, she did not believe Captain Turner to be of their ilk. He was thoughtless, perhaps, as were so many of his sex, but not a bully.

Yet even that accusation now appeared unjust. She had not expected him to show such an understanding of Emily's character. That he had, pleased her, but why could he not speak to the child himself about her father? He had said that he had much on his mind, and she could not help but wonder if what he had discovered that morning as he went over the estate with Mr Rufus Townsend had troubled him. Perhaps he had discovered that it would cost him much more than he had expected to put everything in order, that too might explain his irritation with her. He had offered her a generous salary before he had fully understood his obligations. Well, it could not be helped now, and she was not about to take any less, not when her and Miss Burdock's futures were so uncertain.

When she entered the schoolroom, she was happy to see Barbara and Emily busily copying the alphabet from one of Miss Burdock's books. Each letter had a rhyme below it, and she read it to them after they had completed each letter, asking them to repeat it. They had reached the letter F when Anne approached the table.

"Very good," she said, noticing how carefully Emily's letters had been formed. "I think Emily may be ready for pen and ink, Miss Burdock."

"I quite agree," she said. "I have a notebook she may use for the purpose."

The child smiled, but her eyes held a speculative gleam. "Have we deserved a reward?"

"You certainly have," Anne agreed. "You may put down your chalk, and I will tell you something that I think will please you very much."

"So, Pa was not a bad man?" Barbara said when she had imparted her news.

"Of course he was not," Miss Burdock said. "I wonder what happened to the money?"

Her revelation did not have quite the effect on Emily that Anne had expected. Her eyes filled with tears she refused to shed, and pushing back her chair she ran to the window, her arms wrapping about herself.

Anne went to her and put a gentle hand on her shoulder. "I thought my news would please you, but I quite understand you might be a trifle upset, at first."

The girl whirled about. "I am not upset. I am angry."

"Who with?" Anne asked gently.

"Mr Rogers!" the girl cried. "We was in another of his houses when Pa went back to sea, but he said he could get more rent for it than we were paying. He made us move to a smaller place, and he promised Ma any letters would be sent on to us. He said he would bring them himself." She rubbed at her eyes. "When none came, Ma went first to the post office and then to the old house, but the woman said nothing had come. But what if she gave them to him and he kept 'em? If Ma had got Pa's money, she wouldn't have had to work so hard, and she might never have become ill."

"Was the post usually delivered to your house?"

The girl nodded. "I was only allowed to open the door if there were two knocks, because that was the letter carrier. He wore a smart red coat and carried a bell. If Ma had a letter for Pa, I'd wait 'til I heard his bell ringing and give it to him. But he never came near after we moved."

Anne embraced the child as her tears overflowed, and she began to sob. "I will speak to Captain Turner again. He will investigate the matter further, I am certain."

But she was not to see him that day for he was out both the times she enquired for him.

"I did tell him you wished to see him," Mrs Thirsk assured her. "But he said if it wasn't urgent, it would have to wait until tomorrow as he had a dinner engagement with Mr Townsend. And you never said it was urgent, Mrs Huxley."

She supposed it wasn't, but she was worried about Emily. The girl had clammed up again, and seemed to be dwelling on what might have happened. She could hardly blame her. The thought that her mother had died unnecessarily was a hard blow to absorb, and Anne felt responsible. She had underestimated Emily's native intelligence when she had imparted the information, but how was she to have known that they had changed abode or all that that implied?

Mrs Thirsk had informed her that Captain Turner was an early riser, and so she came down just before seven. She knocked on the library door and waited. When no answer came, she knocked again, and an irritable voice bade her enter.

He did not immediately look up, apparently

absorbed in sorting a pile of papers on his desk. She saw there was an open chest by his desk filled to the brim with them.

"I said I was not to be disturbed, Mrs Thirsk."

"Forgive me for interrupting," Anne said. "But I believe I have some information you will wish to know."

He glanced up, his eyes sharpening. "Come in, Mrs Huxley. I had forgotten you wished to see me."

She glanced at the papers. "I see you did not exaggerate when you said you were busy."

A wry laugh escaped him. "I wish I had been prevaricating or that I had a secretary."

Sensing this was not a propitious moment, she said reluctantly, "Perhaps I should come back later."

He ran his hand through his hair. "Mrs Huxley, it would not matter if you came back on the morrow, or next week for that matter. I fear I will still be elbow deep in paperwork."

"Could you not ask Mr Rufus Townsend to help you?"

"He has enough to do, besides, I do not intend to leave everything to him. This came from the old bailiff's cottage, and it is as well I understand what he was about. What may I do for you, Mrs Huxley?"

"It is rather what you may do for Emily."

He dropped a paper on his desk and came forward, frowning. "You seem concerned. Is something amiss?"

"I am rather afraid that there might be. You mentioned that you had not been able to discover how Mr Proctor's money went astray, and I gleaned some information from Emily that might shed some light on the mystery."

He indicated a chair by the fire. "Please, be seated, Mrs Huxley."

She perched on the edge of her seat and related Emily's story.

"I went to the house they removed from," he said. "And was informed only that Mrs Proctor had gone to the workhouse. There was no mention of her living at another address. When I went to the office where she should have received her remittance, I was told that as I was not family, they could release no information to me. I have written to the admiralty but have received no reply as yet." He grimaced. "I am afraid I am under a cloud at present, and so they may be no more forthcoming."

She nodded. "That is unfortunate. Emily seems to believe that Mr Rogers may have purposefully not forwarded Mr Proctor's mail, and she has retreated into her shell. I believe that the thought her mother died unnecessarily weighs heavily on her mind."

His fingers began to tap on the arm of his chair, his eyes clouding as he mulled this over.

"I can think of a few reasons he may have behaved in such a way, and none of them are palatable."

"I agree," she said. "But is it possible that Mr Rogers may be questioned?"

He startled her by suddenly surging to his feet, a keen fierceness darkening his eyes. She could not help but wonder if that was the look he wore before going into battle.

"You are right, Mrs Huxley. This bears investigating. If an injustice has been done, I would right it. I will go today, as soon as I may pack a portmanteau and dash off a note to Rufus." He gestured to the trunk of papers. "These will still be here when I return."

She rose to her feet, a sudden burst of gratitude breaking through her reserve. "Perhaps I can be of assistance. I think Emily's perturbation will make her unreceptive for the time being. If it would be of help to you, I could go through the papers and at least sort them into categories, such as those that are bills, documents relating to the house or estate, and those which I deem to be of more import than others, and so on. I can bring Emily down with me and give her something undemanding to occupy her while Miss Burdock teaches Barbara."

He stared at her in astonishment, and she feared she had overstepped the mark. In a moment, however, a grin lightened his features, and the astonishment was all hers. It transformed his swarthy harsh features, rendering him almost handsome.

"Mrs Huxley, I would be most grateful. But there is no need to slave away, you know. I imagine I will be away for at least a week, perhaps longer."

She was reminded that despite his unpredictable changes of mood, he was a man of his word. If there was something to be found, she felt sure he would discover it, as she presently explained to Emily. He surprised her once again when he strode into the nursery swathed in his greatcoat some half an hour later.

Emily had been sitting sullenly at the table, but she sprang to her feet and ran to him.

"Captain Turner, if Mr Rogers did it, will you kill him?"

He went down on one knee before her. "I may wish to do so, but if I did anything so rash, I would be hanged."

"What will you do, then?" she asked.

"That depends on what I discover. If he is involved in any way and his actions prove to be anything more than carelessness, you may be sure I will see him punished to the full extent of the law. If not, I may at least give him a bloody nose."

"Thank you."

His eyes widened as she embraced him. He clasped her briefly to him, a small smile touching his lips. "You may thank me by being a good girl for your governesses. Mrs Huxley will be much occupied whilst I am away."

She stepped back. "I will. Be careful. Mr Rogers carries a gun. He showed it to us once, which made Ma very angry."

He rose to his feet, his lips tightening. "I will bear that in mind. You may be sure I will take every precaution, but do not worry; I have been in many battles and know how to take care of myself." He cleared his throat. "You must prepare yourself, however, child. Whatever I discover is unlikely to make you feel better. It will not bring your mother back."

She nodded solemnly.

"Can you describe him to me?"

"He's got a wart on his cheek. When he takes his long hat off, he's got no hair, he wears a long, black coat… and he walks funny."

"Good girl." He ruffled the child's hair, and after

casting a brief glance at Anne, strode to the door. Pausing there, he half-turned, glancing at Nora.

"You need only attend lessons if you wish to or are needed. I feel the girls are in safe hands, don't you?"

"Oh, yes, sir."

He had not stayed to hear her answer, and once more Anne was beset by conflicting emotions. Would she ever understand the man? At one moment, he was cold and abrupt, at another awkward, but he could show a thoughtfulness and sensitivity that made her warm to him. And when a rare smile won through his reserve, her heart thumped in the oddest of ways. It was because she had so rarely been on the receiving end of such a smile from a gentleman, she told herself.

～

The first few days flew by, and Emily's spirits lifted. Whether that was due to the knowledge that something was being done, or a child's natural resilience was unclear, but Anne was glad of it. The girl decided to remain with Miss Burdock in the mornings, and in the afternoon, she would bring her doll, paper, and pen, and sit at a table, studiously practising what she had learned. Now and again, she would talk to the doll.

"Captain Turner will knock Mr Rogers down, and he will be pleased when he sees I know all my letters."

It seemed he had risen in Emily's esteem. And in truth, hers. His absence lessened the impact of his abrasiveness, leaving only the facts to be considered. A man who would rather take in two waifs than leave them in the workhouse, and who would go to so much trouble to right a wrong, must be acknowledged as an honourable gentleman and therefore be admired as such. He might lack the manners of a gentleman born and bred, but he also lacked the duplicity, questionable morals, and absolute sense of entitlement she had too often encountered.

As time wore on, however, Anne found her task somewhat tedious, and at moments regretted the uncharacteristic impulsivity that had led to her offer of help. It appeared Mr Tilbury had had no talent for organisation, and he had seemed to keep everything that had crossed his desk whether it was of import or not. The letters from the departed tenants did catch her interest, however. They clearly outlined their difficulties, growing resentment, and eventual resignation to their situation. She put them in date order in a separate pile so that Captain Turner might easily understand how their situation had unravelled. All landowners had a duty to their tenants, and she hoped that Captain Turner would realise it.

Towards the end of the following week, the desk was covered in neat piles of papers, her back was aching, her eyes sore, and she found herself restless from lack of exercise. It had rained incessantly since the captain had left, but today weak sunshine escaped between gaps in the fast-moving light grey clouds that scudded across the sky.

Anne glanced in the large chest and frowned. How could it still be almost a quarter full? For an instant, she was tempted to tip the rest onto the fire. She had found very little of any great interest, after all. A wry smile touched her lips. She had an inkling that Captain Turner might have done just that, but she could not. As he had sent no word of his return, they could wait.

The rain stopped long enough for them to walk to church. The girls trudged sullenly between Anne and Miss Burdock.

"If you wish to repay Captain Turner for his efforts on your behalf, then I suggest you begin by displaying the good manners you have learned. You will remain by my and Miss Burdock's side at all times, and you will, at least to all outward appearances, seem to be listening to the sermon."

Emily sent her a sly look. "Is that what you do? Only pretend to listen?"

How was she to answer that? The truth would set a bad example and so would a lie. Miss Burdock seemed unhampered by such considerations.

"Sometimes it is all one can do," she said. "An apposite sermon well delivered is a wonderful thing, but one that is poorly chosen and half-heartedly expressed is a trial to be borne." She sighed. "There has been many a time when I have wished that I might have my knitting by me."

Anne smiled at the thought. "I imagine the Lord will forgive his flock's thoughts wandering at some point, but the appearance of propriety must be maintained," Anne said. "It would be disrespectful to do otherwise."

As they came to the village, they attracted several curious looks from stragglers on their way to the church.

"Do not frown, Emily," Anne said calmly. "It is only natural that as myself and Miss Burdock are newcomers to the area, we will attract some attention. Do as I do and pretend not to notice."

"Why do we have to do so much pretending?" the girl asked. "Isn't it like lying?"

Another question that was difficult to answer. "No, think of it as more of a game. We have been play acting as we practise our manners, after all. We do not have to wear our hearts on our sleeve, that way, we do not give people the satisfaction of seeing that they have made us uncomfortable. You cannot control how others behave, only how you do. It is your power."

"My power," the girl repeated slowly.

"It is, indeed," Miss Burdock agreed. "The Lord showed us the virtues of kindness and forgiveness, after all."

Emily cocked her head. "So, if I do not show that I am cross, then I have won the game."

"In a way. It is only natural to feel angry sometimes, but if you allow it to influence your actions, you may behave in a way that is equally wrong. If you do not, you have the satisfaction of knowing that you were the better person and your conduct was that which befitted a lady."

She hunched a shoulder, as she so often did when she felt guilty. "Like when I broke Captain Turner's gifts, and when I made Barbara hide in the woods and she got scratched by the brambles."

"Yes," Anne said softly. "But we are only human, and we all make mistakes. The important thing is that we learn from them."

All the pews towards the back of the church were full. Indeed, they had to walk to the front of the church, and Anne was aware of the eyes that followed them, particularly those of Mr Adams, who stood in his pulpit, clearly ready to begin his sermon.

When they had settled themselves in the pew, she raised her eyes and discovered that he was looking directly at her. His hard brown eyes were set in an austere face, and no hint of a smile disturbed them. His lips turned down at the edges and he began to beat his fingers against the pew. She felt Emily's hand creep into hers, and looking down, gave the child a reassuring smile.

The sermon began unpromisingly and there was nothing half-hearted about it.

"The wicked are like the troubled sea, when it cannot rest, whose waters cast up mire and dirt. There is no peace, saith my God, to the wicked."

As he got into his stride, his attention moved to the rest of the congregation, and Anne allowed the flow of his words to pass over her head. It seemed to her, that he had scoured the Bible for any references to wickedness he could find and tacked them together with no coherent or relevant theme that linked them directly to the people sat before him. If he had tried to balance his rant with the power of redemption and forgiveness rather than dwelling on the fires of eternal damnation, she might have forced herself to concentrate on his harshly delivered words.

Her eyes were drawn to the opposite pew when she heard a sharp shh. A lady in a drab dress bent over a fidgeting girl, whispering something in her ear. When she straightened, she sent the parson an anxious glance. The girl was about Emily's age. Her mouth was pinched, her cheeks pale, and the eyes she cast up at her mama, miserable. She could hardly blame her;

to have to sit through this joyless sermon was a trial for anyone. Anne could only marvel that the church was so full, but then, the poor villagers would probably sustain a visit from Mr Adams if they played truant.

Anne glanced down at her charges and felt a stirring of pride. They were still, their hands clasped in their lap, and their eyes downcast. Her eyebrows rose as she saw them both raise their hands as if in prayer. The reason for it soon became clear, however. With a sleight of hand that a pick pocket might admire, they slipped a small piece of marzipan into their mouths. Her gaze moved to Miss Burdock who looked straight ahead, an attentive expression on her countenance. Her hands, however, rested over a bulging handkerchief. A rueful smile edged Anne's lips, but her head snapped up as the vicar's next words registered.

"A bastard shall not enter into the congregation of the Lord; even to his tenth generation shall he not enter into the congregation of the Lord."

She realised he was looking directly at their pew and anger began to simmer in her veins. How dare he mix and match uncontextualised snippets to suit his purpose? Fortunately, the girls were oblivious to his meaning, and their continued passivity allowed her to resist the impulse to take them by the hand and lead them away from the poisonous parson.

At last, the interminable service came to an end, and they followed the lady and her two children from the opposite pew, down the aisle. The press of people trying to leave was slowed by the vicar, who stood in the doorway to receive an acknowledgement from each passing parishioner. Occasionally, he would select some poor soul to converse with, causing the remainder of the congregation to come to a halt.

In one of these pauses, the child Anne had observed earlier, sagged against her mother. The poor girl was clearly ill. Her younger sister took advantage of her mama's distraction to look around. She offered Barbara a tentative smile. Barbara darted forward and offered her a cube of marzipan. The girl glanced anxiously at her mama but seeing that she was still talking in hushed tones to her sister, took it and popped it in her mouth. Her eyes closed in pleasure as she chewed.

"Thank you," she whispered. "I'm Jasmine. But I'm not supposed to talk to you."

"Why not?" Barbara asked.

Anne tensed, wondering what the girl might say, but her mother turned her head at that moment. The look of horror that crossed her face was ludicrous.

"Jasmine Adams," she hissed. "Come here."

So, this was the vicar's wife. She was surprised. The vicar must be twenty years her senior. Here was her chance to put a dent in the rumours that Captain Turner had assured her abounded, however.

"Good day, Mrs Adams," she said. "I have not yet had the pleasure of making your acquaintance. I…" she indicated her companion with a nod of her head, "and Miss Burdock have been fortunate enough to acquire the position of governess to Captain Turner's wards, Emily and Barbara Proctor."

The woman pursed her lips. "Fortunate? You are living under the roof of a sinner, and as he is tarnished, so will you be."

Anne noticed that several parishioners, still unable

to make their way from the church had turned to listen to this exchange. Well, she would make the most of it.

Anne put back her shoulders and tilted her chin a little, drawing all her dignity about her. "I fear you have been sadly misinformed, Mrs Adams. I can assure you that Captain Turner is a good and honourable man who promised one of his crew that he would care of his wife and children when he lay dying. Unfortunately, he was too late to help Mrs Proctor as he found her gravely ill, but as he is a man of his word, he took pity on the girls. I find your attitude as unfounded as it is uncharitable, and I only hope that if you should ever find yourself destitute, you may lay claim to so good a friend."

There was a murmur of approval from those behind the vicar's wife.

The woman looked at them and back at Anne, uncertainty registering on her face. Anne pressed her advantage.

"If you doubt my word, you might apply to Lady Westcliffe of Westcliffe Park, Somerset. She has been my sponsor and employer and is a lady of the utmost respectability. She would never have recommended me for a post were there any truth to these ridiculous rumours."

Mrs Adams certainly appeared conflicted now, but at that moment, her elder child fell into a dead faint. She wrung her hands, her cheeks turning as pale as those of her daughter's. "Oh dear, Mr Adams will not be pleased."

Anne went down on her knees, touched the girl's forehead, and then felt for the pulse in her wrist.

"I hardly think Mr Adams can blame his daughter for succumbing to influenza, ma'am. Take her home at once and send for the doctor."

A man in rough homespuns pushed through the crowd. "I know as how you suffer with your back, Mrs Adams, so if you will allow, I will carry the child."

"Oh, yes, if you please." Under her breath she added, "I told him how it would be, if only he would listen."

Anne suddenly felt sorry for the woman and her offspring.

CHAPTER 13

The closer he got to Manchester, the more energy Edward felt coursing through his veins. It was a familiar feeling that he had experienced many times when engaging the enemy. It was true that quite who his adversary was remained unclear, but that too was not unfamiliar to him. He had always followed his gut instinct, and it had rarely played him false.

Why had it taken a child, admittedly an unusually perceptive, cynical child, to show him the way? He had suspected that Mrs Morsley, the lady who had opened the door to him was hiding something, but then her eyes had filled with tears, and he had believed that he must have been mistaken. The emotion had been genuine, he had felt sure of it. He still was, yet something told him that she was the key to the puzzle.

When the stagecoach pulled up at the Swan with Two Necks in Market Steet Lane, Edward was both dishevelled and impatient. It was an odd circumstance, but the farther he got from his estate, the more he wished to return to it. It was the first time he had possessed a home he could call his own, and however difficult the transition from sea to land had been, he had, he realised, begun to put down roots. At present, they were tentative and fragile, but they grew stronger every day.

He took his dinner in the coffee room and, unable to settle, went for a walk. He strolled down the broad street of St Mary's Gate and turned onto Deansgate. In a short time, he came to Bridge Street, and the river Irwell. Three gothic arches carried an ancient, stone bridge across the waterway. Both sides of the bank were hugged by looming, tall buildings, a mixture of houses, tenements, and warehouses. The moon escaped a passing cloud, limning the tall tower of a church in front of him. If he were prudent, he would turn back now and wait for daylight as he had originally intended. Even as the thought formed, he moved onto the poorly lit bridge.

Halfway across, he paused, rested his hands on the stone parapet, and idly watched a long, narrow barge propelled by two standing men with long oars approach, a lantern dangling from a hook at each end of the craft. He raised a hand in acknowledgement.

"You would do better with a sail."

The oarsman nearest to him grinned. "We have not far to go."

The man's head turned a fraction, and he squinted as if trying to focus on something else, but then he ducked as they approached one of the bridge's arches.

Instinct warned Edward before he heard the footfall, and he whirled about, drawing the sword hanging beneath his coat. He held it to the footpad's chest, and the man put up his hands and backed away into the shadows.

"I didn't mean no harm. I was only going to ask if you could spare a shilling or two."

His face was half covered by a scarf, and a hat was pulled low over his eyes.

"You are a liar and a thief," Edward said coldly.

It was only as the man flexed his wrist that Edward saw the glint of moonlight on steel. He dropped to a crouch and lunged forward, his blade piercing the man's thigh. The knife sailed over his head and plunged towards the river as the man fell to the ground, clutching his leg.

Edward stood over him, pressing the point of his sword to his throat. "I have a very good mind to finish you off and throw you in after it."

"Stay your hand, sir. What is afoot?"

Edward glanced up to see a stocky man carrying a lantern coming towards him. A wry grin touched his lips.

"It is your lucky day," he murmured to the man on the ground, before withdrawing his sword, sheathing it, and calling to the approaching man.

"Good evening, my good sir. If you are the night watchman, your timing is excellent. This fine specimen of humanity first thought to rob me and then kill me by throwing his knife at me. I have merely disabled him."

The man came up to him and held his lantern over the thief. Edward thought he saw something approaching consternation cross his brow.

"He lies," his attacker said. "I was just making my

way across the bridge when he drew his sword. He is a madman."

The watchman looked up at Edward, a sly look entering his eyes. "How am I to know who to believe?"

So, he knew the man, and if Edward was not much mistaken, he was afraid of him.

"I hope you will take the word of an officer of His Majesty's Navy over a vagabond, sir."

Sweat broke out on the man's brow. "I mean no disrespect, sir, but it does not appear that you are serving at this moment, and I only have your word against his. Can you prove he threw a knife at you?"

Edward turned and looked down at the river. "By now, it is at the bottom—" The boat had just passed under the bridge, and one of the oarsmen waved at him.

"Are you all right? I saw someone moving in the shadows, and then this landed in the boat."

He held up the knife.

"I'm fine," Edward said. "Can you throw it up to me? There is a night watchman here who wishes to see it."

"That's too dangerous, but we'll skull over to the bank."

Edward turned back. "Well, sir. You have your proof. I suggest you go and retrieve the weapon whilst I attend to this villain's leg."

The man hesitated a moment before doing as requested. Edward knelt and untied his neckcloth. Reaching into the pocket of his coat, he withdrew a handkerchief, neatly folded it, and pressed it against the wound. The villain sucked in a breath.

"Mighty kind of you."

His words were belied by his sarcastic tone. Edward wrapped his cravat about the leg, pulling it ruthlessly tight, a cold smile touching his lips when the man gasped again.

"I am merely ensuring that you do not bleed to death before you face justice."

Grabbing the man's arm, he hauled him to his feet as the watchman came up to them.

"He's all yours. What is your name, by the way?"

"Wriggly."

"And who is your superior?"

He did not like the watchman's smile; it was a little too smug.

"The deputy constable, Mr Joseph Nadin."

Edward nodded. "And who does he report to?"

The man shifted uneasily. "The magistrate and reverend, Mr Hays."

That was better. He did not fully trust the watchman, therefore, he was reluctant to trust the man he worked for. "Very good. I shall make it my business to seek him out in the morning. I shall write a statement and hand it directly to him."

"That's a trifle irregular, sir," the man said. "And as the quarter sessions were held last month, he'll likely be at Dukinfield which is all of six miles. It would be easier to leave it in the hands of Constable Nadin."

"Perhaps, but there is another matter I wish to bring before Mr Hays."

The man's eyes narrowed. "And what might that be?"

Edward smiled coldly. "I suggest you take this man to the watchhouse and have his injury looked at rather than standing here asking me impertinent questions. If your superior wishes to speak to me directly, he may find me at the Swan with Two Necks. Good evening."

He turned on his heel and walked over the bridge. Steering clear of the maze of narrow lanes lined with houses and tenements that seemed to have been thrown up with little thought or planning, no doubt to house the ever-expanding workers the mills required, he turned onto the much broader Chapel Street, which gave onto Water Street, his destination. He passed a woollen mill and came to a row of cottages rather better built than others he had passed. Although it benefited from streetlights, the yellow pools of light only served to throw other areas into deep shadow. He sensed nothing amiss, however, and moved confidently towards number thirteen. Noting there was a dim light inside, he raised his hand to knock, but his fist hung in the air as he heard a male voice inside. He could not make out the words, but his tone was harsh, taunting, and undoubtedly threatening.

Crossing the road, he availed himself of one of the pockets of darkness and awaited events. Mrs Morsley was a widow. Had she found herself an abusive protector to save her from want or was her visitor the elusive Mr Rogers? His mouth hardened at the thought it might be the latter. If he spoke like that to Mrs Morsley, he most likely had to Mrs Proctor. It did not speak well of his character, neither did throwing a woman with two children onto the street.

The door opened and the man stepped out. He could not see his face, but as he walked away Edward saw that he fit the description that Emily had given him to the extent that he wore a long black coat, a beaver hat, and walked with a slight limp. Most likely Mr Rogers then.

He stayed in the shadows for several minutes more until the man disappeared around the corner, and then he crossed the road. He knocked on the door and waited. It was not Mrs Morsley who answered, but a pockmarked woman adorned in nothing but a flimsy wrap. Her smile revealed her rotting teeth.

"Well, in't it my lucky day." She stepped back, nodding at a closed door. "It's normally her who gets all the half-decent clients."

His lips tightened as he stepped over the threshold.

"Thank you, but it is Mrs Morsley I have come to see."

The woman tossed her head, turned, and went to the stairs. She paused on the first step and looked over her shoulder.

"She won't like it. You're too early. She don't like clients coming before her girl's abed, and I don't blame her. She's a pretty little thing."

Good God! It was bad enough that Rogers had apparently turned this house into a brothel, but that a child should be reared here was unconscionable. Had he tried to bend Mrs Proctor to this way of life and failed? Had she suffered the workhouse rather than submit? He could only admire her for it. The thought that Emily and Barbara might have been exposed to such a life was intolerable.

He knocked briefly on the door the woman had indicated. He heard footsteps and then the scrape of a key being turned in a lock. The door opened a fraction.

"Go away. I told him not before ten."

Edward braced his hand against the door when she tried to close it. He had come for answers, and he would not leave without them.

"Mrs Morsley, it is I, Captain Turner. We need to talk."

The door opened just wide enough for him to see her. She was as he remembered. Mrs Morsley had once been an attractive woman, but care and want had carved lines into her face, her blonde hair was lank and her figure painfully thin. What looks she had remaining to her would soon be lost.

Her faded blue eyes would not quite meet his, but he saw fear in them.

"I've already told you all I know."

A blur of movement behind her caught his attention, and glancing up, he saw a reflection of what the tired woman might once have been. A girl, who was just burgeoning into a young woman, stood behind her, her blue eyes vibrant, her skin smooth, and her blond hair thick and shiny.

"Ma?"

Mrs Morsley whirled about. "Get to bed and stay there."

The girl's mouth and shoulders drooped in unison, and she disappeared from view.

"Please allow me to enter, Mrs Morsley. I do not intend to leave without answers." When her lips remained tightly closed, he put his instincts to the test. "I know you are in part responsible for what happened to Mrs Proctor, whether by accident or design is as yet unclear to me. You should know that I shall be visiting the magistrate, Mr Hays on the morrow, and I will beg his aid in this matter."

The woman sagged against the door and closed her eyes, a low groan escaping her. "I knew it would come to this, and I deserve it; but what will happen to my poor Susan?" Her eyes sprang open, and she suddenly grasped one of his hands. "Don't do it. Have mercy, sir! If I am not here to protect her, *he* will…" Anguished tears filled her eyes. "He will make her one of us. I know she looks older, but she is but twelve, sir, a mere child."

He squeezed her hand before releasing it. "Mrs Morsley, I have seen many things in my life and hope that I am not unfeeling, but if you wish me to show you mercy, you must tell me what I wish to know. If you speak the truth, I will do all in my power to aid you and your daughter."

She stared hard into his eyes for several moments and then nodded. "I believe you to be honest, sir. What you have done for those poor girls speaks to it."

She stood back, allowing him to enter, before closing and locking the door. He glanced around the tidy but shabby room. It seemed to be parlour, kitchen, and bedroom. Cooking pots hung by the fire, a handloom stood in each of the two corners nearest the window, a small table in another, and along one wall stood a narrow cot. There was a door, which he assumed led to her daughter's bedroom.

She indicated a chair by the table and went to stand in front of the smouldering fire.

"Don't judge me too harshly, sir. It is only recently that I have been brought so low. I had no choice. Mr

Rogers offered me the whole house for a cheap rent. But times is hard; some of the mills have gaslights and power looms so their workers can work all hours and produce more than home workers; although I doubt the quality is as good. Prices have fallen. Or that's what Mr Rogers tells me. He has hundreds of weavers working for him from home and brings us the yarn before selling the cloth on." She drew in a breath, her hands twisting together. "He said he too had been affected, and he must put up my rent, even though he knew I could ill afford it. And when I was deep in his debt, he threatened us with debtor's prison." A half-sob escaped her, but she closed her mouth tight against it. "He made me do it. I didn't want to."

"Do what precisely?" Edward asked.

Her eyes dropped to the floor and her voice took on a dull tone. "He got hold of some papers meant for Mrs Proctor, and he made me pretend to be her so he could get her husband's money."

He felt anger rising within him. "So, when Mrs Proctor came here, you lied to her."

She hung her head. "I had no choice. I had to think of Susan. We had nowhere else to go. He said he had found Mrs Proctor cheaper accommodation and that she had work. He assured me she and the children wouldn't starve."

"And you believed him?" he snapped.

She flinched. "I could not allow myself to think otherwise." She closed her eyes. "He came one day and said that Mrs Proctor was dying in the workhouse, and I would be held responsible if what I had done came out. He said he would protect me if I agreed to live in these two rooms, and he put two harlots in the rooms upstairs." Her eyes filled with tears. "I knew that I could never escape him. He has connections everywhere, both sides of the water. Last month, he insisted that I start receiving visitors." A sob escaped her. "And tonight, he suggested that Susan… that Susan…."

She could not finish, and she did not need to. He was sickened, disgusted, and a cold rage began to run through his veins. None of the scenarios he had imagined were quite as bad as this. He reminded himself that the woman before him was as much a victim of Rogers' iniquity as Mrs Proctor had been.

"You are in a sorry predicament," he said. "Your debt is nothing compared to the crime of fraud. That is a very serious matter, indeed."

Her legs gave way, and she fell to her knees, her hands coming up before her in an attitude of prayer.

"I know it! But what could I do? If it weren't for Susan, I would not have done it. Please, Captain Turner, I have told you everything. Please, help us!"

"You have not told me quite everything," he said. "How did he get hold of these papers? Were they delivered here."

She shook her head. "No, I did not lie when I said nothing had come here. He has the letter carrier in his pocket, and the postmaster for all I know. He makes it his business to find things out that people would prefer to keep hidden, and he blackmails them."

Edward suddenly felt the need for some air. He rose abruptly to his feet.

"Thank you, Mrs Morsley. I will do what I can for you. I believe the magistrate is a member of the clergy, and we must hope he may show you some mercy. If I cannot help you, I will do what I can for your daughter."

She nodded miserably. "Mr Hays in't known for his leniency. But if you can find Susan something, perhaps as a maid where she'll have a roof over her head, that's all I ask."

He hired a horse the following morning and rode out to Dukinfield, arriving there not much after ten. An impressive set of iron gates gave onto a winding carriage drive. He was confronted with a residence far more gracious and elegant than his own. The multi-panelled front door of heavy oak was unusually wide and somewhat protected from the elements by a grand portico, inside of which, stood statues on pedestals. Above it soared a square tower with battlements like the walls. The tall, traceried windows to either side were filled with stained glass. A grand residence, indeed, for a man of the clergy.

He dismounted, walked up the shallow steps, and pulled the bell rope. Its sonorous echoes sounded inside. Should he have sent prior warning? He suddenly doubted that he would be admitted, a depressing thought, for a sense of urgency was upon him. Every delay would mean another day that Mrs Morsley was subjected to her pitiful existence. Presently, he heard a latch being drawn back, and the heavy door opened. A haughty looking butler looked down his nose.

"Good morning," he said, handing over a card. "I wish to see Mr Hays."

The butler took the card, glancing at it briefly before making his reply.

"I do not believe you have an appointment, Captain Turner."

Edward straightened his shoulders, and with the cool reserve he was renowned for, stated his case.

"I have information that any magistrate, or man of God for that matter, will wish to be acquainted with."

The man seemed to waver and then looked over his shoulder.

"Philip, take Captain Turner's horse to the stables."

A footman obeyed the summons with alacrity, passing Edward without a glance. The butler than stood back to allow him to enter. He found himself in a spacious, lofty hall with a grand stairway sweeping upwards, then he was led through a doorway on the right. They passed a chapel and came to a small reception room. The butler indicated a chair.

"You may wait here, while I see if the reverend is available."

Within moments, he returned.

"Mr Hays is expecting you."

Edward stood and nodded, although he could not fathom why the butler had put him through this charade if the magistrate had been expecting him. It appeared either Wriggly, or more likely Constable Nadin had been busy.

He entered the room indicated, and a tall, well-built man, with white hair, dressed all in black, apart from his white shirt and well tied cravat, stood from behind a desk. The spectacles that perched on the bridge of his nose in no way detracted from his gravitas, perhaps because the eyes behind them were as sharp as the knife that he had so nearly avoided the previous evening. Mr Hays' face, whilst cast in a serious aspect, was not unappealing. A long, straight nose led to a mouth whose thin upper lip was ameliorated by a generous lower one.

By the end of the interview, Edward thought that those lips perfectly described Mr Hays' character. He was a curious mixture of the Old Testament and the New.

"Welcome, Captain Turner. I had been warned that I might expect a visit from you. Please, take a seat."

Being a straightforward man, Edward spoke his thoughts. "Then why did your butler think it necessary to keep me in suspense?"

A humourless smile touched the magistrate's lips. "A good butler, Captain Turner, always knows if a person is worthy of an audience. I cannot be disturbed at my home by everyone with a grievance."

His tone irked Edward. "Then you are fortunate to possess one. I do not believe many clergymen can boast of such an acquisition."

He regretted the words almost immediately. He had come to ask for the magistrate's aid in a delicate matter, not to antagonise the man.

"He is not *my* butler, Captain Turner. This house belongs to a generous member of my wife's family who graciously permits us to reside here. Although I find your words a trifle impertinent, I like a man who is not afraid to speak his mind."

"I am glad to hear it, Mr Hays. The story I have to tell, must, I fear, bring you a degree of consternation most unpleasant to you."

An almost supercilious smile edged the reverend's lips. "I hear, Captain Turner, that you did not only invoke my status as magistrate to the butler, but also that of my vocation to the Lord. You may be sure that both duties go hand in hand. As a man of the cloth, I must pray that wrongdoers repent of their sins and turn to God, and as a magistrate I must mete out justice to those who have of their own free will sinned." He frowned, steepling his fingers. "I am afraid that in your case that is not immediately possible. The man who accosted you last evening escaped the watchman."

Edward raised an eyebrow. "Escaped or was let go? I had the impression that Mr Wriggly knew the man and was reluctant to take him in."

The magistrate's frown deepened. "I have it on the authority of the deputy constable, Mr Nadin, that Mr Wriggly was outwitted. Your attacker fainted and being unable to carry him single handedly, the watchman went into a nearby inn to muster help."

"And when he returned the culprit was gone," Edward said dryly.

"Unfortunately, yes, but Mr Nadin has been as effective a constable as he was a thief-taker, and I am sure he will find him."

Edward had no great opinion of thief takers and said so.

"I understand your sentiments, sir, but one must be pragmatic. Where would we be without them? And if, on occasion, they seek to profit from their dangerous profession, though I cannot condone it, I must understand it. To catch a villain, one must, perforce, know their ways. Nadin has a large network of informers and has proved to be most efficient in capturing not only common criminals, but also those who would spread political dissent, which is an increasingly serious issue. Now, I believe there was another matter that you wished to bring before me."

Edward had to acknowledge there was much in what he said. "If this Mr Nadin is so well informed, then perhaps he may prove useful. Has a man named Mr Rogers ever been brought to your attention?"

The magistrate's eyes sharpened, and he leant forward a little. "Now you begin to interest me greatly, Captain Turner. I have heard of this man from several sources. Rumours swirl about him like dirty fog but prove to be just as impenetrable. Apart from a few criminals who have been arrested and have brought up his name in an attempt to clear themselves – unfortunately in these cases the evidence only damned them and so their testimony lacked credibility – no one will speak against him."

"I believe it. You mentioned earlier that it is your duty to mete out justice to those who have of their own free will sinned. It is my hope that as both magistrate and priest, you will show mercy to one who has sinned against her will."

The man sat back in his chair and folded his hands across his stomach. "I will reserve judgement until you have informed me of all the details of the case."

CHAPTER 14

Emily sat curled on the window seat, her eyes fixed on the park as they increasingly were with each passing day.

"He will not come the quicker because you look for him," Anne said gently.

The face that turned to her was not filled with disappointment but excitement. Anne's heart beat a little faster as she glanced regretfully at the chest. However tedious the task, she would have liked to finish it before he came. She had never before been allowed to interest herself in what were considered to be the affairs of men, and she did not wish to appear incompetent.

"It's not Captain Turner. It's Mr Townsend, I think, come to dig up the park. Only he is so far away, it is hard to be sure."

Anne went to a shelf and picked up the spy glass she had moved there to make room for the papers. Returning to the window, she held it to her eye. Mr Townsend appeared to be erecting a large tent. She let out a long, slow breath. How foolish she was to worry about what Captain Turner might think of her. She had given up trying to please men long ago, and besides, she had eased his burden, after all, and he could expect no more of her.

It was the children who were important, and if fostering his relationship with them required her to give more of herself than she would like, then so be it. It meant no more than that. It could not. Her palms suddenly felt damp, and she wished for nothing more than to escape the room she had become far too comfortable in. The schoolroom was her place, not the library.

"Would you like to go and see what he is doing?"

Emily jumped up, her face eager. "Barbara will wish to come too."

"Then let us go upstairs and don stout walking shoes. The park will be muddy."

Miss Burdock expressed her wish to accompany them, and Anne discovered that contrary to the initial impression she had given, she was remarkably spry. When she mentioned this, the lady turned to her, a decided twinkle in her eye.

"My dear Mrs Huxley, when you are as old as I, you must play to the few advantages you have."

A surprised laugh escaped Anne. "I see I must keep my wits about me where you are concerned, Miss Burdock."

She chuckled. "It is advisable to always keep your wits about you, my dear."

Anne raised an eyebrow. "As you did outside the inn?"

Miss Burdock shook her head. "I will admit I was

taken unawares on that occasion, but it all worked out in the end, did it not?"

"Thus far," Anne said.

Miss Burdock wagged a finger. "We must take each day as it comes, Mrs Huxley, and enjoy whatever it offers."

Anne smiled ruefully. "Wise words, Miss Burdock. I will endeavour to remember them."

The girls had been walking a little in front of them, but as they neared the tent, they broke into a run.

"Be careful!" Anne called, leaving Miss Burdock behind as she ran after them. "I do not wish either of you to fall into another rabbit hole."

But it was not the children who were destined to suffer this fate but Anne. Her foot sank into a depression in the ground, causing her to stumble, her arms windmilling through the air as she tried and failed to regain her balance. She heard a crack and then felt a burning sensation in her upper arm as she fell to her knees. She twisted her head to see what might have caused it, gasping as she saw the rent in her spencer and the blood that stained it. A wave of weakness overtook her, and she slumped forwards, one hand braced against the ground.

Miss Burdock's muddied boots appeared beside her. "Oh, Mrs Huxley, you are injured."

"I will be better in a moment," she gasped. "Get the children into the tent, if you please."

A deep voice sounded above her. "They are already there, Mrs Huxley, and will remain there until I say otherwise."

She sat back on her heels and looked into the concerned face of Mr Townsend.

"I have sent two of my men into the woods to discover the culprit, if they can. Rufus has put the word out that any who wish to hunt rabbits may do so for the next week, commencing tomorrow. He intended to come up to the house later to warn you and the children to keep out of the woods for the duration, but it appears someone misunderstood his instructions."

Her dizziness was receding, and she gave a weak smile. "If those who come to shoot the rabbits are as incompetent as the man who grazed my arm, I think we must give this part of the park a wide berth as well as the woods."

He put out an arm as she rose to her feet. "Perhaps that would be best. Come into the tent and I will send to the stables for a suitable equipage to take you back to the house."

"That is not necessary," she murmured. "It is only a scratch."

He frowned. "Nevertheless, I think it would be best—" He broke off as the muffled sound of hooves on turf caught his attention. "Ah, if this is Rufus, he can lead you on his horse."

She turned her head, one glance telling her it was not he who approached but Captain Turner.

~

Edward blinked rapidly, trying to banish the grittiness that blurred his eyes. He had travelled through the night and then hired a horse in Midhurst to bring him the rest of the way. As he rounded the corner of the house, he noticed Mrs Huxley running towards a tent. Who would put up such a monstrosity in the park? Was it gypsies? He turned the horse and cantered towards it. As he neared the governess, a sharp crack rang out, and to his dismay, he saw Mrs Huxley fall to her knees.

A stillness came over him, a cool clarity chasing the fug of weariness from his mind, and he spurred his horse to a gallop. He saw three men emerge from a tent. Two sprinted towards the woods, and one hurried towards the governess. Townsend. His tight grip on the reins slackened as he saw Mrs Huxley sit back on her heels and then take the hand his neighbour offered her.

Relief mixed with anger flooded him. How had this happened? He remembered that he had given Rufus permission to let it be known that any who wished might hunt rabbits in the woods. His mouth drew into a grim line. A stray shot then. What was she about to put herself in danger like that? A diminutive figure moved beside her. Miss Burdock. A spike of alarm shot through him. If they were both abroad, surely the children must be also. His eyes ranged over the immediate area, and as they came to rest on the tent, he saw Emily's head peep around the open flap. They were safe! But, good Lord, they might as easily have been injured as Mrs Huxley.

He jumped from his horse the moment he came up to the governess. Her usually clear eyes were clouded, a small frown puckering her brow.

"Good timing, Turner," Townsend said. "The rabbit cull was not supposed to commence until the morrow, but it seems someone either misunderstood or was a little too eager. I have sent two men to discover the culprit and ensure that no one else has taken such a liberty. Mrs Huxley's arm has only been grazed, but I think she should return to the house immediately and the doctor be sent for. Perhaps you might take her up on your horse."

"There is no need," the governess said. "I am perfectly capable of walking."

Her naturally pale skin had turned the colour of bleached bone, and she was leaning heavily on Townsend's arm.

A spurt of irritation shot through him. "God's teeth, woman. Your composure is in equal parts admirable and foolish. Townsend is right." He turned to his horse and put his foot in the stirrup. "If you will help her mount in front of me, Townsend—"

"No." The word was sharply spoken, as if she were panicked or afraid. Perhaps she had a fear of horses. He removed his foot from the stirrup, turned, and strode to her. "I am not about to stand here and debate with you, ma'am, when it is clear you might collapse at any moment." As she opened her lips to reply, he scooped her into his arms. "If you will not ride, I will carry you."

She gasped, her eyes widening. "Sir! Put me down."

Emily's excited voice carried to them. "Captain Turner! You came back!"

He glanced up to see both children racing towards them.

"Why are you cuddling, Mrs Huxley?" Barbara asked.

Emily gasped, fear filling her eyes. "She's bleeding!"

"I told you to remain in the tent, imp," Townsend said, his voice unusually stern.

The child ignored him, her eyes fixed on her governess's bloodied sleeve.

"Mrs Huxley has suffered an injury and must return to the house, as you must learn to do what you are told," Edward snapped.

"It is nothing serious, Emily," the governess said.

The girl hunched a shoulder. "Then why is he carrying you?"

She forced a smile to her lips. "Because he thinks me a poor creature who will faint at the sight of blood, but you know that I am not."

It should have been him reassuring them, he realised. These children had lost everyone who was important to them, and it was only natural they should fear the worst. When Emily nodded, the governess looked up at him, and he was relieved to see the clouds in her eyes had been pierced by rays of exasperation.

"I will consent to ride before you, sir, if you will but put me down."

"Quite right," Miss Burdock said, drawing Barbara to her side. "You have sustained a shock and now is no time for misplaced modesty. Barbara, Emily, you must remain with me, and we shall look in on Mrs Huxley when she is feeling more the thing."

Miss Burdock's words shed a little light on Mrs Huxley's objections. The thought of being held so close offended her notions of modesty. She was no innocent, however. She had been married. It did not necessarily follow, of course, that she had enjoyed her husband's attentions. He shook his head as if to rid himself of the thought. He should not speculate on such private matters. Setting her carefully on her feet, he went to his horse.

"Come, Mrs Huxley. If you will place your foot on my boot and give me your uninjured arm, I think between us, Townsend and I will be able to settle you without causing you too much discomfort."

She sat stiffly before him as his arm encircled her waist. "Forgive the familiarity, ma'am. It is necessary for your safety; I would not risk you falling."

"Then I hope your riding skill is superior to that of your driving," she muttered.

Surprise made his arm tighten and he heard her gasp.

"I beg your pardon, sir. I should not have spoken my thought aloud."

"Perhaps not," he allowed. "But I would rather hear an honest criticism than a false compliment, although how you can make any judgement on my driving when you have not witnessed it, I do not know."

At least Mrs Huxley was showing a true hint of herself rather than the blandness she often assumed in his company. The notion that she felt bound to hide her opinions because she feared dismissal disturbed him. Wishing to reassure her, he chose to reply with the same candour.

"As it happens, driving does not come naturally to me. I have had far more practise at riding, however. I realised when I was made lieutenant that others, who were there by dint of their relatives rather than their skill, would always look down on me if I did not acquire some of the attributes thought necessary in a gentleman. Whenever I was granted time ashore, I applied myself to learning to ride. I believe myself competent, and even if I was not, this mild-mannered slug would offer only the veriest novice any trouble."

∽

His arm felt like a steel band about Anne's waist, and she felt panic rising within her.

"I believe you are right, Captain Turner," she said, her voice tight. "In which case, I would appreciate it if you would loosen your hold."

His arm immediately relaxed. "Forgive me. I did not mean to alarm you."

The tension left her. He had apologised to her twice in as many minutes, and what is more, he had repaid her snide remark with patience and a degree of honesty she had not expected. In her experience, men did not admit their flaws. She realised that her alarm had been foolish and allowed herself to lean against him. In truth, she had little choice, for she felt light-headed; perhaps that was why a peculiar sensation of safety swept over her. She closed her eyes, wishing to savour the feeling. It had been so long since she had felt it. Her eyes jerked open as she heard his voice.

"Mrs Huxley? Are you still with me?"

She smiled at the gruff concern in his voice. "Yes, Captain Turner. I shall not cause you the further inconvenience of fainting away, I assure you."

As they turned the corner of the house and approached the front door, Rufus came cantering up the drive. He pulled up sharply, his fascinated eyes going to the torn and bloodied sleeve of Anne's spencer.

"I'd get that seen to, ma'am. Flesh wounds can be nasty."

"I assume you have come to warn Mrs Huxley that there will be shooting in the woods, but you are too late. Someone has already started," Captain Turner snapped. "And rather than sitting there stating the obvious, I suggest you ride for the doctor! After you have taken my horse to the stable that is." And then in a softer voice. "I am about to dismount, Mrs Huxley. Hold on."

He slid to the ground, reached up, grasped her about the waist, and lifted her down. Rufus rode forwards and took the reins of his horse.

"I will, of course, but I do not understand how this happened. I made it clear that the cull should not start until the morrow."

"Apparently, not clear enough."

Anne allowed him to draw her hand through his arm and leant against him.

"It is not his fault, Captain."

For the first time she realised how tired he looked. Poor man, to arrive home to this drama. The door opened and Mrs Thirsk stepped through it. She cast one look at Anne and stood to one side.

"You be off to fetch Mr Robart, Master Rufus, and you bring her in, Captain. Sit her down by the fire in the library while I fetch some bandages and water."

"I would prefer to go to my room," she said.

"You don't want to be tackling the stairs just yet, ma'am," the housekeeper said firmly. "I don't know how it happened, but it's plain you've suffered a shock."

"I can carry you," the captain offered.

"No," she said quickly. His nearness was no longer so alarming, but she did not wish to create any more drama than she already had. "The library will suffice."

After seeing her to a chair, he turned and strode to a sideboard. He poured two glasses of brandy and returned to her.

"I realise this may be a little strong for you, but believe me when I say it will make you feel better." He held out a glass. "Come, take it."

"I will certainly take it," she said, accepting the glass and taking an unladylike gulp.

"Have another," he said, kneeling in front of her. "I am going to attempt to remove your spencer, but as the sleeves are so tight, it might be painful."

She did as he requested, her breath hitching in her throat as he began to unfasten the buttons of the figure-hugging garment. His hands were large and calloused but his long fingers nimble, and he managed to open it in seconds, his manner impersonal and his digits barely brushing against her. He eased it off her uninjured arm first, and then as gently as he could, down the other. She sucked in a breath, the soft cloth feeling as abrasive as wire as it passed over her wound. He glanced up, his eyes holding yet another apology as he removed it and dropped it on the floor.

"If you do not object to it, ma'am, I think the sleeve of your dress should be cut away."

She nodded. "Certainly. It is already quite ruined."

It appeared the housekeeper had a similar idea for she came in with a basin of water, cloths, bandages, and sewing scissors. She set all but the scissors on the floor beside Anne's chair.

"We'll have you more comfortable, directly, ma'am."

So saying, she straightened and bent over Anne. Her sleeve was fuller at the shoulder, and it was there she made an incision, cutting around her arm. The material flopped down to where the sleeve narrowed, and Mrs Thirsk cut the material down the back of her arm to her wrist, the blunt edge of the blade cool against her skin. The still wet blood held the fine wool in place, and after gently dabbing a damp cloth around the wound, she slowly peeled it away. Anne dared a glance and saw a shallow, two-inch gash, the blood now only a trickle.

"If you will excuse me, Mrs Thirsk, I would like to see if any cloth has become lodged in the wound."

Anne stifled a giggle as she saw a huge eye bend towards her. "I did not think you the man to use a quizzing glass, sir."

Edward smiled wryly. "Nor am I. This belonged to the admiral. I found it in his desk."

After a close inspection, he straightened. "You may wash the wound, Mrs Thirsk." He glanced at Anne. "Good, you have a little colour in your cheeks, but I would have a little more brandy if I were you. It may sting."

Anne shook her head. "I am already feeling its effects."

She was glad of it, for the housekeeper was quite firm in her ministrations. Her arm felt hot and the bandage tight, but when she mentioned it, she was informed by the captain that was only to be expected.

"Do I take it you are speaking from experience, Captain Turner?"

"I am," he said. "You will have a scar, I am afraid."

"It is of no moment," she murmured.

~

Was her unconcern genuine or a result of the brandy? Sophia would have had hysterics at the thought of a scar on her smooth skin whether visible or not.

As Mrs Thirsk left the room carrying the cloths and bloodied water, fast footsteps sounded in the hall, and Emily's alarmed voice carried through the open door.

"Mrs Thirsk! The basin is full of blood!"

He frowned. "Drat the girl! Can she do nothing she is told?"

"Do not be so hard on her, Captain. She has looked for you every day."

"Because she wishes to know what I have discovered."

She gave a tiny shake of her head. "It is not only that, sir. Her words on seeing you were, *you came back*. But just as one fear was assuaged, another took its place. Mrs Thirsk will explain to her that it is merely stained water in the bowl, but she will need to see for herself that I am well."

Her words disarmed him, and the thought of the recalcitrant child watching for him touched him.

"You have borne your injury with remarkable equanimity, ma'am, but you are not well."

She sat a little straighter in her chair. "There

would have been little point in falling into hysterics. I am injured, not ill."

Her practical observation amused him, and he laughed softly. Her lack of excessive sensibility, the calmness with which she faced adversity was refreshing and quite genuine, he felt sure. It was very different from the blank, wooden expression that had so irked him.

"Mrs Huxley, you surprise me at every turn."

"If I do, it is not my intention. Do not turn Emily away, sir. It is not fair that either of us should keep her in suspense."

He nodded and strode to the door. Mrs Thirsk had put down the bowl and was holding Emily's arm.

"I have no doubt that you have ignored Miss Burdock's instructions, Emily."

The child's shoulders hunched, and Edward again saw the mixture of defiance and fear which had been in her father's eyes when he had lain dying in his arms. His lips twisted.

"But as that can no longer be helped, you may as well come into the library."

She ran past him, coming to a halt in front of Mrs Huxley who smiled reassuringly.

"You see, Emily, I am quite recovered."

"Does it hurt?"

"Yes, but that is only to be expected. The doctor will come presently to check the wound, but I am certain he will think it a trifle."

Seemingly satisfied, the child turned to the captain.

"Did you knock Mr Rogers down?"

His lips tightened, a fierce anger sweeping through him. He pushed it down as the child's eyes widened and she took a step back.

"I did, indeed. Mr Roger and his accomplices are now awaiting their trial for fraud amongst other things, a very serious crime that may see them hanged."

Emily's brow wrinkled. "What is fraud?"

"It is when a person pretends to be someone else to gain some advantage."

The child's face hardened. "Did he take Pa's money?"

"With the help of several others."

His stomach churned at what else he had discovered, but that was not for Emily's ears.

Other footsteps sounded in the hall and Miss Burdock and Barbara came into the room. The lady was breathing rapidly.

"There you are. It was very naughty of you to run away like that, Emily, but I suppose it was to be expected." She smiled at Anne. "She was so worried about you, my dear, that it was quite impossible to stop her."

"Your dress is torn," Barbara said.

"So it is," Anne agreed. "But it is of no matter. I have others."

"Oh, what a waste of a good dress, when all we need do is fashion another sleeve," Miss Burdock protested.

Personally, Edward thought the grey woollen garment drab and would quite happily have consigned it to the fire.

Mrs Thirsk entered the room, a white-haired gentleman in her wake, and Miss Burdock gently shooed the children from the room. After a brief word with the doctor, Edward followed them. He noticed Emily was lagging behind and called her to him.

Going down on his haunches, he put a hand on her shoulder. "I am sorry if I upset you, child."

Her face crumpled and he pulled her to him. She stood stiffly in the circle of his arms for a moment before burying her face in his shoulder. His eyes met Miss Burdock's and at a brief nod from him, she took Barbara by the hand and continued on her way.

Presently, Emily stepped back and although she had not made a sound, he saw her cheeks were damp. He pulled a handkerchief from his coat and dabbed awkwardly at her face.

"It is done, and you must look to the future. This is your home now, and although I can never replace your parents, I will do my best to ensure you and your sister are safe and happy."

"And will you look after Mrs Huxley?"

His mouth quirked up on one side. He felt sure she would bridle at the suggestion. Mrs Huxley, if he knew anything about it, would insist she was perfectly capable of looking after herself. He would admit, if only to himself, that when he had had her up before him on his horse and she had leant against him, he had felt a strong desire to keep her safe.

"I will do my best to protect all my dependents."

"Thank you," she whispered. "I did not mean what I said before. You must have liked Pa to take us in."

He rose to his feet. "And so I did. He was an honest, brave man. I will tell you and Barbara more of him, but perhaps not today. I have much to do. Go to Miss Burdock and try to do as you are told."

CHAPTER 15

He met the doctor at the door to the library and held out his hand.

"Thank you, Mr Robart."

The man shook it, his grip firm. "There was little for me to do, Captain Turner. I have bound the wound tight rather than administer sutures. In my opinion, a scar trumps the risk of infection."

"I agree," he said. "And Mrs Huxley appears resigned to it."

The surgeon smiled. "Indeed, she is a remarkable woman; her fortitude is matched by her calm, good sense. I only hope I do not have a spate of other injuries to see to when the rabbit cull begins in earnest."

Edward had not thought of that, assuming that the country folk would be competent at such a common pastime as hunting their dinner. The events of the day had already proved him wrong, however.

Mr Robart chuckled. "Do not look so concerned, sir. I do not envisage a catastrophic event. Word of

Mrs Huxley's accident will soon get out, and I am sure more care will be taken when there are a number of people in the woods. I think it much more likely that there will be disagreements about who shot the rabbit than a fatal accident. I envisage black eyes, or a broken ankle from tripping over a tree root, or perhaps a foot becoming caught in a snare. I believe the admiral had many set to keep people away."

Edward nodded. "I have employed a man to clear them and tidy up the wood, so the children may safely play there."

Mrs Thirsk appeared, carrying a tea tray. She had a blanket draped over her arm. Edward relieved her of them.

"An excellent notion. I will see to Mrs Huxley whilst you see Mr Robart to the door. Perhaps you would also send some refreshments up to the nursery."

"Certainly."

The doctor put on his hat and nodded. "I shall return in a few days to observe Mrs Huxley's wound. In the meantime, it should be kept clean and bound. I do not envisage any difficulty but send for me if there is any cause for concern."

"You may be sure I will. Thank you for your prompt arrival."

He found Mrs Huxley on her feet. He put down the tea tray and went to her, wrapping the blanket about her shoulders.

"Please, sit down. A cup of tea will make you feel better."

A wry smile tilted her lips. "Ah, the English cure-all. I admit one will be welcome. I could as easily take it in my own sitting room, however." Her gaze moved towards his desk. "I am afraid you still have much to do."

For the first time since his arrival, he glanced at the neat stacks of paper that covered the desk's surface.

"I put those I considered of interest on the right-hand side, and those that might be disposed of on the left. The chest is not yet empty, however."

"Thank you for all you have done, Mrs Huxley. Did you perhaps find the deed to the house?"

She shook her head as she sat down. "I did not. Perhaps you will find it amongst the remaining papers. Is it important that you discover it?"

"Not particularly, I suppose," he said. "But I do not enjoy loose ends."

"No," she said thoughtfully. "Speaking of loose ends, I gained the impression earlier that you had found rather more of them than you had expected in Manchester. When you spoke of Mr Rogers, you looked as if you would have happily placed the noose around his neck yourself."

He grimaced. "You are perceptive, Mrs Huxley, but I am not sure the perfidy I uncovered is any more fit for your ears than Emily's."

She put down her cup. "I am not a child, sir, and I doubt anything you might say will have the power to surprise me. However, as it is curiosity which drives me rather than necessity, I will admit it is not my affair and leave you."

Her tone was wooden once more, and he suddenly knew the urge to dent her impassivity. If what he had to say did not surprise her, she must have led a most unusual life for a gently born lady.

"Mrs Morsley was the lady who moved into the house, and she impersonated the girls' mother, although she did not personally gain from it."

She stared at him, her brow slightly furrowed. "You mean, I suppose, that Mr Rogers coerced her in some way?"

His jaw tightened. "In the worst of ways. He chose his tenants very carefully. He preyed on widowed or abandoned women with children, offering them a cheap rent. After a period of time, he would put it up, and when they could not afford it, he would threaten them with debtor's prison if they did not do as he wished. Once he had them in his power, he would degrade them in the basest of manners."

Her eyes sparked with anger. "So, Mr Rogers was a wolf in sheep's clothing, luring these women into a trap. I assume it was he who kept Mr Proctor's pay?"

"Indeed, it was."

"How did you persuade Mrs Morsley to turn informer? Was she not afraid?"

"Certainly, she was afraid of Rogers, but she was even more afraid of the prospect of her daughter being used as she was."

She sat as stone, her fingers clasped in her lap, only her eyes revealing her shock and disgust. It afforded him no satisfaction.

"How old is her daughter?" she murmured.

He ran a hand through his hair. "Only a little older than Emily."

Her hand rose to her mouth. "What will happen to Mrs Morsley and her daughter now?"

He sat on the edge of his desk. "The magistrate I went to was also a reverend with firm moral views on such activities. Rogers' name was not unknown to him; he had been associated with a host of other crimes from blackmail to theft, but there was never enough proof to bring him to justice. The reverend was prepared to treat Mrs Morsley with leniency if her information led him to Rogers. An acquaintance of his is chaplain at the Magdalen Hospital in London which takes in fallen women who wish to repent their way of life and make a fresh start. He suggested I take Mrs Morsley and her daughter there."

She closed her eyes and nodded. "I am glad." He thought he saw concern in them when she opened them. "You have been gone longer than you envisaged and look quite exhausted. Was it very difficult to catch him?"

Edward's lips curved with grim irony. "The deputy constable, Mr Joseph Nadin, was most helpful. He was a thief-taker at one time and if I am not mistaken is a contemptible fellow who uses the law to his own advantage. He managed to gather a host of information on Rogers with remarkable rapidity which leads me to believe that he was not wholly ignorant of his enterprise." He shrugged. "I would not be surprised if he received bribes to look the other way." He sighed. "Whatever the truth of it, Rogers has been arrested on a number of charges, as have several of his accomplices." He rubbed absently at his knuckles. "Not before I had the pleasure of knocking him down, however."

The edges of her lips tilted up a fraction. "As a rule, I do not approve of violence, sir, but I will admit I am very glad of it."

A brief knock sounded on the door and Mrs

Thirsk came in and announced Mr Rufus Townsend. He strode into the room, a frown on his face.

"They found no one in the woods," he said. "Nor did your man Gibbons see anyone although he was not far away. I shall ask our own gamekeeper to help him keep an eye on things for the next week."

"You relieve my mind, Rufus."

"I shall leave you now," Mrs Huxley said, rising to her feet.

Rufus executed a rather awkward bow. "I hope you recover soon, ma'am."

Mrs Thirsk came forwards. "I'll take you upstairs, Mrs Huxley, and help you out of that dress."

∼

After helping her into a gown with loose full sleeves, Mrs Thirsk left her. Anne was glad of it. Her arm and heart throbbed in unison. Mr Rogers was a villain, indeed. Poor Mrs Proctor. She had worked her fingers to the bone rather than submit to him, and her integrity had been repaid with her and her children being cast on the parish, illness, and death. She covered her face with her hands, wincing as her arm protested. Thank heavens Captain Turner had found them.

A face rose unbidden in her mind. A visage not dissimilar to her own, only the eyes were deep blue, the hair a vibrant red, and the skin smoother and younger. Felicity. She choked back a sob. It would not do to dwell on the past; there lay only heartbreak and despair.

A different image intruded. Captain Turner

putting the blanket around her shoulders with a firm but delicate hand. His fingers had hardly brushed against her, but she had been aware of their nearness. She had felt his warmth, the shelter of his arms behind her, and had known the urge to lean back against him as she had on the horse. She had yearned to once more know that feeling of safety, of being protected and cared for.

She rose to her feet so swiftly the blood rushed to her head. Waiting only for the disorientation to pass, she put back her shoulders and went to the schoolroom. She needed distraction.

"My dear," Miss Burdock said, "you should be resting."

Emily came to her defence. "Mrs Huxley is no weakling. She is strong and brave and..." Her brow puckered as she searched for the word. "Resilient."

Anne laughed, her mood lifting. "Thank you, Emily. Now, let us play a game. I shall call out a letter, and you and Barbara must find as many things as possible beginning with that letter before I can count to twenty and bring them to me. Are you ready?"

The sound of running footsteps and laughter soon filled the nursery, and Anne's mood lightened even further. When she had a large pile of items in front of her, she reversed the game, so that everything was returned to its place. By the time they had finished, it was getting dark.

"Now, go and wash for dinner," she said. "If you are ever to be ready to dine with Captain Turner, we shall need to practise both our table manners and dinner conversation."

As they were forbidden to leave the house the for

the duration of the rabbit cull, Anne interspersed the girls' lessons with play. Both the sisters enjoyed acting; Barbara because she was of an age where the realm of reality and imagination were still closely aligned, and Emily because her sharp observations made her a natural mimic. She used this to her advantage. She and Miss Burdock would enact a scene and they would copy them. It was as good a way to teach them the manners of the day as any she could think of, and she was pleased to find their language subtly altering without them being overly corrected.

Captain Turner would send for them whenever he had a few moments spare, to enquire about their day. This was not done in an interrogatory manner, but gently. They began to take him a piece of their work, and he never failed to praise them. Consequently, they began to look forward to the ritual.

Anne and Miss Burdock would remain in the background, as was only fitting, but whilst Miss Burdock brought her knitting, Anne would remain motionless, her hands folded in her lap, observing their interactions. It brought her great pleasure to see the increasing animation with which the children addressed him. They enjoyed their lessons, taking pride in what they achieved, and the pinched, rather haunted look had left them.

Of course, she could not help but observe Captain Turner too. He was not an easy man to read, his swarthy, rather hard face giving little away, but she slowly began to realise why the children were not put off by his manner. The changes in his demeanour were subtle, mainly in his eyes, which would soften, as would the line of his jaw.

He sent for them late one morning, and they brought drawings of a mosaic they had been working on. After having seen one depicting a dolphin in the book Anne had liberated from the library, they had each chosen an animal to be the feature. Anne had drawn a grid for them, onto which Barbara had drawn a large rabbit, only recognisable by its fluffy tail and long, pointy ears. Emily had revealed herself to be naturally gifted, drawing a very creditable dog. They had used coloured pastels to create the mosaic effect, much smudged in Barbara's case.

When they entered the room, Captain Turner rose from his desk, now denuded of all but a small stack of papers and came around it to greet them.

"Good day, children. What have you brought me today?"

Barbara ran to him and delivered her offering into his hands. He spent some moments studying it before raising his eyes to Anne, a question in them. She mouthed the word rabbit, and he studied the artwork once more.

"The ears are very good," he said at last. "And you have used such an interesting array of colours. I have never seen a blue rabbit, but I am sure he is a splendid fellow."

Barbara beamed. "I thought you might like to put it on the wall. The pictures in here are dull and boring."

Anne smiled as his eyes wandered about the room, a thoughtful frown on his brow. It was true that there were several murky hunting scenes on the walls, but there were also several depicting ships. She was sure he would not think them dull and boring. It was kind of him to at least appear to take Barbara's suggestion seriously, however. Of course, he could not possibly accede to her suggestion. How foolish he would appear when entertaining visitors. She wondered how he would reject the offer without hurting Barbara's feelings. It appeared the thought had also crossed Miss Burdock's mind, for her needles stopped clacking, and she raised her eyes.

"I don't think, my dear—" she began, but the captain forestalled her with a small shake of his head, before turning back to the child.

"How true," he acknowledged. "I had not noticed it before, but the pictures are not at all inspiring. I will certainly keep this, Barbara, and put it in my desk until I have time to have it framed."

Reaching behind him, he laid it on the mahogany surface and held out a hand for Emily's effort. As Barbara skipped to Miss Burdock's side, she came forward, a small smile on her lips.

"You don't need to put my or my sister's work on the wall. It would look funny."

"Let me be the judge of that," he said softly.

∽

He glanced down at the offering, hoping he would be able to interpret it rather more successfully. Emily was far quicker witted than her younger sister, and he would not be able to use the same ruse again.

His eyebrows rose as he studied it. There was nothing crude about this representation of a dog, and she had added quirky details that gave it character. A pink tongue lolled from its mouth, and one ear pointed forwards, the other to the side. It was clearly a terrier of the most disreputable kind. His mouth quirked into a smile.

"Why do I have the feeling you have met this dog before?"

The child's smile was bittersweet. "Ma wouldn't let us have him. She said he was a scavenger and full of fleas, and that we couldn't afford to keep him. But I used to save him some scraps and feed him them when she was out."

The thought of this defiant, resilient little girl reserving food for the animal when she had, he felt sure, so little herself, provoked both his pity and his admiration. His eyes dropped to the picture again.

"Did you give him a name?"

"Patch, because—"

"He has black patches on his coat," he finished for her.

A wistful look entered her eyes. "I hope he didn't starve after we went to the workhouse."

He shook his head. "He looks like an intelligent creature, and I am sure he could not survive on the scraps you gave him alone." He reached out his arm as if he would hand it back but then retracted it. "May I keep it? Or would you like it as a reminder of your old friend?"

She shrugged. "I can make another one."

He placed it next to her sister's picture. "I must think of some way to repay you both for your kindness and hard work."

His gaze went to Mrs Huxley, thinking that perhaps she might offer a suggestion. She did not immediately perceive it, her eyes fixed on Emily, and her lips curved in a proud smile, as a mother might look upon a daughter. Never had he seen such a softened expression upon her face, and something stirred in the region of his heart. He tried to interpret it and decided it must be pity. This woman, who had such a deft hand with children, would never have her own.

"Perhaps you might tell us something about our pa," Emily said.

He glanced down. "He was a good man with a promising future before him. I wished him to make lieutenant, which was not a common occurrence for someone who had come up through his route; but it was possible. He deserved that opportunity, for he was courageous and had the ability."

Emily's head tipped to one side. "Ma said that he might not have left her if she had been better educated."

"But that was not true; he never left her. He wanted to make something of himself, so that he might give you all a better life."

She nodded.

A firm step and cheerful whistle was heard in the hall, and Mr Thomas Townsend strode into the room. He paused, offering a flourishing bow.

"Aha! How appropriate that my two favourite ragamuffins are here just at this moment."

Barbara rose to her feet and curtsied. "We are not ragamuffins but young ladies."

Emily followed suit, and lifting her chin, adopted a haughty attitude. "And it is not at all the thing to come into the presence of ladies in your shirtsleeves, sir."

He shook his head ruefully, his glance sweeping over Anne and Miss Burdock. "Whilst I am in awe of your achievements, I cannot reconcile myself to so drastic a change." His glance returned to the sisters, and he shook his head mournfully. "My two little imps would, I know, like nothing more than to come and see what I have discovered, but these two very correct young ladies standing before me, must, I am sure, consider the prospect of traipsing around a muddy site quite beneath them."

Barbara clapped her hands. "Thomas! Have you found more treasure?"

He grinned. "I have certainly found something of interest."

"Is it a mosaic?" Emily asked.

"It is indeed a fine example of opus musivum," he said. "Although we have only uncovered a small portion thus far, I believe it might prove to be quite spectacular."

Mrs Huxley rose to her feet with the quiet grace Edward was becoming accustomed to. "I think it would be most apt for the children to see it." She glanced at him. "Are you in agreement, sir? We have all been confined to the house and courtyard for the last week, and I am sure we would benefit from the walk."

"By all means. I wish to see this discovery myself."

CHAPTER 16

Whilst the ladies went to don their hats and coats, Edward shared a glass of wine with Townsend. He smiled wryly as he offered it to him.

"You have infected my wards with your enthusiasm."

He showed him their latest work. Townsend regarded the pictures, laughter lighting his eyes. "Why, this is marvellous. But if ever I admit to seeing a blue rabbit, I beg you will tie me up and ensure Rufus removes all the wine and brandy from my house."

Although he smiled, Edward's instincts warned him there was more to this comment than frivolous amusement. Townsend's spirits always seemed high, perhaps too high.

"You may be sure I will do so. Has he ever had to take such a measure before?"

The man looked startled, uneasiness creeping into his eyes. It was gone in an instant, and he laughed.

"Never make the mistake of taking me too seriously, Turner. Except where my work is concerned, of course. By the way, Rufus is impressed by your diligence and attention to detail. He tells me you handled the hideous amount of papers you discovered at Rose Cottage yourself. Did you find anything worth the mention?"

Although he noted it, Edward accepted the abrupt change of subject. "He misinformed you. Mrs Huxley saved me much time. She sorted through the majority of them herself whilst I was away."

Townsend raised an eyebrow. "She is proving indispensable then."

A half smile touched Edward's lips. "She is certainly proving to be very useful. It was interesting to read the correspondence from the past tenants. I hope I will be a better landlord. The new arrivals are to move in next week, and we have hired a man to oversee the home farm. I must thank you for sending me Rufus. He is certainly proving indispensable."

A fond smile touched Townsend's lips. "I am pleased to hear it. He seems content, and there has been no more talk of him moving elsewhere."

Edward considered the man. He now understood Rufus quite well, and although he was everything Townsend had described him as, he did not subscribe to young men being tied to home. Although it was against his own interests, he spoke his thoughts.

"Are you sure it is fair to him to keep him here? He is more than capable, and there is a whole world out there he has never seen. A young man's development must be furthered by experience, after all."

A rare frown touched his neighbour's brow. "For the average young man, perhaps, but you know my feelings on this subject. And Rufus's oddities aside, why should he leave? Lavington House will one day be his, after all."

"You are hardly an ancient," Edward parried, "and I imagine there is every possibility that you will one day marry and produce an heir."

Townsend's laugh was a little harsh. "That is highly unlikely, my friend. At thirty-eight, I am a confirmed bachelor. Unlike you, I have not spent my life at sea and have had myriad opportunities to settle down. Who would put up with me? If my head is not in a book, my hands are in the dirt. No, when he is ready, I will endeavour to find Rufus a young, gentle bride who will not play him false."

Was that a hint of bitterness he heard in Townsend's voice? Had he too fallen foul of an unscrupulous woman? It was none of his business. Indeed, he did not know what he was about to impose on Townsend like this. He had always tried to assist the young men in his charge, but life at sea was different; dangerous and challenging, and they needed guidance.

The housekeeper came into the room carrying a coat.

"Ah," Townsend said. "Mrs Thirsk, thank you for brushing the mud from my coat. It was very kind of you."

He took it from her and shrugged it on. "I will see you at the dig, Turner. Make sure the ladies wrap up warm; there is a cold wind blowing."

Edward's eyes rested on the empty door for a moment. Townsend was a good man, and he hoped, a friend, but there were depths to him he had not fathomed. His eyes fell to the table where the man had left his glass of wine. He had hardly touched it. It seemed Edward had struck a nerve.

He went to his desk and picked up the girls' pictures, a gentle smile he would hardly have recognised could he but have seen it, touching his lips. Between them, Mrs Huxley and Miss Burdock had wrought a miracle. Only a few weeks ago, Emily, at least, had defied him at every turn, and Barbara had looked lost and unhappy. Now, they offered him a gift.

He opened a drawer and placed them in it, beside the two keys he had not yet identified. Picking them up, he threw them gently up and down in the palm of his hand, a small frown etching his brow. He really did not like loose ends. Not only had he not yet discovered the whereabouts of the deed for Rose Cottage, neither had he discovered whatever it was these were meant to unlock. He felt sure the admiral would not have kept them in his drawer for no good reason. Unlike the chaos of Tilbury's study, here everything had been in order, as he would have expected. Something stirred in the depths of his memory. An image of the admiral, or captain as he had been then, standing up from his desk and turning towards the bulkhead behind it. His hand reached towards the picture that hung there.

"Well, Turner," he said, readjusting the painting which had not been quite straight. "In endeavouring to tack after the enemy you find your ship will not stay. What method would you use to get her upon the other tack, losing as little time and way as possible?"

Captain Tewk had been preparing him for his lieutenant's exam in a thorough and meticulous way. If Edward had not understood the destructive power of love, he would have been unable to fathom the man taking his hand off the tiller and allowing such a man as Tilbury to take it. In truth, he still did not completely understand it. His own despair had led him to behave somewhat recklessly, it was true, but not to the extent that he had forgotten his duty. Indeed, his determination to block everything else from his mind had driven him to dedicate himself to his mission with a ferocious fervour.

He put the keys back in the drawer and closed it with a snap. Perhaps he had not been so much in love as he had thought. Perhaps it had been his pride as much as his heart that had been wounded. He had only known Sophia for six months, after all, and then only sporadically when his duties had allowed.

He looked up as a knock sounded upon the door.
"Come."
Mrs Huxley came into the room, her composed visage so different from the one that had just crept unbidden into his mind. Her dove-coloured muslin gown, pale canary spencer, and bonnet trimmed with rose satin spoke of her elegant but restrained style. Not for her the abundance of ribbons, frills, and lace that had always adorned Sophia's clothing. It suited her, reflecting the calm, straightforwardness of her character, as Sophia's overabundance of furbelows had reflected the frivolity of hers.

The face that peeked from her bonnet no longer seemed verging on plain to him but pretty, honest and serene. He could hardly believe that at one time he had suspected her of hiding something from him; it had merely been the natural reserve of a prudent woman in the presence of a stranger.

"The children are ready, but I wished for a

moment alone to thank you for your sensitive handling of the girls. They have come so far in such a short time, but it would be so easy to set them back by an unfortunate misstep."

"Your thoughtful care for my wards is much appreciated, Mrs Huxley, and your and Miss Burdock's progress thus far is promising indeed." He paused, searching for the words to express his thoughts without offending her. "I am curious, however. Miss Burdock's acceptance of the post is understandable; she was quite desperate, but you, I imagine, with your evident breeding and capability, might easily have obtained a post in a far superior household than mine."

Her head dropped for a moment, and when she again raised it, her eyes were troubled. He cursed himself for his clumsiness. He did not wish to disturb the growing rapport between them.

"Sir, I… there is something…"

Were those tears sheening her eyes? The thought that he had brought his redoubtable Mrs Huxley almost to tears appalled him.

"No," he said quickly. "I did not wish to trespass on painful memories. We all have things we would rather not remember. I meant only to say that your kindness, understanding, and unlimited patience with Emily, in particular, is quite remarkable considering—"

She shook her head as if to deny it. "Sir, it is true that I grew up in a genteel household and was taught every accomplishment thought necessary to a lady, but it was done in a rigid, joyless manner that I would not wish on any child. Whatever their backgrounds, every child surely needs understanding, patience, and encouragement."

His lips twisted. "You are correct, of course. Come, let us join the others and go and see what a shambles Townsend has made of my lawn."

~

An uncomfortable mixture of relief and disappointment warred within Anne's breast. He had stopped her from speaking, but a large part of her had wished to unburden herself. The more she knew Captain Edward Turner, the more she respected him. He was unlike any other man she had ever known. Beneath his gruff exterior, lurked a man who wanted to do what was right. When she had encouraged Emily to look at his actions rather than his words, it had been her sense of fairness and a wish to promote a better relationship between them that had prompted her, but she had now seen the evidence with her own eyes. He was a man of action, and if he had floundered like a fish out of water when first he came here and took on so many new responsibilities, he was fast finding his feet.

Miss Burdock and the girls awaited them by the front door. Miss Burdock took Barbara's hand. The child carried her doll in the other.

"For Sally will wish to see it," she informed him.

"Then I hope she is not disappointed."

They had not gone above a hundred yards when the captain looked down in surprise. Emily had taken his hand. Anne was not surprised when an awkward smile touched his lips. She felt a moment's consternation and hesitated for a brief moment when the girl held out her other hand to her, but she could not rebuff the child.

Her eyes met the captain's, and she thought she saw amused understanding in them. She felt her cheeks warm. That disconcerted her; she had never been one to blush. It was merely the awkwardness of the situation, surely.

She glanced away and movement on the edge of the woods caught her attention. It was the man she had seen when she had first arrived. His broad brimmed hat obscured his face. He had an axe in his hand and was hacking at some straggly saplings.

"Who is that man?" she asked.

The captain followed her gaze. "That is Gibbons. He came to the house looking for work shortly after the children had got lost in the woods. Barbara sustained several scratches and so I hired him to tidy it up and make it safe. To clear traps, brambles, and so on." He released Emily's hand. "I wish for a word with him. I will catch up with you in a moment."

Anne watched him go, a small frown wrinkling her brow. She had all but forgot Lady Westcliffe's request that she keep her ears and eyes open whilst she went about her duties. She had seen no evidence that Captain Turner was interested in anything but his estate and the children's welfare. The idea that he was in any way involved in rabble rousing was ridiculous, but she found the timing of Gibbons' arrival interesting. Could he be the agent who had followed him into Sussex? She would write to Lady Westcliffe and warn her that she thought the man, whoever he might be, was wasting his time.

Inside the large tent Mr Townsend had erected, eight square feet of earth had been carefully dug out to a depth of three feet. He knelt in one corner on a small square of carpet and was delicately brushing tesserae of green, brown, and white, which had been fashioned into interlocking curved lines that reminded Anne of a neat row of multicoloured stitches. Her lips parted on a soft gasp; to see such images in books was one thing, but to witness the uncovering of such an ancient artefact was quite another.

He turned his head and smiled, his eyes alight with pleasure. Getting to his feet, he set his hands on his hips. "Well, imps. Is it not beautiful?"

Barbara whispered something into her doll's ear and then put the toy to her own and nodded solemnly.

"We think it would be better if it were an animal."

"It is only the edge, silly," Emily said. "All the mosaics in the book had patterns around them. It might have people, animals, or other patterns on the inside."

"I see you are a Roman scholar, Emily," Mr Townsend said, before winking at her sister. "You must wait and see what remains beneath this mud, Barbara, but I must warn you; it will be a slow business. I will not risk damaging it and so the mud must be gently scraped and brushed until all is revealed."

In truth, Edward had very little to say to Gibbons, but the blush that had crept into Mrs Huxley's cheeks had had the oddest effect on him. His heartbeat had seemed to slow and thump heavily in his chest, and he had been glad that she had looked away for he had not been able to wrench his gaze from her face.

"How goes it, Gibbons?" he said, as he came up to the man.

"As well as can be expected with only me to do the work, sir. Not that I'm complaining, but a few extra hands wouldn't go amiss."

Rufus had suggested that he take on four groundsmen, a gamekeeper, and a stable boy. He knew Mrs Thirsk would also be grateful for a little more help in the house. He remained reluctant to take on so many extra costs until the estate became more profitable, however. He had already turned away several men from the village and had encountered some surly looks when he had passed through it as a result. Hopefully, allowing them to hunt rabbits on his land had softened their resentment.

"In time, Gibbons, in time."

"Very well, sir." He held up his axe. "This is as blunt and chipped as an ancient's tooth. It's not fit for purpose."

"Very well. Take it to the stables and give it to my groom. I shall go into Midhurst this very day and deliver it to the blacksmith. He will make it good as new."

Gibbons grinned. "Thank you, sir." He rubbed his shoulder. "It would be much appreciated."

Edward turned and made his way to the tent. "While I appreciate you wish for some protection from the weather, Townsend, this eyesore—" He broke off abruptly as he saw the mosaic. "Good Lord! It almost looks as if it were only laid last week."

Townsend grinned. "And in order that we preserve

it, the tent will have to stay. I may have to erect several others if the finds prove extensive, at least until a more permanent structure can be built."

Edward's eyebrows rose. "A more permanent structure?"

"Come, man. Surely you do not wish to cover it all up again. People will pay you for the privilege of coming to view this villa. They need not disturb you."

"I am not sure I wish a host of strangers tramping over my land."

Townsend chuckled. "Spoken like the lord of the manor. It is far too early for such discussions, however. Let us see the totality of the remains before we discuss it further. Now, if you will all excuse me; I have work to do."

Edward nodded. "And I need to go into Midhurst."

He glanced at Mrs Huxley, and a slight smile tilted his lips. Her rapt gaze was still fixed on the mosaic. A thought occurred to him, and before he could consider it, it formed into words.

"If you are not too afraid of my driving, perhaps you might come with me, Mrs Huxley. I am sure there must be an item or two that you or Miss Burdock requires. There is a haberdashery shop in Midhurst where you may find material for a new dress to replace the one that was ruined."

She glanced up, her eyes widening. "That is not necessary, Captain Turner."

"Perhaps not," he said. "But the garment was damaged on my land whilst you went about your duties and so it is my responsibility to replace it."

"That is fair," Miss Burdock said. "And it will be my pleasure to make it up for you."

"Miss Burdock needs some more wool," Barbara said. "I saw that her basket is almost empty."

Edward glanced at the little lady. "Then it must be replenished, but I am curious, what is it you are always so busy knitting?"

She smiled at him. "I am knitting you a pair of slippers. It will soon be winter, and there is nothing so comfortable as a pair of warm, knitted slippers when one sits by the fire in the evening."

Edward's amazement was apparently shared by his neighbour. Townsend hastily covered a laugh with a fit of coughing. Miss Burdock cast him a concerned look.

"You must take more care of yourself, Mr Townsend. I shall knit you an undershirt to protect your chest from the chill. We would not like you to suffer an inflammation of the lung, now, would we?"

It was Edward's turn to feel amused. "A fine idea, Miss Burdock. I shall certainly ensure you have enough wool for the purpose. If you inform Mrs Huxley precisely what you require, she will purchase it for you this very day. I am sure Mr Townsend's need is greater than my own. Indeed, I think you should make it your first priority."

CHAPTER 17

Anne was touched by the captain's thoughtfulness but was reluctant to be alone with him. Not only did she not wish to give rise to more gossip, but she did not fully comprehend the effect he had on her. Why had she blushed? When Emily had taken both their hands, she had felt the oddest sense of connection to him, as if the child had been a conduit that allowed something undefined to flow between them. It had felt strangely intimate and unsettling. She could not rebuff his generous offer, however, nor deprive Miss Burdock of her wool.

"You are very generous, Captain Turner, but I have another scheme that might solve several matters in one swoop. You mentioned that you would like to repay the children for their kindness, and Miss Burdock is very particular about the quality of the wool she employs. Perhaps we might all go to Midhurst. That way, Miss Burdock may select for herself her preferred yarn, and the girls might like to choose some ribbons to furbish up their bonnets or wear in their hair."

She thought she saw a flash of disappointment in his eyes, but the next moment a lazy smile she had not seen before touched his lips. It suited him.

"You think of everything, Mrs Huxley. I shall have the carriage made ready. When you have concluded your business, go to The Spread Eagle Inn where I will hire a private parlour so that we may all enjoy a nuncheon."

The children were in high spirits during the carriage ride.

"I shall have blue ribbons," Barbara said. "Blue is my favourite colour."

Emily smiled at her younger sister. "I believe you would have blue hair if it was possible."

"Well done, Emily," Miss Burdock said. "That was very nicely phrased. I am thankful that it is not possible, however. Blue hair would be so very deleterious to the complexion."

Barbara's eyes widened. "What is complexion?"

"I am talking of the appearance of your skin. It would make it look most odd, positively ghoulish, in fact. Very pale and unnatural."

Emily cocked her head to one side. "Deleterious," she said slowly, as if savouring the word. "I think… believe, I know what you mean."

Anne smiled. Emily soaked up words like a sponge did water. "Can you put it in your own sentence?"

The girl's brow puckered in thought, and then she grinned mischievously. "Mr Adams' sermons are deleterious to the ears."

Miss Burdock sighed. "I should not say so, but I

quite agree. Perhaps Captain Turner will allow us to attend the church in Midhurst tomorrow."

Emily gave one of her sly looks. "Will we still get marzipan?"

Anne raised an eyebrow. "Too much marzipan is also deleterious to the complexion. Girls who eat too many sweets suffer from unsightly spots."

Barbara pouted. "I wish to see Jasmine."

"That reminds me," Anne said. "I really ought to call on Mrs Adams and see if her elder daughter has recovered from the influenza."

Emily looked confused. "Why should you call on someone who doesn't like any of us?"

Anne smiled ruefully. Would this child ever stop asking awkward questions? "She cannot dislike us because she does not really know us. She has been given a false impression, and the only way to remedy that is to show by our actions who we really are."

Both Barbara and Anne were to get their wish. Their business at the haberdashers was soon completed, and whilst they were waiting for their items to be parcelled up, the tinkle of the bell above the door announced another arrival.

"Jasmine!" Barbara cried, running over to the girl.

Anne moved forward, fully expecting Mrs Adams to rebuff her, but to her surprise, she said nothing.

"Mrs Adams. We were speaking of you and your daughters only a bare half an hour ago. I had meant to call on you to enquire after your ill daughter."

The woman's eyes held both apology and shame.

"That was a kind thought, but it would not have been wise. My husband... well... he...."

Anne put a gentle hand on her arm. "You do not

have to explain." She glanced gratefully at Miss Burdock as she guided Emily towards a display of hats.

Mrs Adams took a deep breath. "You are kinder than I deserve. Dianna is much improved though sadly pulled." She glanced towards the corner Jasmine and Barbara had retreated to. "It is such a shame they cannot be friends, but believe me, it is impossible. When Mr Adams gets an idea in his head, it can be very difficult to shift. But I want you to know that I believe what you said."

The bell tinkled once more, and Mrs Adams glanced over her shoulder. A soft gasp escaped her, and she moved past Anne, murmuring, "I am sorry, Mrs Huxley, but I know that woman and cannot be seen speaking with you."

As their parcels had been tied, they took them, left the shop, and climbed into the waiting carriage. The town was not large, and it took them only a few minutes to reach The Spread Eagle Inn. As they stepped down from the carriage, Captain Turner came out to greet them.

"Well met. I did not expect you to complete your purchases quite so expeditiously."

"I am glad we have not left you waiting too long, sir," Anne said.

Barbara skipped up to him and took his hand. "I saw Jasmine Adams. She wishes to be my friend." Her mouth drooped. "She says her papa is very strict, and she can't because you are a bad man. I told her it wasn't true."

The smile faded from his lips. "Thank you, Barbara."

Emily rolled her eyes. "Mr Adams thinks everyone is bad."

He turned abruptly and led them to a parlour at the back of the inn, holding the door open as they entered. Anne brought up the rear, and he delayed her by laying a light hand on her arm.

"How came this about, Mrs Huxley?"

She watched the children run to the table adorned with bread and butter, cheeses, ham, fruit, and little iced cakes. Miss Burdock followed, seemingly as keen as they to enjoy this bounty. Keeping her voice low, Anne told him of their experience at church and that day.

"Mrs Adams believes me but is afraid of her husband, and I believe some of those who overheard me in church have been given food for thought, but they all appear in thrall to that poisonous parson."

Despite the consternation in his eyes, a reluctant grin touched his lips. "Poisonous parson; how very apposite. I shall not subject any of you to his sermons again; we shall come into Midhurst from now on. It is what Townsend frequently does."

"I think that might be wise. But I do not think it would be prudent to keep away from the village altogether. If they see us often enough, the novelty of the gossip will wear off, and they will see how respectable we are."

A raised voice from somewhere in the inn made her heart thump and her tongue dry.

"Landlord! Do not keep me waiting!"

Her ears strained to hear it again.

"Landlord!"

Dizzying relief flooded through her. She had been mistaken; it was not his voice.

"Mrs Huxley?"

She felt Captain Turner's hand on her arm again and the world steadied.

"Forgive me, sir, I was woolgathering. What did you say?"

His penetrating grey eyes bored into hers. "Nothing at all. That was no mere daydream. You looked as if you had seen a ghost."

She swallowed. "It was a distant memory, sir, that is all. It is strange how a sound or smell can conjure them."

He nodded briefly. "I understand."

She saw that he did. There was more than comprehension in his shadowed eyes. It was only natural, she supposed, that he had witnessed many things he would rather forget.

Laughter came from the table and a smile tugged at his lips. "Come, let us join the children and banish this unpleasant memory."

Anne was unsurprised to discover it was Miss Burdock who had caused the hilarity. When she had taken a bite of her cake, the icing had somehow lodged itself above her lip.

"Miss Burdock," Emily gasped. "That moustache does not suit you at all and is most deleterious to your complexion."

"Oh dear," she said, raising a napkin to her lip. "I am sure you are quite right. How clumsy of me."

"Think nothing of it, Miss Burdock," the captain said. "I was once at a dinner where a gentleman slumped forward and fell face first into his soup."

The girls thought this very entertaining, but when their laughter had abated, Emily became alarmingly proper.

"Forgive us, sir. It is unbecoming for a lady to laugh with her mouth full, or even at all at the table."

A shout of laughter escaped him. "Perhaps it is not wise to laugh with a mouth full of food for it presents a risk of choking as well as being unsightly, but I do not object to laughter at my table." His lazy grin once more made an appearance. "As long as the laughter is not directed at me, of course."

Barbara considered him with large eyes. "Not even if you do something funny?"

He shook his head. "Especially not then, for I never intentionally do anything amusing."

"Why not?" Emily asked.

His lips twisted into a smile of gentle self-derision. "Because I am a dull fellow who does not know how."

The softly spoken words held complete conviction. He really did think he was dull, Anne realised.

"Amusing rattles are vastly overrated, sir."

"Indeed," Miss Burdock concurred. "They can speak for minutes at a time without ever saying anything of substance. I have never had the felicity of being entertained by one, of course, but I imagine it must become extremely wearisome. You, at least, talk sense, Captain Turner."

"And you did make us all laugh," Emily pointed out.

"And you have a nice smile," Barbara added for good measure.

He regarded them silently for a moment and then gave an embarrassed laugh. "Well, now we have established what a fine fellow I am, let us enjoy our food."

They had barely left the village on the return journey when they passed Mrs Adams and Jasmine walking along the lane. The woman was limping. Putting her head out of the window, Anne requested that the coachman stop. She walked back to meet them.

"You are hurt, Mrs Adams."

The lady peered over her shoulder.

"There is no one there, ma'am."

"It is nothing," she said.

"Mama fell down the stairs and hurt her ankle," Jasmine said.

An image of a gracious sweep of stairs came unbidden to Anne's mind, and she felt the dizzying sensation of falling. Banishing it, she summoned a smile.

"Then you most certainly must not walk the three or four miles to Hayshott."

"It is shorter cross country," Mrs Adams said mulishly.

Jasmine groaned. "But it is still a long way and my legs are tired."

Mrs Adams once more glanced over her shoulder at the sound of an approaching vehicle.

"It is only Captain Turner," Anne reassured her.

When he pulled up beside them, she sought his support.

"Add your voice to mine, sir. Mrs Adams has an injured ankle and should not walk so far."

"No, indeed," he agreed. "I am sure that Mr Adams could not object to such an errand of mercy. I do not know what he was about to let you walk in this state."

Mrs Adams bristled at this direct attack on her husband. "It is not his fault. He had need of the gig, and my ankle felt much improved. It only began to throb so a few minutes since."

Anne attempted to soothe her ruffled feathers. "Please, let us at least take you some of the way. We can set you down before the village. It will be a little crowded, but…"

"It need not be," Captain Turner interjected. "You may come up with me, Mrs Huxley, and as my groom appears to have disappeared on business of his own, advise me on my driving." He smiled ruefully. "You cannot do a worse job than him; he is the unhandiest of grooms. If he were not so cheap, I would not keep him."

Jasmine tugged at her mother's sleeve. "Please, Mama. My feet hurt, and I won't say anything, I promise."

The last of Mrs Adams' resistance crumbled. "Very well, if you are sure it is not too much trouble."

Captain Turner climbed down from the curricle, took her arm, and helped her and Jasmine into the carriage. Closing the door behind her, he returned to Anne.

"Well, ma'am? Are you ready to put your courage to the test?"

She could not help but respond to his rallying tone. "Perhaps you should let me drive, sir, so that I may show you the way rather than offer advice. Few men like to be instructed by a woman, after all."

He handed her up into the curricle, jumped in beside her, and offered her the reins.

"I warn you, ma'am, they are a testy pair."

She felt a thrill of excitement shoot through her. Her father had been a great whip and one of the few times they had been in accord had been when he had imparted some of his skill to her. Not that he had wished to or expected her to succeed, of course. She had always been a sad disappointment to him; the undistinguished child of his first loveless marriage with nothing remarkable about her.

One night at dinner, he had lamented that he had no son to pass his skill on to. One of his cronies, who was a little worse for wear and in the dismals, had posited that life was full of disappointments and at least he had saved himself the mortification of discovering that his son was cow-handed and he unable to do anything about it.

Her father had responded that that was nonsense and that he could impart his skill to anyone if he so pleased. Apparently not liking his opinion being so summarily dismissed and knowing that her father had no great opinion of ladies driving, much to her dismay, the man had challenged him to teach Anne.

"I will lay a pony on the chance that after a period of, shall we say, six weeks, she will be unable to drive your pair of greys."

Anne had goggled at the thought. They were known to be extremely temperamental.

Her father had given a harsh crack of laughter. "Are you quite mad? She'd ruin their mouths."

"I did not say you had to teach her with that pair, only that she must be able to drive them after the set time. Come man, I have been more than reasonable in suggesting six weeks. However, if you are afraid to put your conviction to the test, so be it."

In that moment, Anne's heart had sunk for she knew her father's pride would ensure he took the bet, and she would be subjected to his unremitting scrutiny. She had surprised them both.

"Mrs Huxley? Shall I take the reins?"

She suddenly laughed. "No, you will not, sir. Let us put *your* courage to the test."

She took the whip from him, and with a light flick of her wrist, allowed it to wisp over the horses' backs. She approached the carriage within moments and swept past it. By the time she pulled in they were approaching a bend, checking her speed only a little, she sent her whip past the ear of the left horse and feather-edged it. A grin of pure delight curved her lips. The road straightened for some distance, and she gave the horses' their heads.

"Captain Turner," she cried, "these are a fine pair of horses. They are so responsive."

She turned her head to see an uncharacteristically wide smile on his face and admiration glowing in his eyes. Never had a man looked at her in such a way. She felt the heat rise in her cheeks and only hoped he put it down to her exhilaration.

"Before this moment, Mrs Huxley, I had thought them a bad-mannered, mismatched pair with a mind of their own, but I see I was mistaken. It is I who was lacking, not the horses. Bravo, ma'am, bravo!"

She turned her eyes back to the road. "It is only that my father taught me well. If you put me behind the wheel of a ship, I am sure our roles would be reversed."

But Captain Turner seemed to be possessed of an equal exhilaration that would not be silenced.

"That is not a fair comparison, ma'am. I was on the sea shortly after I turned eleven, but you could hardly have been put in charge of a pair of horses at so tender an age. You are that rare specimen of womanhood that does not put herself forward to display her accomplishments at every opportunity, and yet there can be no doubt that you possess many."

Anne did not know how to respond to such an encomium, nor did she need to, for the sharp retort of a gun cut the air, several pheasants burst from the hedge, and all her attention was devoted to the panicked horses. Sweat beaded her brow as they bolted. They approached another bend at break-neck speed. Never had she thought she would be grateful to her father, but she was then, for his words came back to her just in time to avert a sure disaster.

"The more excited they become, the calmer you must be. Use your whip judiciously and do not allow too much tension in your hands. They will know it. They must remain stern but soft, as must your voice."

She spoke to them, calming sounds issuing from her lips, and they responded, slowing, and obeying her whip. Yet even as they turned the bend, the wheels of the curricle hovered for a moment over the ditch before they were in the rough grass and then once more upon the road.

They were not far from home when she brought the horses to a stop, her pulse still keeping time with their wild charge. That was nothing compared to the tumultuous feelings that overwhelmed her when Captain Turner suddenly took her in his arms and pressed his lips to hers. He aroused feelings she had never before encountered or imagined. The blood was humming in her veins, leaping to the beat of her racing heart. Every instinct urged her to melt into his arms, but she would not, could not. Yet neither could she separate herself from him until she heard the distant rumble of carriage wheels. She jerked away, picking up the reins that had fallen from her nerveless fingers. She set the horses to a gentle walk, not trusting herself to do more just yet.

Captain Turner cleared his throat. "Forgive me. It was the relief... the exhilaration. If I had been driving, we would have undoubtedly had an accident. You were magnificent, ma'am."

"I merely did what was necessary, sir. We shall forget the kiss. I am only grateful that there was not a soul to witness it."

CHAPTER 18

Mrs Huxley spoke with her usual good sense, only the swift rise and fall of her chest and the lingering dusky rose in her cheeks speaking of her agitation. And yet Edward did not wish to, nor did he think it possible, to forget the kiss. It had been as much of a contradiction as the woman herself. Even while her body had remained rigidly unyielding, her lips had clung to his. Her control and self-mastery were formidable, but not complete. Some part of her had responded to him and absurd as it was, the thought pleased him. More than pleased him. He had wanted to draw her in and deepen the kiss, revel in the sensations of heat and fire that moved like quicksilver through his veins.

He shook his head as if to clear it. He was being foolish. Her response had been a balm to his pride after Sophia's rejection, that was all. That lady's cruel words echoed in his mind.

"I merely took pity on you, Captain Turner, but surely, you cannot have thought that my affections were engaged? Why, you have neither family, countenance, manners, nor charm to recommend you. It amused me to see if I could bring such a taciturn creature as you around my thumb, but it was only a game."

Well, he had a family now, and one that would have horrified Sophia. *It does not horrify Mrs Huxley. She would be a good mother to the children.* He blinked slowly, considering the thought. Could such a union work? He wished for a family of his own, after all. His lips twisted ruefully. What a pathetic creature he was. The first moment a woman showed him the slightest sign of affection, it went to his head. Mrs Huxley might be a governess, but how could a woman so gently bred admire him?

He remembered her blushes, those lips clinging to his. It might mean that she was not wholly impartial to him, but by the same token, it might mean only that she had been shocked and embarrassed. He could make no assumptions on so little evidence. Besides, he remained the man Sophia had described, and he did not wish for a woman to accept his hand merely that he might preserve her from want.

One thing he was certain of, however, was that he did not wish what had happened that day to result in the awkwardness of their early interactions. He had seldom spent so pleasant an hour as over luncheon. He could hardly believe that he had jeopardised the chance of experiencing another by behaving in such a rash, unconsidered manner. He did not know what had possessed him.

No, that was untrue. He had experienced a burst of admiration, an intoxicating excitement so strong that he had acted upon it without thought. He must try to put it right. She had said that they would forget it, but she had not said that she forgave him.

"Mrs Huxley, I am truly sorry that I used you in such a way. Believe me when I say that I am not the type of man who... who—"

"I believe you, sir," she said sharply. "Please, let us say no more about it. I accept your apology and understand that people frequently behave out of character after a moment of crisis."

The captain was generally never more himself than at such a time, but he let her statement stand. Where was Dickson? If his groom had been present, it would never have happened. It seemed Mrs Huxley had had the same thought.

"Where is your groom, sir?"

"I wish I knew," he growled. "I sent him to the blacksmith, and he never returned. I have a good mind to turn him off." His brows snapped together. "I hope you do not think that I purposely left him behind so that I might importune you."

It appeared that she did not as she seemed to regain her equanimity. The rigid set of her shoulders eased, and the slightest of smiles tilted her lips. He glanced away not wishing to dwell on the softness of those lips.

"Not unless you possess a crystal ball, sir. You could not know that I would stop the carriage to pick up Mrs Adams, after all."

She was right, of course. His wits had well and truly gone begging. The furrow on his brown deepened.

"It was damned careless of someone to shoot at

pheasants so close to the road. What if it had been the carriage's horses who had been spooked? The children might have been injured."

"I quite agree. I can only assume it was a poacher. Someone with so little regard for someone else's property can hardly be expected to follow etiquette. Perhaps you should mention it to Mr Rufus Townsend; he will know who to inform."

"I certainly will. I am not perfectly sure, but I think those fields belong to the Walthamstow estate. I do not believe Sir Anthony Fairbrass is in residence, in which case, his steward and gamekeeper should be alerted."

He glanced up in surprise as Gibbons appeared through a gap in the hedge in front of them. The man nodded and touched his cap.

"Pull over, Mrs Huxley. Perhaps Gibbons saw the culprit."

The man came panting up to them. "I'm that glad to see you and Mrs Huxley are uninjured, sir. I was up a tree, cutting away a dead branch that looked like it might fall when I heard the shot and racing hooves and realised what must have happened." His eyes widened as he saw it was Mrs Huxley who held the reins. "Lordy, ma'am. Don't tell me it was you who was driving?"

Edward frowned. "Never mind that. Did you see the culprit? He needs a flea in his ear at the least and hauling up before the magistrate at worst."

Gibbons shook his head. "No, sir."

Much later, when she lay in bed gazing at the sickle moon and Venus shining brightly above it, Anne remembered that kiss. Her fingers fluttered to her lips and she closed her eyes. She would permit herself to think of it only this once; to do otherwise would be madness. The captain had acted on a moment's impulse, of course, and it meant nothing. None knew better than she that affection and urges of a physical nature did not necessarily go hand in hand.

It had not been her first kiss, but how she wished it had been. She could not be sorry that she had at least once experienced the intoxicating feeling of knowing she was wanted, if only for a moment. She sighed. One kiss that would have to last her a lifetime. Her eyes roamed once more over the night sky. Was it just the lack of clouds that made everything seem brighter or was it this strange awakening that made her feel more connected to the world about her?

She yawned, her eyelids fluttering closed, a secret smile curving her lips. Perhaps for this night only, she would also allow herself to dream of how different her life might have been if she had loved and been loved in return.

But dreams were fickle, ungovernable things and she awoke some time later with her heart racing for an entirely different and far less pleasant reason. It had been some time since she had suffered a nightmare. It had most likely been prompted by her imagining she had heard *his* voice.

Throwing off the bedclothes, she swung her feet to the ground, donned her dressing gown, and pulled the sash tight. A glass of warm milk usually settled her and allowed her to sleep once more. She slipped her feet into her slippers, lit her candle, and made her way down the servants' stairs to the kitchen. In the larder, she discovered a covered jug of milk, poured some into a pan, and rested it on the embers of the fire.

She heard the faint chimes of the long case clock. It was three o'clock in the morning, a lonely time to be the only one stirring. Turning, she went to a sideboard and reached for a glass. She nearly dropped it as a sudden rattling noise made her jump. Her eyes swivelled towards the small porch that gave onto the kitchen garden. She was sure it had come from that direction. Had someone tried the door handle? Surely not. Who would attempt to gain entry to the house at such an hour?

Her eyes widened as a scraping sound followed. She picked up her candle, her eyes falling on the rolling pin and basin that lay on the table. She grabbed the former and went slowly towards the alcove. A mew greeted her, and a black cat appeared from behind a pewter pail. A soft laugh escaped her, and she returned to the fire.

She poured a little of the milk into a saucer and placed it on the floor.

"Not that you should be rewarded for giving me a fright, but I will concede it was not entirely your fault. My imagination is playing tricks on me today."

And so, when she reached the top of the stairs and thought she heard a groan, her usual calm good sense reasserted itself and she told herself it was only the wind. But she had gone no more than a few steps before it sounded again. The noise was louder, anguished, and most definitely human. Retracing her steps, she turned the corner and walked slowly down the hallway. This was Captain Turner's wing. The groan came again, and her steps quickened. Could he be hurt?

She paused outside his chamber and harsh, bitter words reached her ears.

"It should have been me!"

She rested her palm against the door and closed her eyes. It seemed she was not the only one to suffer a nightmare that night. She wished she could go to him, wake him, and release him from his torment, but not only would that be wildly improper and imprudent, she did not think he would thank her for it. He would not wish her to see him in so weakened a state.

❦

They attended the morning service in Midhurst. The white-haired, bespectacled vicar treated them to a gentle, meandering sermon touching on the themes of human frailty, repentance, mercy, and forgiveness. Anne's eyes strayed several times to Captain Turner and dwelt on the shadows under his eyes, the same question echoing in her mind. What was it that he could not forgive himself for? It was a fruitless exercise, of course. He must have made hundreds, if not thousands, of critical decisions in his time, and it could not be supposed that the outcome had always been as he had wished.

Her eyes dropped to her hands. Did she not know that to her own cost?

The church gave onto the market square, and after the service, many of the congregation gathered there, exchanging greetings and news. Mr Townsend had not made an appearance, and not having any acquaintances, they skirted the crowd and went straight to the carriage.

Captain Turner had indeed turned off his groom when he had given him no acceptable excuse for his tardiness. Indeed, he had blithely said he was whetting his whistle in another of the town's inns, almost as if he wished to be relieved of his duties.

Captain Turner had decided to accompany them in the carriage and sat wedged between Emily and Barbara. As they were so slight, their close proximity was not an issue of space but of choice. Barbara slipped her hand into his and rested her head on his arm, whilst Emily merely huddled against him. Anne could not blame them; there had been a frost on the ground that morning, and they had been able to see their breath in church.

He appeared unconcerned, merely laying his head against the squabs, and closing his eyes. The girls' glanced up at him and after exchanging a grin, relaxed against him once more and closed theirs. Anne allowed herself a long, lingering look.

Her eyes ranged over his dark, slanting eyebrows, his long eyelashes, the hard edge of his jaw, and came to rest on his nicely shaped lips. His nearness to her was both awkward and yet comforting. Not wishing to chance him opening his eyes and catching her staring, she turned to the window.

She sat bolt upright, icy fingers of dread and fear spiralling down her spine. She did not have a clear view of the gentleman who entered The Spread Eagle Inn; there were people behind him, but the tilt of his head and the set of his shoulders were familiar. Horribly familiar.

She closed her eyes for a brief moment and looked again. He had disappeared. Her lips opened on a soft gasp as she drew in a much-needed breath. Her eyes darted back to Captain Turner, but he remained as before. It was Miss Burdock who had noticed her odd reaction. She leant towards her.

"What is it, my dear?"

Anne shook her head. "It is nothing. I merely thought I saw someone I once knew, but it is impossible. He could not know… does not know anyone in this part of the country. It is my mind playing tricks on me. I only saw him from behind."

Miss Burdock touched her arm. "Then I am sure you are correct. How are you to tell one gentleman from another when they dress so similarly, after all? Unless they are an out and out dandy, of course, but other than that, one beaver hat is much like another as is a coat."

Miss Burdock's prosaic observations soothed her, and she gave a relieved smile. "Yes, you are right. It is the strangest thing, for I am not generally prone to odd fancies, but for the past day or two, they have stolen into my thoughts."

Miss Burdock's eyes flicked momentarily towards the dozing captain, and then she took Anne's hand, patting it gently, her eyes a little distant as if she were searching for the right words.

"I find that the imagination is often stimulated when one is suffering from some strong emotion such as love, hate, guilt, or fear. If you are troubled by anything, you may talk to me at any time and be assured of my discretion, my dear."

∼

Edward did not mean to eavesdrop. He had fallen into a light doze, a state somewhere between sleeping and waking that he had cultivated over his years at sea. There had been times when he had needed to rest but also be able to leap into action at a moment's notice. He was floating in this halfway place when the hushed voices slithered into his consciousness.

It is nothing. I merely thought I saw someone I once knew.

There was a faint trace of panic in her voice. It troubled him that Mrs Huxley was still reluctant to meet anyone from her former life. Was she still not completely reconciled to her position? Perhaps it was only natural that she was not, for however fond she was of his wards, to lose one's place in the society she had been born into could not be easy.

It is the strangest thing, for I am not generally prone to odd fancies, but for the past day or two, they have stolen into my thoughts.

His heart gave an odd kick. Was it only since their kiss that these odd fancies had taken root? Could it be possible that the thought she might raise herself up had crossed her mind?

I find the imagination is often stimulated when one is suffering from some strong emotion such as love, hate, guilt, or fear.

How well he knew it. He was certain that Mrs Huxley did not hate or fear him, however, that left only guilt or love. But why should she feel guilty? She had not been responsible for the kiss and there was little she could have done to avoid it. That left only love. Again, he remembered those soft lips clinging to his. Was it possible that he could have ignited some spark of affection in her?

His eyes sprang open as the carriage suddenly lurched and tilted. He wrapped his arms about the children, holding them firmly against his side. Mrs Huxley had clasped Miss Burdock to her. Fortunately, they had been approaching a sharp bend, and the horses had been going at little more than a walk. The children looked surprised but not alarmed.

"Is the carriage broken?" Barbara said.

"It would appear so," he replied.

"And now we will have to walk," Emily grumbled.

Anne raised an eyebrow. "I thought you liked to walk."

The girl pouted. "I do, but I was warm and cosy, and it is cold outside."

Anne smiled. If she was not much mistaken, Emily had been enjoying being snuggled up against the captain. "Never mind. We have not far to go."

The coachman appeared at the window. "It's a broken axle, Captain, although how it should happen, I don't know. I give her a good going over every few weeks, you may be sure."

"Never mind that now. Open the door and help the ladies to alight."

He climbed out after them, turned, and knelt on the road, examining both ends of the axle carefully. He drew in a sharp breath, his eyebrows snapping together.

"This was no accident," he growled, rising swiftly

to his feet. "It had been cut almost half through, and the weight of the carriage did the rest."

Miss Burdock had drawn the children away and they were amusing themselves by chasing a pheasant along the verge, but Mrs Huxley was staring at him aghast. He could not take the words back, however, and the coachman confirmed them.

"Well, dang me. You're right, sir. But who would do such a thing? There's only me and Dickson who hangs about the stables, oh, and Mr Gibbons often takes his meal and a tankard of ale with us." His eyes moved to the road. "And bless my soul, here he is now."

The man was running towards them. "Sir! What happened?"

"Perhaps you can tell me, Gibbons?" the captain barked. "Someone tampered with the axle. Do you know anything about it?"

"Me? No, sir. I've just been to church and thought I'd take a stroll is all, and I came round the bend and saw the carriage." He frowned. "If you can find him, I'd talk to Dickson. I went into the village for a tankard of ale last night, and he was at the inn saying some downright nasty things about you. Said as how you had turned him off without a reference, and that you were tight-fisted. Then he laughed and said you were ham-fisted too, and he wouldn't recommend anyone to apply for his position because they would likely end up with a broken neck when you overturned your curricle." He glanced at Anne. "He also made some grubby insinuations that I won't repeat in front of a lady."

"Did he now?" Captain Turner said in an icily soft voice. "And have you any idea where I may find him?"

He shook his head. "I asked him where he was agoin', but he just looked at me all surly and marched off. It was late, though, so I doubt he got any farther than Midhurst. He were going in that direction."

"Then get yourself there and see if you can discover his whereabouts."

The man looked uneasy. "It'll be like looking for a needle in a haystack."

The captain was fast coming to the conclusion that whatever the cost, he must hire some reliable servants. "Just do your best, Gibbons. And while you are there, get someone to come out and fix this axle."

He turned to the ageing coachman. "Well, Robert. Will you be able to see to the horses on your own?"

The man looked affronted. "Of course, I can. Haven't I been handling horses for the last fifty years?"

CHAPTER 19

Anne looked at him with wide eyes. "Sir, did Dickson know that you were intending to travel in the carriage today?"

"Yes," he said curtly, taking her arm and all but marching her towards Miss Burdock and the children. "When he deigned to make an appearance last evening, I was informing Thomas of it. One of the pair that pulls the curricle has a strained hock. I did not mention it as I did not wish you to feel in any way responsible."

"I do not feel responsible," she said, pulling her arm from his grip. "Only sorry that such a thing should have happened. But, Captain Turner, would Dickson really have done such a thing only to get back at you?"

He glanced down at her, his eyes stormy. "I cannot think of another with so strong a grudge against me, ma'am, but that he would have chosen a method that might have injured us all is despicable." He drew in a breath as if to calm himself. "Mrs Huxley, I must insist you, Miss Burdock, and the children remain indoors until this miscreant is caught and questioned. If anything should happen to any of you, I would never forgive myself."

He looked haunted by the thought, and she swiftly agreed, as much for his sake as for hers. "But what of you, sir? Will you also stay indoors?"

A cool smile touched his lips. "I doubt he meant to kill me, Mrs Huxley, merely to dent my pride and injure my person, but he will discover that I am a difficult man to best."

She stopped suddenly, a strange panic rising within her. "Sir, you cannot know his intentions. The precautions you wish to put in place on our behalf are prudent, I urge you to follow your own advice."

His eyes searched hers so intently that she felt the heat rise in her cheeks.

"You are worried for me," he said slowly.

She was, horribly so. She dragged her eyes from his and walked briskly ahead. "Of course, I am. The children have become attached to you, and to lose yet another they have come to depend on would be a severe blow to them."

He walked silently beside her until they had almost caught up with the others. She dared not look at him in case he saw that it would also be a severe blow to her.

"And I have become fond of them," he said at last.

There was no time to say more as Emily came rushing back to them.

"Did you see the pheasant? Was it not pretty?"

"The males are certainly very colourful," the captain admitted.

Emily cocked her head. "But males should not be pretty."

The tense line of his jaw relaxed. "No, so it would be more apt to say it was a handsome pheasant."

"Very well. I saw a handsome pheasant and I wish to draw one. Miss Burdock has helped me learn part of a poem so I may remember its colours." Her mouth moved as if she were silently rehearsing it and then she nodded. "*His purple crest, and scarlet-circled eyes, The vivid green his shining plumes unfold, His painted wings, and breast that flames with gold.*"

Anne's heart swelled with pride. How far this child had come in so short a time. "Well done, Emily. It is from a poem by Alexander Pope, I believe."

Captain Turner's smile was gentle. "You spoke it very well, child. Very well, indeed. Perhaps we might find it in the library, so that you might learn the remainder of it."

She grinned. "Yes, then I will copy it out."

As she skipped away, Anne sent him a sideways glance. "Perhaps it would be better if she did not find that book."

He looked enquiringly down at her. "Why ever not? Is it perhaps a very long poem that you think would defeat her?"

"*Windsor Forest* is indeed a very long poem, but even if she were to copy only the verse pertaining to the pheasant, it would, I fear, fill her with dismay."

When he still appeared confused, she recited the other lines.

See! From the brake the whirring pheasant springs,
And mounts exulting on triumphant wings:
Short is his joy; he feels the fiery wound,

Flutters in blood, and panting beats the ground.
Ah! What avail his glossy, varying dyes…

"Ah, indeed," he murmured. "Thank you for preventing me making a misstep. If the volume is in my library, I will find it and hide it." He grinned. "Emily may then while away her hours of confinement by searching for it."

Anne could not share his amusement, nor approve his scheme.

"Sir, how can you change from righteous anger to flippancy in a heartbeat?"

He shrugged. "My anger was not because of what happened to me, but what might have happened to the rest of you. That danger has passed, and I have taken action to ensure you all remain safe. It is but a precaution, you understand. Now that my head has cooled, I do not expect Dickson will be found. If the man has any sense at all, he will be long gone. He has done his mischief, I believe."

She could see the logic of his words, but her heart remained troubled. He seemed to sense it.

"Come now, Mrs Huxley. You assured me you were not a poor creature and have shown me the truth of it on several occasions. You made no fuss when you were wounded by a stray bullet or when the horses bolted, do not fail me now."

She cast rueful eyes up at him. He was right. Her fancy was getting the better of her once more. Dickson had spread his poison and extracted his revenge from a distance. A cowardly act. It would make no sense for him to remain; he must have known the blame would fall on him.

"Very well, sir. I acknowledge that my fretting will help no one."

"Good girl. Now, do you perhaps know the title of the volume this poem resides in?"

She smiled wryly. "It has appeared in several, I believe."

He sighed. "Well then, I think it highly likely that I will not leave the house for the remainder of this day, at least. I shall be too busy becoming intimately acquainted with my library." One eyebrow rose as if a thought had just occurred to him. "I shall make amends for my underhand tactics by presenting Emily with a painting of two pheasants. There is one in my bedchamber. The colours are a little faded, but it will give her something to work from."

When they entered the house, Mrs Thirsk was waiting for them.

"I saw you coming up the drive. Has there been a mishap with the carriage?"

"It broke," Barbara said promptly.

Her brows rose. "Oh dear, how unfortunate, but then it was left unused for years so perhaps it is not surprising, although I know Robert has tried his best to maintain it. I hope he has sustained no injury?"

"None. He is seeing to the horses," Captain Turner said.

"Well, I am relieved to hear it, for he is such an old friend." She smiled at the girls. "Look how pink your noses are. No doubt you are frozen. Why do you not come and warm yourselves in the kitchen? I am sure cook will give you some milk."

"Can we have it in the schoolroom?" Emily said. "I want to draw a pheasant."

The housekeeper sent the captain a glance Anne could not quite interpret. He looked at her blankly.

"Come down just for a few moments." She sent the captain another glance. "Cook has a *surprise* for you."

It appeared comprehension had struck because he suddenly smiled.

"A splendid idea, Mrs Thirsk. Come along, everyone."

Anne and Miss Burdock glanced at each other, a question in their eyes. Anne took her arm.

"Let us hope it is a pleasant surprise, and remind me, Miss Burdock, that if I ever need someone to take part in a ruse of any kind, never to ask Captain Turner to aid me."

The little lady smiled. "I see what you mean. He is clearly complicit in this surprise but had forgotten all about it. He can hardly be blamed, however, after the shocking events of this morning."

Anne raised an eyebrow. "I did not think you had heard."

Miss Burdock smiled. "I will admit my eyes are not what they once were, but my hearing is extremely acute, my dear. I did not hear the whole, of course, but enough. We will discuss it later."

The girls' squeals of delight had them hurrying into the kitchen. Nora rose from the table, and cook cast a benevolent smile on the girls, who were huddled over something in the corner.

"Be gentle now, or you'll frighten him. He's only a pup, after all."

Emily glanced over her shoulder, one hand still stroking a black and white whippet puppy.

"Thank you, Captain Turner. What is his name?"

"That is for you to decide." He bent and stroked the dog's ears. "You may take him up to the schoolroom, but he will sleep in the kitchen for the time being and remain here until you have completed your morning lessons."

"I quite agree," Miss Burdock said. "He is delightful, of course, but would be such a distraction."

Anne went to the animal and scooped him up. His muzzle was white, as was his chest and abdomen, but his eyes were circled by black hair that extended over his head and down his back. She smiled. "He looks as if he is wearing a domino."

Emily's brow wrinkled. "What is that?"

"At a masquerade ball, one dresses up and goes in disguise. A domino comprises a black mask and cloak."

The child grinned. "He does look like he is wearing a mask. We shall call him Domino."

Anne glanced at the captain. "Where did you discover him?"

"Rufus. This is the runt of one of Townsend's tenant's dog's litter."

She stroked his head. "Then we shall have to take very good care of you. I am sure cook will feed you up." She smiled at her employer. "It was a kind thought."

~

Edward dragged his eyes from Mrs Huxley's sweetly smiling lips. "Well, I will leave you to your day. I have much to do."

"You should not work on a Sunday, sir," Miss Burdock said gently. "You look as if you need a rest."

"Old habits are difficult to break, Miss Burdock. Wars and storms do not abate because it is a Sunday."

He turned, a frown gathering on his brow as he left the room. He had done his best to abate Mrs Huxley's fears, with mixed results, he thought, but he was not as insouciant as he had tried to appear. It had not escaped his notice that her life had been placed in danger not once, but three times, and it was hardly surprising she was rattled. He was rather shaken himself. The first two incidents had appeared to be random accidents, and surely, they must have been, and today's misadventure had clearly been aimed at him, yet he could not help but feel that there was more to it than that.

What were the chances that a governess, living in a retired situation in rural England, should suffer three accidents in the space of a few weeks? The probability seemed slim to him. Either she was extremely unfortunate, or there was something else at play here. He racked his brain to think what it might be but could come up with no adequate explanation. He ran his hand through his hair and strolled over to the bookcases. The only thing he was certain of was that Mrs Huxley was becoming ever dearer to him. Perhaps it was this partiality that drove his disquiet.

Dare he hope that it was her partiality for him that also drove hers, or was her concern merely for the children as she had claimed? Another question he could not yet answer.

There were several shelves devoted to poetry, many of them compilations of various poets, but before the hour was out, he had found the only two that contained the poem. He took them over to his desk and opened the drawer which held the girls' pictures. He had made two simple wooden frames himself and placed the girls' drawings in them the evening before.

Anger once more rose within him. How dare Dickson put his girls in danger! He hoped that against all odds Gibbons would find him. He would very much like to get his hands on the man and make him sorry he was ever born.

His brow gentled as he once more regarded his wards' offerings. A low laugh escaped him as he removed them from the drawer. There was no doubt any visitors he entertained from now on would think him quite mad, but he found he did not care one jot.

Turning, he reached for the painting behind the desk. It depicted a ship; a man of war. As his hands closed around the gilded edges of the frame, he had another vision of Captain Tewk straightening the picture in his cabin. It was superseded by another. An enemy ship had been spotted on the horizon and the first lieutenant had ordered him to inform the captain. He had raced to his cabin and, in his excitement, had forgotten to knock. The captain had been in the act of re-hanging this very painting.

He had turned on him roaring, "What do you mean, boy, by bursting in on me like this? You deserve to be flogged. Whatever it is you saw, forget it."

"But I didn't see anything, sir," he had replied.

Although that had not been strictly true, he had not been precisely sure what it was he had seen. He had been but twelve, after all. He was sure now, however.

A grin touched his lips as he lifted the painting from the wall. And sure enough, he was confronted with a locked panel. A safe. Spinning around, he retrieved the unidentified keys from his desk. The larger one went smoothly into the lock and turned just as easily. He pulled on it gently and the panel swung open. The recess was deep, a shelf dividing it into two parts. The lower section was filled with a variety of newspapers. It seemed an odd thing to keep locked away. He grabbed a handful and spread them on the desk.

They comprised of *Steel's Navy Lists*, articles from *The Naval Chronicle*, *The Gazette*, and various other publications. They spanned a period of ten years. Had the admiral missed his life at sea so much that he had relived it through reading these articles? He supposed it was only natural that he should retain an interest in what was going forward in the world, but why keep them?

As he looked closer, he realised that marks had been made in black ink around some of the entries. He leant closer, the better to read them. His eyebrows rose, and he grabbed another handful of papers, dropping them on top of the others. Some half an hour later, he sat back in his chair and regarded them in some bemusement. Admiral Tewk had followed his career from the moment they had parted after the Trafalgar action.

He had apparently devoured news of every ship Edward had been assigned to, every engagement he had been involved in, and which prizes he had taken, and he had underscored any and every article in which his name appeared. His lips twisted. Not all of the articles were to his credit; one outlined the details of a three-day court martial where he was severely reprimanded for removing his ship from its station and acting on his own initiative rather than awaiting permission from the admiralty. He could only be thankful that his latest trouble had not come to Tewk's attention.

The admiral had been a bluff, taciturn man, more likely to reprimand than praise. It had not been until he left Edward Hayshott that he had understood quite how fond he had been of him.

He gathered the newspapers into a neat pile and turned back to the safe. Dozens of small leather bags lay behind where the newspapers had been. He pulled one out and weighed it in his palm. Good God! He loosened the drawstring and turned it upside down. A shower of golden guineas raced across the surface, before spinning and coming to rest, some of them spilling onto the floor, bouncing and rolling across it.

An astonished laugh escaped him. He collected the stray coins and counted them all. Fifty guineas! He swiftly counted the bags. There were twenty-five of them. The top compartment was above his level of sight. He crossed the room, retrieved a footstool, and returned. Climbing on it, he saw several items. Another key, a long rectangular box, and a similar number of leather bags. Another snippet of memory came back to him.

He had received his first prize money of any note, which as a midshipman was not a huge amount, although it had seemed so to him at the time. Captain

Tewk had taken one glance at his face and given him some advice.

"If you are prudent, you will save not spend, and neither a borrower nor a lender be. We have both come from nothing, and only on ourselves may we depend. Do not trust the banks, however. I have known more than one to fail. And if you must have an agent; choose him carefully. There are many charlatans out there."

He had heeded the advice, keeping only a moderate sum in an account, the rest had been invested in the funds. He had assumed the admiral would do the same, that he would consider it the safest course. It seemed, however, that the admiral had not trusted that option either. Reaching into the safe, he removed the key and box. The key was too large for the box, and so he tried the smaller one he had found in his desk. It was a perfect fit. Inside he found two folded pieces of parchment. The first was a letter, and the second the deed to Rose Cottage. It was not made out in his name, however, but to a woman named Susanna Croft.

He had never heard of her. Frowning, he turned to the letter.

Hayshott, March 1815

Edward, I am failing. I know it and do not expect to last much longer. I had hoped that I would have a son to succeed me, but it was not to be. Take that as a warning, and do not wait too long to find a wife. I had nearly said love, but perhaps it would be better if you used your head rather than your heart. Love is a blessing and a curse. It confounds all reason, offering an ecstasy of feeling that sweeps all else before it but leaves only the darkest abyss when it is lost. I can only liken it to being elevated to a heavenly height only to be cast into the pits of hell.

I have followed your career with interest, and it has thus far played out much as I expected. You have done well, but the reports and divisions of opinion that surround you only reinforce what I have always known. While your genius, bravery, and ardour for your country should propel you towards a prosperous path, your dangerous self-assurance and headstrong nature might as easily lead you to disaster.

I have long been your mentor, however, and have used my influence on your behalf when possible. You are, in short, the closest thing to a son I possess, and so I shall leave you Hayshott. I trust the lawyers as little as I trust the banks, however, so I have taken steps to protect what is mine, and now yours. Why have I not made it easy for you to discover my secrets, I hear you cry. Have I not always tested you? Have I not always taught you that you must think beyond the obvious?

I am afraid you will find the estate neglected, as Tilbury is hardly capable of administering it, but as shameful as it is, I find I cannot rouse myself enough to care.

You will find the deed for Rose Cottage with this letter. Susanna Croft is my beloved wife's younger sister. She must be in her late twenties by now, and I believe is likely to be poverty stricken as was her sister, Elizabeth, when I met her. A reversal of fortunes in the family made it necessary for them to make their own way in the world, and to my wife's enduring regret, they lost contact.

She was last known to be working at a mantua makers in Bruton Street, but the shop has changed hands and the current owner, Madame Lafayette, claims to have no information as to her whereabouts. I know how dogged and determined you can be and would request that you see what you can discover. The money you will find in this safe is for her. If, of course, you discover that she has departed this world, it is yours to do with as you will.

I can only imagine your disappointment on finding such riches only to have them snatched away, but I feel sure that it will soon be ameliorated.

Richard Tewk

Edward leant forward and dropped the letter on the desk. So, he had solved one mystery only to be presented with another. He *was* disappointed; the money would have been extremely useful. He scanned the second half of the letter again, and two lines jumped out at him.

The money you will find in this safe is for her.

I can only imagine your disappointment… but I feel sure that it will soon be ameliorated.

Why say this safe rather than the safe? His eyes fell on the new key he had discovered, and a dry laugh escaped him. His eyes went to the portraits that adorned the walls. Several of them were of ships, the others dull hunting scenes. Grasping the key, he stood and went to the first one that depicted a vessel. He took it down, and sure enough, there was another panel with a lock. Another safe. He eagerly inserted the key. If he was correct, then he would be able to give Rufus permission to hire all the men he desired, and Mrs Thirsk might also hire more help.

CHAPTER 20

⁂

It was not until they were facing each other across the tea tray in their sitting room that evening that Anne had the chance to speak privately with Miss Burdock. Although the children and puppy had proved a great distraction, she had not been able to rid herself of a creeping sense of foreboding. In the rare moments of quiet, her thoughts had turned inward, and vivid images had flashed before her; her bloodied sleeve, the horses bolting, that kiss, the man walking into the inn, and Captain Turner's thunderous, upturned face when he realised the axle breaking had been no accident.

"My dear," Miss Burdock said, as she handed her a teacup. "You look tired, worn, and worried. Will you not share with me what most concerns you?"

Anne sipped her tea as she tried to assemble her thoughts.

"I must say," Miss Burdock continued, her attention seemingly on her knitting. "I am not surprised you are feeling a trifle worn down. It seems that hardly a day goes by without you suffering some accident. It is most disconcerting."

Anne put down her cup. "If it were just the accidents, but it is not. When we were at the inn yesterday, I thought I heard a voice I recognised, and today I thought I saw the possessor of that voice."

"Ah, and it is this gentleman who concerns you most?"

Anne nodded.

"And has he seen you?"

"No, that is, I do not think so."

Miss Burdock glanced up. "It seems to me that whether there is a gentleman visiting The Spread Eagle whom you wish to avoid or whether there is not, all you need do is remain indoors and there is not the remotest chance you will encounter him. I cannot think he will be making a long stay. Midhurst is a pleasant enough town, but it is hardly a fashionable resort."

How Anne wished it were that simple, but she could not speak the words only half-formed in her consciousness. Not yet. If she did, her deepest fears would seem only too real.

She rose to her feet. "Excuse me, Miss Burdock. You are right; I am tired and will retire. A good night's sleep will, I hope, restore my mind to its natural calm."

Miss Burdock smiled. "Quite right. I shall sit up a little longer, for I have nearly finished Captain Turner's slippers."

Despite her misgivings, Anne could not repress a smile. The item taking shape under Miss Burdock's sure hands was nicely formed but fashioned in a vibrant spring green. Would he wear them? She had an inkling that he would, at least once, to please Miss Burdock. Under that gruff exterior lay a kindness she had rarely encountered in a gentleman.

Her bed brought her no rest, her dreams a tangled web of images past and present. In one of her many waking moments, she tried to find some commonality between the accidents, and it was then it struck her. Mr Gibbons. He had been in the wood when that shot had been fired, and he had made an appearance shortly after the other two incidents. It was only his words that had incriminated the groom, but what if he had lied and she had been the target all along? A cold dread settled in her stomach, and there was only one way she knew how to dispel it.

She rose and dressed early, waiting only for the sky to lighten before she slipped from the house. The servants would be taking their breakfast in the kitchen, including Robert coachman and Mr Gibbons.

She walked quickly down the avenue, entering a tunnel of flame-coloured leaves. She was so preoccupied she barely noticed them. In the depths of the night, she had been almost certain this was the right thing to do; the only thing to do, but the brightening sky cast doubt on her convictions. Surely, she was imagining things. The first two accidents had been just that: accidents. They might have happened to anyone. Yet some instinct warned her it was otherwise.

The loud crack of a twig snapping jerked her out of her reverie. She paused, closing her eyes, her ears straining. Nothing beyond the rustle of wind-touched leaves and the twitter of birdsong. She untied the ribbons of her bonnet, removed the veiled, wide-brimmed hat that obstructed her view, and cast a look over her shoulder, but the path was empty.

Whatever the truth of the matter, she must know who the gentleman staying at The Spread Eagle in Midhurst was. If she had been discovered, she must leave Hayshott Hall at once. She could not risk anyone else being injured. It was why she had gone strictly against the captain's advice and ventured out alone. Placing the hat back on her head, she reached for the ribbons. A gust of wind took it before she could grasp them, and it flew from her head. She reached up an arm, but it rose beyond her reach and caught on an overhanging branch.

Casting a regretful glance at it, she went on. She could not risk Gibbons discovering her in the woods. She hesitated at the gate, poking her head through so she could ensure the road was clear. She crossed it quickly and climbed the stile on the other side, ducking behind the hedge for several minutes, peeping through the gaps to see if she had been followed. She was quite prepared to crouch and hide in the water-logged ditch in front of her if that proved to be the case. As she had told no one of her plans, she thought it highly unlikely, but she would take no unnecessary risks.

When no one appeared, she rose, turned, and strode briskly away, her steady pace and pelisse keeping her insulated from the chill air. Her eyes ranged over the rolling countryside before her, noting landmarks that would ensure she stayed on a straight course; an interestingly shaped tree here, a farmhouse there, or the curve of a ribbon of water. It would have been a very pleasant walk if she were not so anxious.

She found herself looking over her shoulder frequently, but other than a sheep or cow, there was nothing to be seen. She had never suffered from a nervous disposition and berated herself for jumping at shadows.

Her heart began to race, however, when halfway up a gently sloping hill, she heard hooves on turf. Two horses if she were not mistaken. She knew the urge to run but banished it. It did not sound like someone in hot pursuit but the rhythm of a gentle trot. How foolish she would appear if it were merely an acquaintance; Mr Rufus Townsend and his brother perhaps. Besides, she could not outrun whoever it might be. Turning, she waited for them to appear over the brow of the hill.

It was not the Townsend brothers but a lady and gentleman. They altered their course, slowing their horses to a sedate walk as they came towards her. She put her hand to her eyes, and a gasp escaped her. The lady possessed dark hair and eyes, the youthful bloom in her cheeks deepened by the exercise. She had seen that face before, and yet it seemed unlikely that Lucy should be here. She had recently married, and had not Lady Westcliffe said that Mr Ashton hailed from Yorkshire?

As they drew closer, she saw that the lady held herself with a confidence that Lucy had never possessed. She had a somewhat militant sparkle in her eyes, but there was no sign of recognition. There was only one conclusion to be drawn: Lucy had a sister.

Her gaze moved on to the gentleman. He sat tall on his large steed, a smart riding coat bound to his broad shoulders like a second skin. He was handsome in a rugged way, with a square jaw, strong nose, and eyes of a grey blue not dissimilar to her own, except they held a piercing clarity. He looked rather formidable and certainly not the type of man to be brought to his knees by a musical performance as Lucy's husband had been.

"Good day, ma'am. I am Sir Anthony Fairbrass, and this is my wife, Lady Abigail Fairbrass."

She performed a neat curtsy. "Good day, sir, ma'am. I am Mrs Huxley."

The gentleman frowned as if trying to place her and then smiled ruefully.

"I do not believe I have the pleasure of your acquaintance, but then I have been at home so little that is hardly surprising. I did not see you in church yesterday, but are you, perhaps, a neighbour?"

"In a way, sir. I have come from Hayshott Hall. I and my colleague, Miss Burdock, are governesses to Captain Turner's two wards."

She thought Lady Fairbrass stiffened, her suspicion confirmed when her horse shook its head and sidestepped. Her husband put out a large hand and gently placed it over hers.

"You are holding the reins too tightly, my love."

Anne could not imagine what she had said to cause the young lady to bridle, unless…

"If I have accidentally trespassed on your land, sir, I am sorry for it. I am on my way to Midhurst and thought only to take the most direct route."

"Not at all," Sir Anthony replied. "This is my land, but you are welcome to cross it."

Her heart sank. There was only one other reason Anne could think of that the lady might be regarding her with such coldness. She lifted her chin and met her frosty gaze. It was too bad that Mr Adams, a man of the cloth, should spread his malicious rumours. Neither Captain Turner nor the children deserved it. She had undertaken the task of dispelling them, somewhat unsuccessfully, but she would try once more.

"I think you may be suffering from a misapprehension, Lady Fairbrass," she said coolly.

The woman's eyebrow arched. "Am I? And what might that be?"

Anne met the challenge in her eyes calmly. "Miss Emily and Miss Barbara Proctor are most certainly Captain Turner's wards and nothing more, whatever slander you may have heard. They were the children of the master's mate on his ship, and he undertook to care for them after he and their mother died. They have suffered a difficult life but are good girls, and they do not deserve to have their reputation so sullied, any more than the captain does."

Her words seemed to have some effect. The lady's eyes softened.

"I have no idea who any of these people are," she said, "but if the case stands as you present it, I quite agree. Who is it who spreads such rumours?"

She realised her error. It was not that which had caused the lady to stiffen, after all. Perhaps she merely looked down on governesses. Whatever the case, as the foremost lady in the immediate neighbourhood, she could do no more for the girls than to somehow garner her support in the matter.

"Yes, pray, do tell us," her husband said, frowning a little. "We have not long arrived at Walthamstow, and I have had no time…"— he paused, his frown vanishing as he offered his wife a devastating smile—"or desire to catch up on the doings in the neighbourhood."

The lady's eyes sparked with pleasure. This was a love match, then. A pang of something that might have been envy smote Anne's heart. She straightened her shoulders and cleared her throat. Even though he deserved it, she could not help but feel like a telltale for informing on the vicar. She had been brought up to respect the clergy. But then, she had been brought up to respect many things that had been proven to be unworthy of it. That being said, Sir Anthony was perhaps the best man to rectify the situation; it was likely he or his father had given the man the living.

"I am afraid it was Mr Adams, the vicar at Hayshott."

Husband and wife exchanged a glance she could not quite interpret, but she thought she saw something approaching triumph in the lady's eyes and chagrin in her husband's. He glanced at her.

"I shall look into this, Mrs Huxley."

Mischievous dimples appeared in Lady Fairbrass's cheeks. "I am glad to hear it, sir." She glanced at Anne. "I would meet your charges, Mrs Huxley. They sound quite delightful."

Anne responded to her light-heartedness, a chuckle escaping her. "That is not quite the epithet I would ascribe to them, but for all that, they have their charms."

Lady Fairbrass laughed softly. "You have made me only more determined to make their acquaintance."

Sir Anthony turned his head, regarding his wife with a strange mixture of admiration and warning.

"Then I shall make Captain Turner's acquaintance as soon as I am able." He regarded Anne once more. "I shall leave you to continue your journey, ma'am. Although my wife shows impressive aptitude, she is still a novice on a horse, and I would not wish her to suffer any unnecessary discomfort."

Lady Fairbrass's head snapped towards him. "I am not so poor a creature, sir."

Anne bit back a smile, the echo of her own words striking a chord. "I am sure you are not, ma'am, and neither do I consider myself one, but I remember how sore I became when first I began to ride." She dipped into another curtsy. "Good day."

She strode on, a small smile playing about her lips. They were newly married, if she was not much mistaken; the lady spirited and elegant, the gentleman older and wiser. He would need to take a firm hand with her, no doubt. Her smile slipped, and she reminded herself that where there was love a firm hand might be wielded in a velvet glove.

How strange it was that two sisters so alike in appearance should be so very different in character. She drew in a shaky breath. She and Felicity had not been at all alike, but then she had only been her half-sister. Anne had loved her, however, and it grieved her still that she had been unable to protect her.

Pushing these painful thoughts aside, she concentrated on the landscape before her. She soon saw a church steeple some way ahead and realised she was nearing Midhurst. The river blocked her way, however, and seeing no bridge, she was forced to return to a farm track she had crossed. It brought her to the road. She soon entered the village and found herself on South Street. She passed several attractive cottages bordering a large pond, and a little farther ahead, perceived the sign bearing an eagle.

How she wished she had her bonnet and veil at this moment. Taking a deep breath, she pressed on. If her fears proved to be nothing more than morbid fancy, she was in no danger. And even if they were not, she had chosen her timing carefully. The man she had known would not leave his room before noon.

The Spread Eagle was on the coaching route from Chichester to London, but it was quiet as she approached. Entering a large hall, she saw a fine oak staircase ascending to the first floor, to the left of it a large desk, presently unmanned. On the shelf behind it the residents book leant at a drunken angle. Could it be that simple? As she walked quickly towards the desk, the quiet murmur of subdued conversation issued from behind a closed door. Early risers enjoying their breakfast in the coffee room, she presumed.

She moved quickly behind the desk, but as her hand reached for the book, the rattle of wheels on cobbles reached her. Voices and footsteps sounded, and she just had time to retreat to the other side of the desk before a door opened. A man in shirt sleeves and a leather waistcoat stepped into the hall. He was followed by a waiter carrying a breakfast tray.

"You take that up to Mr Randall and be quick about it. He's one of our best customers. We'll have the folk from the stage in at any moment."

Suddenly noticing Anne, he approached quickly, a frown puckering his brow. One quick assessing glance at her trim pelisse and upright bearing had clearly convinced him she was worthy of notice, but the mud on her boots and the damp hem of her dress, never mind the lack of a maid or companion, clearly gave him pause.

"I am Mr Dingle, the landlord. How may I help you, ma'am?"

Having prepared for this eventuality, she smiled in a confident manner. "Good morning, Mr Dingle. I fear I have intruded upon you at an inconvenient time, but my business should take but a moment. I have been expecting a visit from my dear friend, Mrs Langley, this past week or more. She had meant to put up here. Can you tell me if she has arrived?"

His brow cleared. "I do not recall that name, ma'am, although we've more than twenty guests so I can't be certain."

As the stagecoach customers began to come through the door, he turned away.

"Perhaps you might look in the hotel register?" she suggested gently. "Or, if you are in a hurry, which I can see that you are, perhaps I might look."

Nodding, he darted behind the desk, plucked the register from the shelf, and dropped it on the desk.

"Thank you," she murmured, as he hurried away, ushering his guests into the coffee room.

She opened it, her finger not quite steady as she ran it down the list of names. It came to an abrupt halt, and she inhaled sharply. He was here. He had not used his official title, but he was here; she was sure of it. She snapped the register shut, spun around, and marched quickly from the inn. It took a few moments for her to regain her equanimity, and she realised that in her turmoil, she had gone in the wrong direction. She found herself on the edge of the market square.

She was about turn round when her arm was taken in a firm grip, and she was pulled into an alley. A hand covered her mouth, and a soft, rough voice spoke in her ear.

"Forgive me, ma'am, but I couldn't risk you screaming."

Recognising the voice, she nodded. The large beefy hand was removed. She glanced over her shoulder. "It is not my habit to scream, Finn, however startled I might be."

He grinned. "Spoke like a right 'un. Although what such a level-headed lady as you is doing coming into town alone, I don't know."

He pulled her farther into the shadows and she tensed as a familiar figure sauntered by. *His* valet, Timble. The man's presence left her no room to doubt her suspicions.

"Thank you, Finn. I am grateful to you for saving me from an unpleasant and potentially dangerous encounter."

"There's no potentially about it, ma'am. It's why I'm here. To put a stop to all these accidents that keep befalling you."

She felt a sharp pain lodge under her ribs, the truth of the matter knifing through her. "There is only one way to stop it. I must leave."

"It might come to that, but you'll be forever looking over your shoulder." He glanced up as another figure passed the alley.

"Gibbons," he called.

She grasped his arm. "You don't understand, Finn. I suspect that Gibbons—"

He grinned again. "You suspicion wrong, ma'am.

It's Gibbons who has kept Lord and Lady Westcliffe informed of what's been going on. That's why I'm here."

The supposed woodsman came up to them, holding her hat in his outstretched hand.

"You were following me!" she said, taking the hat, the knowledge that she had not been imagining things giving her little relief.

"I've been trying to watch you, ma'am, but it has not always been possible."

"I do not understand," she said. "If Lady Westcliffe had some knowledge that I might be in danger, why did she not alert me?"

Finn put his hand inside his coat and pulled out a letter. "She sent this. I believe it will explain everything, but allow Gibbons to escort you back to Hayshott before you read it, and I suggest you put your hat on. I know where that rogue of a valet has been and need to discover what he was up to."

CHAPTER 21

As he had suspected, Gibbons had found no trace of his groom. The knowledge could not dent his good humour, however. There had been other safes behind the three remaining paintings of ships, all filled with bounty, including countless guineas and several examples of very fine jewellery. He was looking forward to Rufus's arrival. He would be able repair all the cottages, as well as ordering the hiring of the staff. He would ask him to give first priority to those who lived nearby, which should solve two problems.

The resentment that both the parson and Dickson had cultivated must die down when they were given employment, and they would see for themselves what manner of man he was. He chuckled. He might even stretch to a butler and a couple of footmen. Townsend was right. He was becoming more like the lord of the manor every day. Just as it had taken many hands to run his ship, so it would to run his estate and house, especially a house with two ladies, one of which he very much hoped would consent to be his wife.

Reading all the reports the admiral had kept had reminded him that his lack of birth had not defined him but only made him more determined to succeed. He had forged his own path once the admiral had set his feet upon it, and he must continue to do so.

His experience with Sophia had dented his confidence, made him doubt his instincts, but during the night they had spoken clearly to him. Mrs Huxley's lips had clung to his, the anxiety in her eyes had been for him, and the sweet smile she had offered him whilst holding the puppy, the softness of her eyes, had spoken of her affection and approval for and of him.

He sent for the children after breakfast, wishing them to see that he had kept his word, and wishing to see once more the approval in Mrs Huxley's eyes. He had not been able to place their pictures behind his desk as had been his first intention, for they would not have completely hidden the panel behind, and so they had taken the place of one of the dull hunting scenes that hung beside the fireplace. In effect, he had made them as prominent as they could wish. That is where he positioned himself so that they must immediately see them.

But Mrs Huxley did not come down with the children; Miss Burdock brought them in. The sharp pang of disappointment that smote him was ameliorated by Barbara's squeal of delight.

"That is much better," she cried, turning to her sister. "Isn't it, Emily?"

The child grinned. "I'd like to see your friends' faces when they see them."

Edward tugged at a lock of her hair. "Doubter! Mr

Townsend has already approved of them. I believe the word he used was magnificent."

"I am sure he did," Miss Burdock said. "He is such an enthusiastic gentleman."

"How right you are," Edward agreed. "I see that Mrs Huxley has not come down. I hope she is well."

The lady smiled. "Oh, I am sure she is, but she was so fatigued last night that I think she must have overslept. I saw no reason to disturb her."

A movement in the doorway caught Edward's eye and he saw Rufus standing there, his eyes fixed on the children's work.

"I've just seen her coming from the woods. She was heading towards the kitchen. At least, I think it was her. She had the right height and build, but there was an ugly hat with a veil obscuring her face."

Edward's good humour fled. She had gone out, alone, when she had promised him she would remain in the house. His eyes swivelled to Miss Burdock.

"Did you know of this, ma'am?"

The woman looked flustered. "No! I felt sure she would not go out, but… oh dear… perhaps I misread the situation."

"Why are you cross?" Emily said. "Why should Mrs Huxley not go for a walk? She is very fond of walking."

Even as a cold anger filled his veins, he forced a smile. "So she is. Go back up to the nursery with Miss Burdock, if you will. Nora may bring the pup—"

"His name is Domino," Barbara interrupted.

"Very well, Nora may bring Domino to you presently."

As they trailed from the room, Emily glanced over

her shoulder, a frown upon her brow. The child sensed his turmoil.

"Sir, why have you children's work on the wall? The dog is quite a good effort, but a blue rabbit?" asked Rufus.

"Never mind," he snapped. "You have my permission to hire whatever help you feel necessary and to put in train any works that need doing on the cottages. Now, if you will excuse me, I have an important matter to attend to."

"Very well," Rufus said, dragging his eyes from the artwork. "And may I stick to the budget I outlined."

"Yes, yes."

"It's just as well, sir. I found a farm gate broken, a fence pulled down, and Thomas's tent has been stolen. It is just as well he is laid up with a head cold or he would be outraged."

At any other moment, so would Edward have been, but his most prominent desire at that instant was to see Mrs Huxley. "Send him my best wishes for his recovery. Now, be on your way, if you please."

Unlike Emily, the young man appeared impervious to his mood and merely nodded and strolled from the room. Edward followed him, raced up the stairs and along the corridor, his long strides bringing him within moments to Mrs Huxley's rooms. She would, he felt quite sure, come up the servants' stairs in an effort to remain unseen. His chest tightened as he heard a soft tread. She appeared and came to an abrupt halt, her eyes widening.

"Captain Turner."

His gaze raked her from head to toe, taking in the wet and muddied hem of her skirts. It appeared she had gone some distance. Had she no regard for her safety or respect for his orders? He opened the door to her sitting room and gestured for her to go in.

The blood seemed to drain from her face, but she lifted her chin and did as he requested. He followed her, snapping the door shut. As she removed her hat, he noticed that her hands trembled. She went to the fire and held them to the blaze.

"It is no wonder you are cold, ma'am," he said bitterly. "Judging by the state of your dress, you have walked some distance. A circumstance I find quite baffling when I thought we had agreed that you would not go out for the time being. Have you no regard for your safety?"

She turned then, and he saw tears sheening her eyes. His anger fled and he went to her, taking her hands in his.

"Forgive me. I am a brute. You bring out the worst and yet the best in me. I did not mean to hurt you. Indeed, I wish only to cherish you—"

She shook her head, a half-sob escaping her. That he had made his redoubtable darling cry, filled him with remorse. He pulled her to him, wrapped his arms about her, and would have kissed her but she turned her head away and pressed her hands against his chest in an attempt to escape.

He released her at once, the rejection of his embrace stinging him as surely as if she had slapped his face. He had got it wrong, just as he had with Sophia. What else had he got wrong? He remembered her words in the carriage and the strange hitch in her voice as she had uttered them. *It is nothing. I merely thought I saw someone I once knew.* Perhaps it had not been panic he had heard but excitement. A spasm of jealously shot through him.

"Was it to Midhurst you trudged, Mrs Huxley? Perhaps to see the gentleman you thought you saw there? Am I to believe, that like another I once knew, you have shown me one face while possessing quite another?"

Her downcast head reared upwards, her expression earnest. "I never wished you to see me at all. I desired to remain in the background as governesses are wont to do. I never sought nor wished for your admiration, and if…"—her voice wavered—"if I have somehow captured it, I am sorry, for whatever my feelings for you, I am not free, nor will I ever be, to reveal them." She spun around, her shoulders heaving. "I have deceived you, Captain Turner, although I have not liked to. I nearly told you all one day in the library, but you forestalled me. You said you did not wish to tread on painful memories."

In the library? Ah, yes, he remembered it. She had seemed distressed, and even then, he could not bear it. He suddenly realised that she had not denied her feelings for him, only stated that she was not free to reveal them. He tried to make sense of it all but could not.

"Mrs Huxley," he said, bemused. "Why are you not free to speak?"

She turned back to him, her eyes anguished.

"Because, however much I wish it were not so, I am already married, sir."

He staggered back as if he had received a facer. His words seemed to come from far away. "I had not thought myself stupid, but I do not understand you, ma'am."

"Brandy," she croaked. "If I am to get through this interview, I need brandy. We both do."

He sank into a chair. "That, Mrs Huxley, is the first thing you have said that makes the remotest sense to me. You will find a decanter and glasses in my room."

～

She went quickly away. How bitterly she regretted not speaking the truth earlier. If he had deemed her unfit to care for his wards and sent her away, at least it would have saved them both this heartache. And if he had not, surely knowledge of her circumstances would have prevented him developing any affection for her. He certainly would not have kissed her, and then she too might have resisted her own inclinations.

She entered his chamber, her eyes searching for the brandy. There it was, on the dresser. Quickly crossing the room, she picked up the tray. As she turned, her eyes fell on the portrait above the fire. The woman was handsome rather than beautiful, with dark blonde hair and soft brown eyes. At first glance, she bore a striking resemblance to Sukey, only when Anne looked more closely, she saw her lips were a little thinner, her nose slightly larger, and her jaw more angular. Shaking her head, she left the room. It seemed highly likely that she would see her friend once more in the very near future. What a pity it could not be in happier circumstances.

He had not moved, but still sat in the chair, his eyes closed. Setting the tray down, she poured the brandy and went to him, placing the glass on the table beside him. Taking the seat opposite, she took a gulp of the amber liquid, wincing a little as it burned her throat.

Now that the moment was upon her, a detached calm descended. The captain took a swig of his drink, set it on the table, and leaning his head back, once more closed his eyes.

"Go on, Mrs Huxley." He frowned. "Tell me, is that even your name?"

She sighed. "My husband is the Earl of Rothley, and I am Lady Annabel Rothley, but for my own protection, and because I have come to despise his name, I go by Huxley. It is the name of my family. My father is Lord Huxley, a baron."

An ironic smile twisted his lips. "Why am I not surprised that you are a member of the aristocracy, no less. I wish to know everything from what made you fall in love with this man to how you came to be estranged from him. Leave nothing out."

She folded her hands in her lap and stared into the fire. "I was never in love with him. I merely wished to escape a household where I was not valued. He seemed a reasonable gentleman when first I met him, and I thought having a house and children of my own preferable to being treated like a drudge."

She glanced up and saw a muscle twitch in his jaw.

"And did this gentleman have a fortune?"

"What gentleman of birth and fortune would have looked at me? I had neither beauty nor vitality on my side, and at five and twenty was firmly on the shelf. He needed some money for a venture he was interested in, and I brought a generous dowry with me."

"Did your father approve?"

A bitter little laugh escaped her. "When I accepted the proposed match with nary a complaint, I believe it was only the second time in my life I ever had his full approval."

"The first being when you proved such an accomplished whip?"

"Correct."

She once more sipped her drink and then leant back, closing her eyes. It would be easier if she did not see his reactions to her sorry, sordid tale.

"For the first year, things went much as I expected. We were polite to each other, and I did not interfere with his pursuits nor he mine. He was often in Town on business. He did not believe women should bother their heads with men's affairs, and so it was not until later I discovered what that business was."

"And what was it?"

She paused. "He had a stake in several slave ships."

She heard his sharp intake of breath. His voice, when it came, however, was low and expressionless. "And how did you feel about that?"

"I was horrified that the money I had brought to the marriage was being used in such a way. Things had already been strained between us for some time, and they only became worse. He was disappointed that I had not become enceinte, among other things."

"What things?" he demanded.

She gasped. "Sir, some things are too private to speak of. Suffice it to say that he had a string of mistresses, which I had half expected, what I had not expected was him to bring one into our house."

There was a long silence.

"And is that why you left him?"

She winced. "I wish it were."

Opening her eyes, she reached for the brandy. "I have a younger, and far prettier half-sister, Captain Turner. Her beauty and taking ways ensured she was cosseted and indulged from an early age."

"You were jealous of her?"

"No. I loved her as well as everyone else, although that is what my parents implied when I informed them that he had seduced her."

His eyes snapped open. "How old was she?"

"She was but fifteen, sir."

Pain lanced though her. She would never forget the rage and dismay she had felt when on the last night of Felicity's visit, she had discovered him coming out of her room.

"It is a pity you are not more like your sister, wife."

She had flown at him then, beating her hands against his chest. He had taken her wrists in a cruel grip and sneered.

"So, at last my wife shows me some feeling, some passion. I never knew you had it in you, dear, but perhaps you might save it for the proper time and place."

He had walked calmly away, and she had found her sister sobbing.

"I did not mean things to go so far, Annie. I did not understand. I thought he just wanted a kiss."

Captain Turner suddenly leant forward, removed the brandy glass from her fingers, and took her hands in his. "I am sorry."

She shook her head. "Save your pity for poor Felicity. I packed my things and returned home with her. She denied it, of course. She could not bear the thought of losing Papa's affection." She grimaced. "But she could not deny it when it was discovered she was with child."

"And so you left him."

"I never returned to Rothley Court after that day, much to my father's dismay."

"Good God! Surely, he could not expect that of you."

Her fingers returned his clasp. "He feared scandal, of course, but I promised him a scandal worthy of the name if he did not arrange a private separation agreement between us." She smiled wanly. "I took legal advice, pretending I was enquiring on behalf of a friend and was informed that I had grounds for divorce for the crime of incest, and that the courts would also look unfavourably on a man bringing his mistress to the house in which his wife resided."

He pulled her closer so that their noses were but inches away. "You still do! Divorce him and we can be together. I will fund the case."

She shook her head. "I cannot. I would never have acted upon my threat. Our dirty laundry would have been hung out for the world to view. I could not and cannot bring such shame on my sister. She was young, spoilt, and foolish, but that is a fault of her upbringing. I had no excuse when I married such a man. My poor choices led to the mess, and I must accept my portion of the blame."

He took her face between his hands and pressed the gentlest of kisses to her lips. "No, you are blameless." He released her so suddenly that she nearly tumbled from her chair. He stood and began to pace around the room.

"Did he ever raise a hand to you?"

"No. I did tumble down the stairs on one occasion, and for a moment thought that he had pushed me, but he scoffed at the suggestion and claimed it had been an accident." Her fingers twisted together. "Now, I am not so sure."

He ran a hand through his hair. "God's teeth! What did you hope to achieve by going to see him? Am I to expect him on my doorstep?" He laughed wildly. "I rather hope he will come, for if you will not divorce him, there is only one thing to be done. You must become a widow."

She rose swiftly and went to him, placing her hands on his chest. "Edward, no! I did not go to see him, but only wished to be certain that he was or was not there. I saw the name Mr Coalville in the register. Baron Coalville is one of his lesser titles. I am afraid, very much afraid, that he has an ambition to become a widower."

His eyes glowed like heated steel. "Anne, you only bolster my resolution."

"I see I have come just in time, for as admirable as your sentiments are, Captain Turner, it would be a shame to put a noose around your neck just when your name is about to be cleared. Not to mention the irresponsibility of leaving those poor girls without a protector."

"Lady Westcliffe!" Anne gasped.

"Yes, as you see. Do not tell me you were not expecting me? Have you not read my letter?"

"No. Finn gave it to me earlier, but I have not had the opportunity to read it."

"He is losing his touch, I fear. You should have had it yesterday. Never mind, I shall explain everything to you. I am only sorry that I have put Mrs Thirsk to the blush. My woman is helping her sort out our rooms." She turned to Edward. "I have met your wards, sir. How very charming they are. But do not let me keep you waiting, Lord Westcliffe is expecting you in the library."

CHAPTER 22

Edward blinked. Was he being dismissed in his own house?

Lady Westcliffe offered him an understanding smile. "I know you have many questions, Captain, but my husband is more qualified to answer them than I. Especially the ones concerning you. He and the admiralty have been working quite closely together."

He looked at the handsome, elegant woman for a moment, turned and went to the door.

"Bye the way, Captain Turner, I thought your choice of art in the library very interesting, but I rather think I like it. I did not think I had misjudged you, and it is so very gratifying to realise I was not mistaken."

He walked slowly down the stairs, feeling as if his world had been turned on its head. At that moment, he knew only two things; Anne returned his regard, and he must find some way out of this coil. Lady Westcliffe was right, however. He would cut his nose off to spite his face if he did what he most desperately wished to do.

That his Anne had been put through such turmoil and humiliation scoured his soul. He had less sympathy for her sister; she sounded too much like Sophia, who had been the daughter of a Spanish delegate who had come to Sierra Leone when the Vice Admiralty Court had been replaced by the Mixed Commission Court in 1817. She too had been spoilt and cosseted all her life. He allowed Felicity some grace, however. She had been very young and no doubt ignorant of the ways of men, whereas Sophia had been only too well aware and had plucked their strings as if they had been violins, knowing how to wring from them a sweet or discordant note.

He knew now that he had never truly loved her but had been spellbound by her beauty and flattered by her attention like some green and callow youth. In truth, despite his age, he had been little more where women were concerned, for his life had been devoted to his profession and he had given little thought to aught else.

He stared in astonishment as he found a tall, liveried footman waiting by the door. The man bowed and held it open. Stepping into the library, he discovered Lord Westcliffe seated behind his desk. Unlike his wife, his appearance was undistinguished. He was the sort of man you might pass in the street and barely notice. As he got closer, Edward amended his view. He might pass notice unless you looked in his eyes. He thought them cool, hard, and penetrating, and felt certain that Lord Westcliffe was not a man to be trifled with. Well, neither was he.

Strolling to the desk, he held out his hand. He would not be made to feel like a visitor in his own home. He took his visitor's hand in a crushing grip.

"Welcome, Lord Westcliffe."

A spark of amusement brightened his visitor's eyes. "You must forgive me for descending on you with so little warning, Captain, and for taking the liberty of treating your library as if it were my own. I find I think more clearly when seated behind a desk."

Edward waved his hand towards the chair. "Then please avail yourself of it. I have always thought better when standing, so forgive me if I remain so."

"As you wish." Lord Westcliffe rested his arms on the mahogany surface and clasped his hands. "You may expect a letter from the admiralty any day now. It will contain an offer of a ship, and inform you of your promotion to Post Captain."

This would have been music to Edward's ears a few months ago, but he discovered it made very little difference to him now.

"I would rather discuss Mrs… Lady… Anne's affairs."

Lord Westcliffe regarded him closely and then an understanding smile tilted his lips. "Ah. I see neither Gibbons nor my wife were mistaken. Lady Westcliffe rarely is. You have fallen in love with the lady. You have my sympathy."

Edward's fingers curled into his palms. "I do not wish for your sympathy only a solution." He frowned as Lord Westcliffe's words fully registered. "What the devil has Gibbons got to do with anything?"

His visitor steepled his fingers. "Gibbons is an agent for the Home Office." His smile turned wry.

"He is not by any means the most able, but he is enthusiastic and honest, at least."

A maid Edward did not recognise brought in a tea tray.

"Ah, Mary. You may bring it to me."

The girl walked slowly to the desk, carefully placed the tray on it, and offered a rather awkward curtsy.

"Thank you, Mary. That will be all."

Edward again felt that he was the guest in his own house.

"I hope you do not mind, Captain Turner, but Mary is one of our orphans who has been training to be a maid, and we thought it would be good experience for her to see how another house runs. Besides, we felt that bringing one or two servants with us was the least we could do when we descended on you with such short notice."

"I do not care if you have brought a dozen servants with you, sir. I beg you will explain to me what an agent of the Home Office is doing masquerading as my woodsman?"

Lord Westcliffe prepared the tea and pushed a cup across the desk. "Calm yourself, Captain. I intend to explain everything, but I wish you to have a clear head. If I am not much mistaken, I smelt brandy fumes on your breath."

Edward took the cup irritably and threw the scalding brew down his throat. "There."

"Very well. As I said, Gibbons is not one of our brightest stars, but a dogged individual. He was investigating certain political gatherings in Manchester when he saw you at a meeting."

Edward's eyebrows snapped together. "I have

never attended any… oh, wait. I did happen to be in the coffee room of an inn where a group of men were gathered to discuss political reform. They had my sympathies truth be told but not my affiliation. I neither spoke with them nor listened to them above half. After the third glass of daffy, they made very little sense."

An ironic smile tilted the earl's lips. "Indeed, I find that so often to be the case. There was something about you, Captain, that made Gibbons think you a rather brooding, sinister figure, and in his wisdom, he followed you into Sussex and applied to you for work so that he might keep an eye on you."

Edward was not amused. "And you sanctioned this?"

Lord Westcliffe shrugged. "He did not ask anyone's permission, sir. The agents are rewarded when they bring us actionable evidence, and they use their own initiative to discover what that might be."

Edward began to pace up and down, his hands clasped behind his back. "Well, he cannot have discovered any, so what is he still doing here? Or has he suddenly discovered a burning desire to chop wood and clear shrubs?"

Lord Westcliffe sighed. "You are not a restful person at all, Captain Turner. I wish you will stop pacing, it is making me feel quite bilious."

Edward snorted but came to a halt by the wall, leant his shoulder against it, and folded his arms. "Please, continue. I am all ears."

"It is true that Gibbons found very little, apart from you enduring a visit from Sir Godfrey Webster."

A wry laugh escaped Edward. "You do not like him either."

"Not very much, I admit. As to what kept Gibbons here; have I not already said he is dogged? And we really must be very grateful for that fact. When he realised that far from trying to stir up resentment towards the establishment, you, as a member of it, were the target of ill feeling, he realised his mistake."

"Resentment fuelled by Dickson, my groom, and Mr Adams, the vicar." He smiled ruefully. "Or the poisonous parson as Anne would say."

"It was Gibbons who alerted us to the odd accidents that have befallen Lady Rothley, and he was assigned the task of protecting her as best he could."

"Which means not at all," Edward said dryly. "But, at last we come to what concerns me most. Anne thinks that her villainous husband might be responsible for at least the first two incidents, the third was aimed at me."

A rather wintry smile touched the earl's lips. "You are mistaken, sir, all of them were aimed at you, and the second two at you both."

Edward strode to the desk and laid his hands palms down on it. "Explain. If I have understood you correctly, sir, you are saying that I was the original target."

Lord Westcliffe sat back. "Do not loom over me, sir."

Edward turned and drew up a chair. The earl waited until he had seated himself to continue.

"I believe Mr Dickson came with the curricle?"

He nodded and then groaned. "It was brought through an agent of—"

"One Mr Coalville, and you were offered a reduced price if you would take the groom."

Edward stared, comprehension dawning in his eyes. "Good God! I led Rothley to her!"

"Indeed, you did. Dickson was hired after Lady Rothley had left her husband and so had never seen her. But I imagine that when he reported that his first attempt on your life had gone awry and it was a Mrs Huxley who had been injured, Rothley saw a way to rid himself of you both."

"But what did he have against me?"

Lord Westcliffe raised his brows. "Come now, sir. Is it really necessary for me to tell you?"

Edward stood once more and resumed his pacing. After a few moments, he whirled about.

"Slave ships! Do I take it that I inconvenienced Rothley by taking some of his ships?"

The earl nodded. "But it is more than that. Your nemesis, Captain Filcher, was in his pocket and it was in his best interests to get rid of you. It was Filcher who persuaded Sophia Perez to play her little game, and he who provoked you to go beyond the line. Indeed, you acted in the precise manner he wished you to."

Edward ran his hands through his hair. "Of course, I did. For heaven's sake, the man came alongside and boarded my ship, ordering me not to take a vessel flying a Portuguese flag when I had reliable intelligence it was a British vessel. I could not delay because the cold-hearted villains who run such ships throw the slaves overboard rather than surrender their vessels!" He closed his eyes. "They did anyway, and Filcher then forbade me to make any rescue attempt.

It was then I locked him in my cabin and lowered the boats. There was a child, a girl, no more than six, and as I reached for her a wave hit us, and I went overboard. I got her into the boat, and Proctor offered me his hand to pull me up. The boat tipped and he plunged into the water. By the time I had scrambled in, a shark had him. We fought it off with the oars, but he had lost his leg by the time we pulled him up, and he had lost too much blood."

The earl looked down at his hands, giving Edward a moment to gather himself.

"The accusations he brought against you were not widely believed, but the admiralty had to impose some sort of punishment upon you for your actions towards a senior officer. It was also necessary to get you out of the way so that Filcher might feel confident enough to continue his activities. He paid his crew well enough for them to be loyal, but after your accusations, a man was planted amongst them. A competent seaman with an apparently besmirched reputation."

"Just the sort he liked," Edward said dryly.

"Indeed. The admiralty is grateful that you brought the problem to their attention. It is a great embarrassment to them that after our country has led the charge for banning the trade in slaves and encouraged so many others to do so, that such corruption should be found in their ranks. They hope that you will give evidence at Filcher's trial. As you will be the most senior ranked officer to do so, your testimony will carry the most weight. Rothley's part in it will be uncovered, which is an embarrassment, but the failure of his business interests is of even greater concern to him. Captain Filcher has many influential relations, and Rothley will hope that with you out of the way, they might exert what influence they can and see his name cleared."

"Rothley wishes me out of the way." His eyes blazed with a cold anger. "As I wish him out of the way. I assume you have Dickson, and he has bleated like a lamb. Can we have Rothley hanged for attempted murder?"

The earl sighed. "As you probably know, a peer of the realm may only be judged by his fellow peers, and then only for certain crimes. Attempted murder is a serious offence indeed, but it is not murder, and there is simply not enough evidence against him. His valet was his go-between. The confessions of Dickson or his man will not be enough. Rothley will deny everything. To hang Rothley would set a dangerous precedent as far as his peers are concerned. If the word were to be taken of any disgruntled servant with a grievance against his master, which is what he will claim, then they would all be in the basket."

"But then what are we to do?"

A wry smile twisted Lord Westcliffe's lips. "You have a reputation for having a mind of your own, sir. Of thinking... shall we say... of original solutions? I admit, I very much hope you may think of one now, for my wife is very invested in this case, and I do not like to see her unhappy. Particularly not at this moment, for although she has tried to hide it from me, she has not been in the most robust of health recently. Indeed, I must insist we impose on your hospitality for several days, for I wish her to be well rested before we make another journey."

"Forgive me if I pace again, Lord Westcliffe, but I find that it helps me think."

The earl opened a beige folder. "Then, by all means, but do it at the other end of the room, if you will, I have some reports to read."

~

Lady Westcliffe took Anne's hands. "My dear. I can quite see why you have fallen in love with him. He has quite a presence."

"How did you know?" she said dully.

"Your letter, extolling his virtues, my dear. I am quite practised at reading between the lines, you know. I never believed he was a rogue; a little hot headed at times, perhaps, but not a rogue. My request that you keep your ears and eyes open was as much for your sake as for his."

Anne's eyes widened. "Do you mean you expected some trouble?"

"Not expected, precisely. But a few days before you left, news reached me that Rothley's mistress was now a wealthy widow. Not at the hands of your husband, I am afraid. That would be all too simple a solution. But it occurred to me that he might feel it expedient for him to do away with his wife if he could find her." She raised an eyebrow. "Westcliffe told me I was being fanciful, that peers did not go about murdering their wives, and then I heard, to, I am sure, Rothley's great mortification, she had thrown him over for a wealthier paramour. I thought the danger had passed. Westcliffe then discovered that Rothley's business ventures are about to come crashing down about his ears, and that you had been injured in a freak accident, and I begged him to look into things further."

Anne listened with growing amazement as she explained that Edward had been the initial target and that her whereabouts had been discovered quite by chance. Once she gave the matter some consideration, however, she found she was not surprised. Even if Rothley's business ventures had not been threatened, he had spite enough when crossed to cause any amount of mischief.

"I wish that I had never met him," she said bitterly.

"That is perfectly understandable, but then you would not have met your captain, my dear."

Tears sprang to her eyes. "But it is all in vain."

"Nonsense," Lady Westcliffe said firmly. "It will not be easy to bring Rothley to justice for he has done nothing directly, but I am sure two such resourceful men as my husband and the captain will think of something."

Lady Westcliffe led her to the sofa. They had barely sat down when she pulled a face. "I can quite see why you might have needed something to bolster your courage before baring your soul, but would you mind moving those glasses, dear? The smell of brandy is making me feel nauseous."

Anne sprang up and took them to the tray. When she returned, she noticed that Lady Westcliffe was still rather pale and had a handkerchief pressed to her lips. After a few moments, she removed it and drew in a deep, slow breath.

"That is better."

A sudden notion entered Anne's head. "You were suffering from nausea when last I saw you at Ashwick Hall." Her eyes widened. "Lady Westcliffe, could it be that you are expecting a happy event?"

The countess smiled softly, her hand briefly touching her stomach. "I did not think it possible and have taken such pains to keep it a secret. I must beg that you will also. I am six and thirty, after all, and I do not wish my lord's hopes to be raised until I am sure that nothing is likely to go awry." She sighed. "I am afraid that I will not be able to keep him in the dark much longer, and when he discovers the truth, he will wish me to take a far less active interest in Ashwick Hall."

"And he will be right," Anne said. "Indeed, was it wise of you to travel?"

Lady Westcliffe smiled wryly. "My dear, do not begrudge me one last adventure before I am kept closeted at home." She looked dismayed and reached out a hand. "Forgive me, my dear. I know this is no mere adventure for you."

"If your confidence is not misplaced, it might be the beginning of a very great adventure," Anne said softly.

"That is the spirit. Now, if you will excuse me, I shall lie down for a while."

Anne's brow wrinkled. "Of course, but what will happen to Sukey, Beth, and Flora if you are not on hand to help them?"

"I must do what I can for Sukey whilst I still may. As for Beth, I have a feeling Flora may well take her under her wing."

"Flora? How can she help her?"

Lady Westcliffe laughed softly. "I shall let you into another secret, my dear. Flora has been a patroness of my charity for several years, and she is the only one of my ladies who chooses to be at Ashwick Hall. She could leave at any moment, but she is a stubborn creature. I believe she will return to society for Beth's sake, however. She has become very fond of her." She sighed. "I doubt very much I shall be taking in any more ladies for some time to come."

It seemed it was a day full of surprises. Anne had often wondered what had brought Flora to the hall, but she had never imagined that she had chosen to be there.

"It is just as well, then, that I did not send Miss Burdock to you."

"Indeed, it was. I can see she is very happy here, and I am not at all surprised. She informed me that she had once worked for Lady Bellstaff, who, I must say, is one of the most unpleasant women I have had the misfortune to meet. She has the looks of an angel but the disposition of a harpy. It is hardly surprising that her offspring are reported to be ungovernable. By the way, the children you sent to me are doing very well." She rose to her feet. "I shall leave you now. Perhaps you too should get some rest; you have had a very trying morning." She paused in the doorway. "Oh, I had almost forgot." She removed a letter from her reticule and held it out. "Susan asked me to give you this."

Anne smiled and took it. It was a brief missive, merely informing her that the child was well and that she hoped Anne was enjoying her new position.

She returned to her seat by the fire, a thoughtful look in her eyes. The name Lady Bellstaff sounded familiar. An image of a dainty woman with blonde ringlets, blue eyes, and cupid's bow lips swam before her. She grimaced as she recalled the circumstances of their meeting.

It had been the only occasion that she and Rothley had attended a house party together. The Bellstaffs had also been invited. Sir Rupert Bellstaff had been regarded as an amiable dimwit, but even he had noticed the flirtation going on between Rothley and his wife. Only the resigned, sympathetic glances he had sent her had given him away. She had felt so sorry for him.

All the visiting children had put on a sketch the evening before their departure. It had all been going swimmingly until the Bellstaff daughters had fallen out. Some pushing and shoving had occurred, and they had both fallen into the painted scene behind them, causing it to crash to the ground. Chaos had ensued as some of the smaller children had started to cry. Amid all the gasps and whispers, a little lady had rushed forwards and tried to remove her charges, only to receive a kick in the shins for her trouble. Anne had only caught a brief glimpse of her before various other governesses and nurses had rushed forward and she had disappeared from view. She had heard the next day that the governess had been dismissed.

Anne now knew why she had thought she recognised Miss Burdock when they had first met. She had been that unfortunate lady. And as she knew she herself had been the subject of much gossip and pity, she was reasonably sure that the lady had known precisely who she was. Why had she not said anything? A moment's reflection gave her the answer. Miss Burdock would not have wished to have caused her any discomfort or embarrassment.

CHAPTER 23

Edward's brow smoothed as the path became clear to him. He marched back to the desk.

"Has the valet been taken yet?"

Lord Westcliffe looked up. "No. I did not think it wise to alert Rothley that we were on to him."

"Then it must be done. If both his accomplices disappear, he will be forced to take action himself."

"Or he may merely return to his estate and disclaim all knowledge of their activities," the earl countered.

"No. He will not. This man is vindictive. He may not be stupid enough to step foot on my estate, but he will not be able to resist an opportunity if it is given him and he feels there is no risk to himself."

Lord Westcliffe steepled his fingers and brought them to his lips, a thoughtful expression descending on his brow.

"Am I to assume you wish to put yourself in his way?"

An anticipatory, rather wolfish grin touched Edward's lips. "I insist upon it."

"It will be dangerous. However well made our plans, you will be exposed to a great deal of risk."

Edward raised an eyebrow. "Come now, Lord Westcliffe, is that not why you have laid all this before me? This is what you hoped would transpire from this interview. And you have precisely what you want; I take the risk, and you may say with perfect truth that the idea was wholly mine."

The earl smiled wryly. "I will admit only to this; that I cannot see another way to catch him red-handed apart from putting Lady Rothley in his path, and that I will not entertain."

Edward slapped his hand on the desk. "Neither will I. I have faced the enemy many times for my country; it was my duty and my honour, but I face this enemy for duty, honour, and love, and however high the stakes, it will be worth it." Edward pulled his chair a little closer to the desk. "Now, let us formulate these plans."

The earl held up a hand. "Do not be so hasty. You must consider the children."

"I do not envisage failure, my lord, but I will, of course, make a will. Anne will be my sole beneficiary, and she, I know, will ensure that Emily and Barbara are cared for." His eyes hardened. "Whilst I am prepared to take all the risk in this endeavour, you must promise me that you will ensure Anne neither gets wind of our intentions, nor is put in the slightest danger."

Lord Westcliffe gave a brief nod. "I think you will

discover that my wife will keep Lady Rothley fully occupied."

"Good, because I am not prepared to wait a moment longer than necessary. We must act in the morning. Do I take it you have some men we may rely on?"

"We have Gibbons, Finn, who you have already met, my coachman, and Jack, the footman."

"Very well. Now, let us consider the possibilities."

~

Not only were Anne and Miss Burdock invited to dine with their guests, but so were the children. They were to meet in the drawing room at six o'clock.

"You must be on your very best behaviour," Anne said, as she led them downstairs. "It is not every day you dine with an earl and a countess."

"Lady Westcliffe was nice," Barbara said.

"Oh, indeed, so very gracious," agreed Miss Burdock.

Anne glanced at Emily, who was unusually quiet. "Do not be nervous, my dear. You will acquit yourself admirably, I am sure."

The girl took her hand. "You sent the boy who tried to steal Miss Burdock's money to her orphanage."

Anne suddenly understood. She squeezed the girl's hand. "You must know she has not come to take you there. She takes in those who do not have a home or anyone to care for them, and you have both. Captain Turner would never allow anyone to take you away."

"Do you promise?"

Anne bent and gave the child a brief hug. "Of course, I promise. Lady Westcliffe is the one who sent me to you. She is my friend, and one of the kindest ladies I know. She thought both you and your sister charming."

Emily smiled. "I will try to be."

"Just be yourself, my dear."

It seemed Barbara had no notion of being herself. They were met at the drawing room door by a tall, young man dressed in livery.

Anne smiled and nodded her head in acknowledgement.

"Who are you?" Barbara asked.

He bowed. "I am Jack, and I am to announce you."

"Why?" Emily asked. "Everyone knows who we are."

He leant forwards, murmuring, "Because I am training to be a footman, and hope one day to become a butler, so I have to practise many things."

He stepped into the room. "Mrs Huxley, Miss Burdock, Miss Emily Proctor, and Miss Barbara."

As Emily executed a very creditable curtsy, Barbara tugged on the footman's sleeve and gestured for him to bend down. She whispered something in his ear, and he straightened, his face wooden.

"Go on," she hissed.

His startled glance went to Lady Westcliffe.

"Yes, do go on, Jack," she said with a small smile.

"Princess Barbara," he amended.

"Oh dear," Miss Burdock murmured, "perhaps we should not have play acted quite so often."

Lady Westcliffe laughed softly. "Come and sit with

me, Princess, Miss Emily. Once I have introduced you to my lord, I wish to hear more about Domino."

Anne's eyes met Edward's and they shared a smile. Miss Burdock's discreet cough reminded her that she must not wear her heart on her sleeve. Not yet. Perhaps never. She took the lady's arm, and they went forward to meet Lord Westcliffe.

As the earl politely drew Miss Burdock into conversation, Anne turned to Edward. There was a bright, keenness in his eyes that she had seen once before. It had been the moment he had decided to return to Manchester in pursuit of Mr Rogers. A mixture of fear and excitement gripped her.

"Edward," she murmured. "Lady Westcliffe was confident that you and the earl would discover some way to wrong foot Rothley. Have you?"

"We have discussed several ideas, but none are yet carved in stone."

She raised her hand as if she would touch him but recollected herself and let it drop. "Promise me you will not do anything to endanger yourself."

The footman just then announced dinner.

Edward gave the lazy smile that did something strange to her insides.

"We cannot discuss this now. Do not fret, however. When there is something worth the telling, you will know of it."

She nodded. "Very well."

Two leaves had been taken from the dining room table and they made a cosy party. Anne was particularly proud of Emily when she turned to Lord Westcliffe.

"Did you have a good journey, sir?"

"Why, yes, thank you, although I think my wife found it a little tiring."

Her eyes turned to the countess. "Did you come far, Lady Westcliffe?"

The lady answered with gravity, but her eyes smiled. "We have been two days upon the road."

Emily nodded. "At least the weather was fine."

"So it was."

Emily looked down at her soup, her lips moving as if she were rehearsing a word. Smiling, she glanced up.

"But it has been very cold, which can be deleterious to the complexion. It makes my nose go red."

Edward smothered a laugh, and Anne sent him a frowning glance.

"You may be sure I had a blanket and a hot brick to keep me warm."

Anne could see that Emily had all but used up her stock of polite conversation, so perhaps it was just as well that Barbara interrupted.

"What is this? It is the colour of the slippers Miss Burdock has made for Captain Turner." She was stirring her soup with her spoon, and it was in imminent danger of slopping over the sides of her bowl.

"It is pease soup, and it is not polite to play with your food, Barbara," Miss Burdock said gently.

The girl put down her spoon. "Princesses don't like pease soup."

"Then you must sit quietly until it is removed," Anne said.

"What is it princesses like?" Lady Westcliffe enquired.

She answered without hesitation. "Rabbits."

Lady Westcliffe chuckled. "Of course. I saw your depiction of one in the library."

Barbara smiled. "Thomas has found a mosaic in our garden, and I am hoping he will find a rabbit when he has finished brushing the mud off."

"How interesting," Lady Westcliffe said. "I believe the Romans sometimes depicted hares in their mosaics, which are very like rabbits. I should very much like to see it. Perhaps you might show it to me after you have completed your morning lessons."

Anne glanced at Edward, unsure if he would approve them leaving the house. He smiled.

"An excellent idea. Our neighbour Mr Townsend is very excited about it, Lady Westcliffe."

~

Edward had no qualms in them viewing the mosaic because he knew all the villains of the piece would be either incapacitated or fully occupied.

When he strolled into The Spread Eagle Inn just after ten o'clock, the innkeeper was dealing with a customer who was settling his bill, but he glanced up and nodded.

"I'll be with you in a moment, sir."

"Don't trouble yourself, Mr Dingle. I've only come for a coffee to chase out the cold."

"Right you are, sir."

He strolled into the coffee room with all the insouciance of a man without a care in the world, but his blood was thrumming through his veins. The game was afoot.

As the waiter approached with the pot of coffee, an irritated shout came from above.

"Landlord! Have you seen my man?"

The waiter placed down his tray with a roll of his eyes.

Edward raised an eyebrow. "It appears you have a difficult customer."

"Mr Coalville is that right enough. Nothing's good enough for him, and his valet is not much better. He thinks himself as high as a duke!"

"Landlord! Did you not hear me?"

"I should think there's not a soul who did not hear him," the waiter muttered, pouring the coffee into a cup. "I don't know how he can bear to shout; he was dipping deep last evening. He went through the best part of three bottles of wine and fell asleep in his parlour."

Good. He would not be thinking clearly. As hasty footsteps sounded on the stairs, Edward took a few gulps of the dark brew.

"You were there all the time! What do you mean by it, man?"

"Why nothing, Mr Coalville. I was busy dealing with another customer."

"Where is my man? He neither put me to bed nor came to shave and dress me this morning."

Edward's lip curled. The man sounded like a cosseted, arrogant fool.

"I don't know, sir. He went out to blow a cloud, must have been after eleven last evening, and I haven't seen him since. He was a bit on the go, mind you. Perhaps he went for a walk and is sleeping it off somewhere."

Edward smiled. Bless the landlord; he could not have said anything more to the purpose.

Another voice joined the conversation. Finn's voice.

"Excuse me for interrupting—"

"You can wait your turn, man. What do you mean by interrupting your betters?"

"I didn't mean no disrespect, sir. I was in the tap room, just whetting me whistle, and couldn't help overhearing. I don't know if it's your man, but when I went for a stroll earlier, I saw someone lying near a stream. He had fawn britches, a red waistcoat, a black tailcoat, and he was snoring like a hog."

"That's Timble. Show me where he is, man."

"I'm sorry to disoblige you, sir, but I've got an appointment. I can take you part of the way and then point you in the right direction from the road. At least, I think I can. One stretch of countryside looks the same as any other to me."

Edward stood, threw a few coins on the table, and strolled from the room. "I'd have the man flogged."

"And who the devil are you?"

Lord Rothley was a handsome man, possessing classical features marred only by his bloodshot narrowed eyes and sneering lips. Edward could not decide if his chestnut locks were purposefully disordered or if the man was merely incapable of brushing his own hair. He certainly did not appear able to don his coat for he stood in his shirt sleeves.

Edward bowed. "Captain Turner at your service."

Something shifted behind the man's eyes, and he inclined his head.

"Mr Coalville. Forgive me for being rude, Captain."

Edward smiled. "Do not give it a thought. It sounds as if you have been put to a great deal of inconvenience. Perhaps I might be of some assistance as no doubt I know the land hereabouts a little better than this good fellow." He glanced at Finn. "Were there any particular features that might help me? A strangely shaped tree or a farmhouse, perhaps?"

Finn scratched his head and appeared deep in thought. "Aye," he said slowly. "Now you mention it, I believe there was a spinney, and there was a wooden footbridge over the stream."

"I know the place," Edward said. "It is not far from the Selham Road, about half a mile from here. As it will not take me far out of my way, I would be glad to show you, Mr Coalville. Or perhaps you would prefer to wait for your man to come to his senses and return. I do not see why you should be put to so much trouble, after all."

"Neither do I, but I will accept your offer, sir. I do not choose to wait on the convenience of my valet, nor do I wish him to freeze to death. If you will just give me a few minutes to finish dressing, I would be grateful." He glanced at Mr Dingly. "Dare I hope you have a decent horse that I may hire?"

"I'll send a message to the stables directly, sir."

"Thank you, and send someone up to help me into my coat, will you?" He nodded at Edward. "I should not be above ten minutes."

As he made his way upstairs, Edward and Finn strolled outside. A stable boy caught the coin Finn flicked towards him and ran under the arch that led to the yard. Finn climbed into the waiting covered cart as Jack came from the yard.

"Did everything go as planned?" Edward asked.

"Yes, sir," the footman said.

"Jump up," Finn said. "We must away." He glanced at Edward. "Be careful, Captain. I don't like to leave you alone with him."

"Take up your position, Finn. I can handle myself. He is not going to attempt to kill me in the open, the danger will come when we leave the road. Even then, I do not think I will be imperilled. He is a man who never does anything himself if someone else will do it for him. He will wish to enlist his man's help, perhaps even have him do the deed, and certainly get rid of the body."

Finn shook his head, but there was a glimmer of amusement in his eyes. "I like your spirit, Captain, but this is no laughing matter."

"No," Edward said grimly. "It is not."

Fifteen minutes later, he and Rothley trotted under the arch.

"This is really very good of you, Captain Turner."

"Think nothing of it, Mr Coalville. Are you making a long stay?"

He laughed dryly. "I think not. These provincial inns are so tiresome."

"I am sorry you think so. I have found Dingly to be most hospitable."

"Then I suspect, sir, that you are an easy man to please."

He had not quite managed to keep a trace of sarcasm from his voice, and Edward sent him a sideways glance.

"I do not believe that is my reputation."

When his companion turned his head, he smiled. "I will admit, however, that almost any inn must be more comfortable than a ship."

"I would not know, but I shall take your word for it."

They turned onto a farm track just beyond the village, and Edward dismounted to open a gate. "It is only a few minutes ride from here."

The man tipped his hat as he rode through.

Edward did not wish to linger; he thought his reading of the man was accurate, but he would take no unnecessary risk.

"This is a fine stretch of country, Mr Coalville. What say we put our horses through their paces?"

The earl smiled. "After you."

Edward had tried to allow for any eventuality and was not about to chance being shot in the back. Rothley had a good seat and the confidence of one almost born in the saddle. "I find myself in need of a little sport. Let us make a race of it." He pointed his whip at a large tree several hundred yards ahead. "The first to that oak is the winner."

Rothley's eyes brightened with the glow of a habitual gambler. "How much?"

"Ten guineas."

His companion laughed. "Come, sir, that is hardly a wager. Make it fifty."

Edward produced a leather pouch and dangled it from his fingers. "I have only thirty about me."

"Very well, sir. Thirty it is."

The man had barely finished uttering the words before he took off, throwing up clods of earth behind him. Edward gave chase, knowing he would not catch him. The knowledge did not dismay him; he wished for the greater prize. The stream was not far from the tree. The moment was almost upon them.

He pushed his horse as hard as he dared, however, for he wished Rothley to win by as small a margin as possible. He could as easily shoot him in the front as the back and pocket the money. When the earl pulled up, he was only ten yards behind, a distance covered in a matter of seconds. He tossed the purse to him and dismounted.

"Thank you, Captain. You put up a better challenge than I had expected; your mount was the inferior horse."

"And I the inferior horseman."

Rothley's brow rose. "You are modest, Captain Turner."

"Not at all. I am merely aware of my limitations." He smiled. "Come, Mr Coalville. It is only a step to the stream."

"Good. I shall reward this surprisingly decent horse with a drink. I may even offer to purchase him." He suddenly laughed. "I may even forgive Timble for his laxness."

Edward led him towards the spinney. The stream crossed their path just before they reached it. The footbridge consisted of no more than two planks that had been thrown across it. On the other side, under the shelter of the trees at the edge of the spinney, lay a man. He was face down, his head resting on one arm.

"If you will wait here, Captain, I shall wake my man."

Edward grinned. "A good kick should do it."

"My, what a violent man you are, sir. First you wish me to whip him and now kick him. I must admit that I prefer rather less crude methods. You may be sure he will know I am displeased, as he will know I will punish him in my own way and in my own time. The waiting, the not knowing, can be far more torturous than the event itself."

Edward felt his fingers twitch. How much he would like to knock him down. That is how he had treated Anne, and each punishment he had meted out had been crueller than the one before until Rothley had finally gone too far. As he had now.

As soon as he reached the other side of the stream, the earl deposited the leather purse in his greatcoat pocket, whirled about, and withdrew his hand. He held a duelling pistol. His lips curled in a feral smile.

"Do not make a move, Captain."

Edward feigned surprise. "Is this some sort of joke? If it is, it is a poor one."

The man laughed, walking slowly backwards towards the prone body. "It is no joke, sir. I would recommend you believe me; you are so poor a gambler, after all. Honest men so often are."

Edward frowned. "I do not understand you, sir. What have you to gain from my death?"

The man paused by his valet and gave a harsh laugh. "You, Captain Turner, have long been a thorn in my side. I have lost more than one ship due to your self-righteous zeal, not to mention their cargos. Captain Filcher did what he could to damage your reputation, and yet you still threaten to compromise my business. If that were not enough, you have given shelter to my dull, faithless, and disappointing wife."

Edward took half a step forward, but a movement in the trees reminded him he had not yet completed his task.

"I have only ever carried out my duty. There is nothing personal in that, Mr Coalville. As for your wife, sir, I do not know of what you speak."

The earl's lips thinned. "No, you are as much of a dullard as she. Your governess, Mrs Huxley, is my wife, Lady Annabel Rothley. Can you believe she ever thought that a woman so plain and cold as she could ever satisfy me? Did she really expect me to stay faithful or think that she could desert me, making me a laughingstock? She is my property, and you have stolen her, Captain. You deserve to die as does she." He drew in a breath. "You have both proven very hard to kill, but you, at least, will not escape this time." He nudged his valet with his foot.

Edward's eyes widened as if he had experienced an epiphany. "You mean when that shot spooked my horses, when my axle broke—"

"That is precisely what I mean. Perhaps it is as well it came to this, for Dickson has proven an ineffective tool." He did kick his man now. "Wake up, Timble, you fool."

The man groaned.

"Good God! I am surrounded by idiots."

Edward judged the time had come. He raised his hands and moved slowly towards the bridge. "Come now, Coalville. You cannot mean to kill me. Why, the landlord at the inn heard our conversation. When I am found murdered at the very spot I was leading you to, the suspicion will fall on you."

"Simpleton!" the earl spat. "I shall not leave you

here. You led me to Timble and went on your way. You will be found some way from here, and I will leave the magistrate to make of it what he will. No one is going to suspect that a peer of the realm would be involved in so sordid a business. You are so very unpopular that I am sure there might be any number of suspects." He smirked. "And then I shall turn my attention to my wife. I shall take her home where she will suffer an unfortunate accident."

Edward wanted nothing more than to leap over the stream and throttle the man, but he needed one more thing from him.

"I do not believe you will do it," Edward said, stepping onto the bridge.

Rothley raised the gun a little higher, aiming it at Edward's head. "I see you are as arrogant and cock-sure as reports would have it."

He pulled the trigger. There was a light click. He tried again to no avail. He kicked his valet once more. "You idiot! I have told you to always keep my pistols loaded."

Relief swept through Edward; until that moment, he had not been certain that the man had not checked his pistols before venturing out.

"They were," he assured him, "but I arranged for them to be unloaded."

He crossed the bridge in two long strides, pushed the gun out of the way, and planted the man a facer.

"Who is the idiot, now?"

The earl had fallen to the ground, but he sprang up, a trickle of blood trailing from his nose. Edward raised his fist to hit him again, but a cool voice stayed his hand.

"Enough. You played your role very well, Captain, but your part is done."

Rothley whirled about. "Westcliffe!"

Lord Westcliffe gave a wintry little smile. "As it is your peers who will judge you, Rothley, I thought one had better be present to witness your confession and murder attempt. You may as well have some dignity and come quietly, for if my coachman has fulfilled my orders, which no doubt he has as I choose my servants very carefully, you will find the magistrate and two of his constables waiting for us at the inn."

Gibbons, Finn, and Jack stepped from behind a tree.

"You may tie him up and put him in the wagon with Dickson and his man."

The valet rolled over, groaned, and drew all eyes as he started to retch.

A look of distaste crossed Lord Westcliffe's face. "I think you must have been a little heavy handed with the brandy, Finn."

As they approached, Rothley turned, kicked the legs from under Edward and ran.

CHAPTER 24

Edward cursed, pushed himself to his feet, and sprinted after him. One of the planks spanning the stream tilted and he slipped into the water. It came just below his knees and slowed his momentum giving Rothley the chance to spring onto his horse. By the time he had mounted his own, the earl was galloping away. He gave chase, and to his surprise, although he did not close the distance, neither did he fall farther behind.

He turned his head as he heard the thunder of hooves coming up beside him. Lord Westcliffe.

"His mount is a showy piece but lacks stamina."

Dread settled in Edward's stomach as he saw Rothley change direction. He kicked his heels, urging his horse on. "I hope you are right, sir, because if I am not much mistaken, he is heading for Hayshott Hall."

"Good God! I think you are right. Come on, man!"

"You may pack away your things," Anne said. "I shall see if Lady Westcliffe is ready to come into the garden."

Miss Burdock pulled her shawl closer about her. "Are you sure we should, my dear? It is bitterly cold outside."

Barbara went to her and embraced her. "Domino will wish to see the mosaic, but you need not come. I shall tell you all about it."

The little lady stroked her hair. "I shall insist on it."

"I'll come if you like," Nora said. "That way, if it proves too cold for the girls, I can bring them back in."

Anne smiled. "I would be very grateful, Nora."

She went to her room, donned her warmest cloak, and opened a drawer to find a pair of fine woollen gloves. As she removed them, she uncovered the reticule Sukey had given her. She smiled and picked it up.

"That is very pretty."

Anne turned to discover Lady Westcliffe standing in the doorway wrapped in an ermine lined cloak, her hands buried in a muff.

"Yes, it was a gift from Sukey."

"Then why do you not use it? It is a shame for something so lovely to be kept tucked away in a drawer."

"I thought it too fine for a mere governess," Anne admitted.

"It is only a reticule, Anne."

"Yes, I suppose so, and it does seem a pity… very well, I shall use it."

She hastily pushed a handkerchief and a couple of hairpins in it and slipped it over her wrist.

"I am ready. Let us wait for the children downstairs. I thought I might see if Ed... Captain Turner might like to join us."

Lady Westcliffe took her arm. "The gentlemen are very busy hatching their plans, I believe. We shall leave them in peace for just a little longer."

Mr Townsend glanced up as they approached. He was swathed in a great coat and a thick scarf was wound about his neck. At sight of Anne and Lady Westcliffe, he rose hastily to his feet, brushing at his knees.

Barbara picked up the whippet pup and ran forwards.

"Thomas! Meet Domino!"

He rested one hand on the grass and vaulted from the pit.

"He is a tiny fellow," he said, scratching behind the puppy's ears.

Barbara peered around him and pulled a face. "Eugh! Why are there worms coming out of that lady's head?"

He chuckled. "They are not worms, but snakes. She is called Medusa, and anyone who looked upon her was turned to stone."

Barbara's eyes widened. "But I haven't turned to stone."

Emily nudged her. "It is only a story, silly. She is not real."

Barbara pouted. "Well, I don't like her."

"Neither do I," agreed her sister. "Her eyes are wonky."

The nurse stamped her feet and rubbed her hands. "Well come away then and leave Mr Townsend to his work. Cook had just taken some tarts out of the oven when I fetched Domino."

"Perhaps it would be better if you returned to the house," Anne said. "You have quite exhausted that pup already. It was quite a long walk for such a scrap of a thing."

"And he only has a thin coat," pointed out Lady Westcliffe. "He is shivering."

She smiled at Mr Townsend as the girls retraced their steps, and Anne made the introductions.

"May I see?" asked Lady Westcliffe.

"Of course."

He stepped aside.

"Why, it is quite wonderful," Lady Westcliffe exclaimed.

Mr Townsend stuck the fine brush he held behind his ear and regarded it thoughtfully. "When I uncovered the first small section, I was pleasantly surprised by its good condition, but if you look closely, you will see the surface is uneven in places, and many of the tesserae are loose. I shall have to seek some advice on the best way to preserve it."

Lady Westcliffe nodded. "I quite agree. It should certainly be covered in some way."

He sighed. "It was, but there have been several occurrences of petty vandalism on the estate, and my tent was one of the casualties. I came to check the culprits had not also damaged the mosaic."

Anne gasped. "I did not know of this."

He smiled wryly. "Perhaps I should not have

mentioned it, but do not concern yourself, Mrs Huxley. Rufus has been given free rein to hire as many people as he thinks necessary, and the tenant farmers will arrive this week. I am sure things will settle down." He glanced over their heads. "It appears you have a visitor."

An unusually tall, well-built man strode towards them.

"Good Lord. It's Sir Anthony Fairbrass, I believe." He surged forward to meet the man, his hand outstretched. "How are you, my boy? It must have been all of eight years since I last set eyes on you."

Sir Anthony smiled. "Mr Townsend. I would have known you anywhere. You haven't changed a bit."

The amateur antiquarian clapped the newcomer on the shoulder. "I cannot say the same for you, young man. The stripling has turned into an oak! Let me introduce you to the ladies. This is Lady Westcliffe, and this is—"

Anne inclined her head. "We have already met. Good day, sir."

Sir Anthony bowed. "Mrs Huxley, Lady Westcliffe."

The countess regarded him with some interest. "I am delighted to make your acquaintance, Sir Anthony. I have heard a little of you from a mutual acquaintance, Lady Frampton."

He grinned. "Need I be quaking in my boots? Has she shredded my character with that sharp tongue of hers."

Lady Westcliffe laughed softly. "I doubt you know how to quake, Sir Anthony. However, you may rest assured that I have heard nothing that need alarm you."

Anne smiled. "You have made good your promise to make Captain Turner's acquaintance, I see."

He laughed. "My wife was so keen to meet the children, I brought her with me and have left her in the nursery talking to Miss Burdock." He smiled wryly. "You must forgive her if she was a little sharp with you, ma'am. She has no reason to love governesses. It is a pity that Captain Turner is not at home, for there was a matter I particularly wished to discuss with him. However, my disappointment is ameliorated by the prospect of seeing the mosaic Miss Burdock mentioned. Will it rival those at Bignor, do you think?"

"If I can protect and restore it a little, perhaps. But come, see for yourself."

As the men peered into the pit, Anne murmured, "For a moment, I thought Lady Fairbrass was Lucy, but it took only a few moments for me to realise that I was mistaken. They are very different in character, although the resemblance between them is quite remarkable."

"They are twins, my dear. I do not believe she has spoken of her stay at the hall, however, and so we must be careful what we say. It is widely believed that she was in France with Lady Frampton."

Then the full import of Sir Anthony's words registered. "Lady Westcliffe, he said Edward was not at home, surely—"

She broke off as the rhythmic pounding of hooves on hard turf came to their ears. Edward and Lord Westcliffe were galloping towards them.

"You see," Lady Westcliffe said, "he has returned.

There seemed no point in worrying you unnecessarily. Look how quickly the captain approaches, perhaps he has good news he cannot wait to impart."

"Good Lord!" Mr Townsend said. "Are they having a race?"

Another horse broke from the trees, swerved, and bore down on them.

Anne stumbled backwards, horror writ large on her face. "It is Rothley!"

Sir Anthony moved quickly, wrapping his arms about the ladies, and sweeping them forwards.

"It is not a race; it is a chase. Move Townsend! This way. We must move to the other side of the pit."

They barely made it, before the horse was upon them. Anne's knees trembled. Rothley's face was covered in livid scratches and his bloodshot, wild eyes were fixed only on her. He looked like the devil in human form. She raised her hands in a futile gesture even as the poor horse stumbled into the pit. Sir Anthony turned, covering their bodies with his own as a shower of mud and tesserae flew through the air.

∽

They had almost caught him when he had turned from the road and headed into the woodland.

Lord Westcliffe looked over his shoulder, shouting, "We will lose our advantage if we follow him. We will head him off on the park side."

Edward nodded. Rothley would have to contend with shrubs, fallen logs, and low-hanging branches. He stroked his sweating mount's neck.

"Good boy, come on, only a little farther."

The tight knot of fear that bound his heart relaxed a fraction as they came into the park, and he saw the small group of figures in the distance. He crouched over the horse's neck, urging him to one last push. An anguished groan escaped him as Rothley burst from the trees ahead, but then he saw a large gentleman bundling the ladies to the other side of the pit. He knew in an instant what he intended, and a burst of wild elation swept through him. The next moment the horse fell, and a high squeal rent the air. The poor beast.

Leaping from his horse, he ran to Anne, sweeping her into his arms. Lord Westcliffe had also clasped his lady to him and their eyes met over their heads. A silent acknowledgement passed between them of all that had passed, and Edward knew they would be bound in friendship from that day forward.

A deep voice recalled him to his surroundings.

"Get the ladies away, they do not need to see this."

Still not quite ready to release Anne, he held out a hand. "I do not know who you may be, but you will forever have my gratitude."

The man grasped it. "Sir Anthony Fairbrass."

"I am recovered," Anne said quietly. "Is he dead?"

"Undoubtedly," Sir Anthony said.

Lady Westcliffe stepped from her husband's embrace and held out her hand. "Come, my dear. We shall go back."

Edward's instinct was to insist he carry her on his horse, but he knew his Anne was stronger than he could ever have imagined when first he met her, and he let her go.

As they walked slowly away, the gentlemen gathered around the pit. Both the horse and Rothley lay unmoving. The earl sprawled where the depiction of Medusa had been, his neck at an unnatural angle. A hollow had opened up beneath him, revealing the slim stacked stones of a hypocaust, and his head rested upon them, blood pooling on the uppermost one.

CHAPTER 25

Anne stood by the library window, a small smile edging her lips as she watched Lady Fairbrass, or Abigail as she had insisted she call her, play with the children and Domino. She was making a valiant attempt to sculpt a figure from the light dusting of snow on the ground. A futile effort she feared. She was grateful to her, however. She seemed hardly more than a child herself and yet nothing appeared to have the power to discompose her. She had come every day, helping distract the children, giving Anne time to reflect on all that had happened. Whilst she could not be sorry that she was now a widow, neither could she rejoice at the death of a man, however despicable he may have been.

Anne's eyes rose, scanning the driveway. She wondered if Edward would return today. She had scarcely seen him since that horrid day, for once he and Lord Westcliffe had finished dealing with the magistrate, doctor, and coroner, they had gone to

London, Edward to the admiralty, and Lord Westcliffe to the Home Office.

"I hope you are not brooding, my dear."

She turned and smiled. "No, not really. I cannot help wondering if Edward will be tempted to go back to sea, that is all." She bit her lip. "He has said nothing about the future." A sniff escaped her, and she rummaged in her reticule for a handkerchief.

Lady Westcliffe came and stood by her side, bending to pick something from the floor. "He has hardly had the opportunity, and it would have been quite inappropriate to have spoken so soon. But I think his actions speak for him, do not you? He all but crushed you when he discovered you unharmed, after all."

"True," she admitted. "And I know it is too soon, but if he should speak, what am I to do? I do not think I can bear to wait a year or more when I cannot find it in my heart to mourn Rothley for even a day."

Lady Westcliffe touched her arm. "No, and I doubt very much the captain will either. As you have been separated from your husband for over a year, there can be no question of you carrying his child, but a hasty marriage will still be frowned upon."

"I know it," Anne said. "Edward will not care a jot about appearances, and I don't think I do anymore. I do not believe Mr Townsend, Sir Anthony, or Lady Fairbrass will turn a hair."

Lady Westcliffe smiled. "Well then, perhaps you need wait only a few months, and then have a small, private ceremony, perhaps by special license. You should keep things quiet until nearer the time, however. You are living under his roof, after all." The countess touched her stomach. "I have decided to tell Westcliffe about the baby when he returns. It seems my attempts to hide my bouts of illness have not gone completely unnoticed, and he threatened to consult a doctor whilst he is in Town."

Anne nodded. "I think that wise."

Lady Westcliffe held out her hand. "You dropped this."

It was a folded piece of paper.

"I do not think it is mine."

"I saw it drop from your reticule, my dear."

Anne sat on the window seat and unfolded it. It was a hastily scribbled letter, little more than a note.

Portsmouth, June 18

Dearest Sukey,

Why have you not replied to my last letter? I hope you are well. I have almost saved up enough to come to London for a few days if I am very frugal, and the thought that I might once more see you fills me with joy. I have so much to tell you but would rather do it in person.

I have to go for there is a gentleman come to take me for a drive! I will tell you all about him when I come, perhaps next month.

Your loving sister,

Lizzie

Anne held out the note. "I left Ashwick Hall in such a rush that I fear Sukey gave me the reticule completely forgetting that the letter was there. Would you return it to her for me?"

"Of course."

A carriage passed the window, and Anne's heart leapt, but it did not bear Lord Westcliffe's crest. It was

Sir Anthony's carriage. Footsteps were heard in the hall and Jack announced him.

"Good afternoon, Sir Anthony," Lady Westcliffe said. "You have come to claim your wife, I presume." She gestured at the window. "I think you will discover she is not quite ready."

He bowed, greeted them, and paced to the window. The gentlest of smiles touched his lips.

"Then I shall give her a few minutes more."

Lady Westcliffe glanced up and saw the footman still hovering by the door. "I see you have anticipated my requirements, Jack. Perhaps you would send for some tea."

They moved to the chairs set around the fireplace.

"I am afraid Captain Turner has not yet returned," Anne said.

Sir Anthony crossed one leg over another. "My news will wait."

Lady Westcliffe raised an eyebrow. "News? You should know better than to drop a word like that into the conversation and not expect a lady to try and worm it out of you."

A voice was heard in the hall. "Thank you, Nora. Goodbye, children."

Lady Fairbrass came into the room, the tip of her nose and her cheeks pink from the cold.

"Have you told them the news? I know Anne will be pleased. She thought him horrid too."

Sir Anthony stood, kissed his wife's hand, and offered her his seat. "Have you forgotten, my love, that I thought it best I speak to Captain Turner first?"

She wrinkled her nose. "Pooh. I am sure he won't mind."

"What won't I mind?"

Edward and Lord Westcliffe strolled into the room as another carriage passed the window. The latter went to his wife and bent to kiss her cheek. "Do not get up, my dear."

Anne had risen and stared at Edward, drinking in the harsh, swarthy features she had come to love so much.

"Did everything go well?"

He smiled. "They feel they have a strong enough case to bring against Filcher."

The tea tray was brought in, and more chairs were pulled to the fire.

"You are come in good time," Lady Westcliffe said. "Sir Anthony has some news he wishes to impart. We are all agog, but he would insist he wished to tell you first."

Sir Anthony looked heavenwards. "I see there is no hope of a private interview."

"Come now," Lady Westcliffe chided, "are we not all friends?"

He smiled ruefully. "Very true. My news will be of more interest to some than others, however, and I did not wish to bring up unpleasant memories." He glanced at Edward. "I have persuaded Mr Adams that he should remove to a more retired situation and install a curate in the parsonage. He arrives tomorrow." He sighed. "I was never very well acquainted with him, and my father would always look the other way rather than face any unpleasantness. It was very wrong of the parson to spread malicious rumours and stir up resentment towards you, but it was not only his ill-nature that prompted him, although it was that weakness that allowed him to be so gullible. Mr Dickson was very busy whilst he was here. He started and then stoked the fire of these rumours and, as he was your groom, Mr Adams thought that they must be true."

His good wife sent him a sparkling look. "I told you after the first time he called on us that he gave me the shivers."

"It his wife and children I feel sorry for," Anne said.

"Let us hope he has learned the error of his ways," Lady Westcliffe said. "When this parson no longer has a congregation to inflame with his righteous wrath, perhaps he may become less inflamed himself."

Sir Anthony stood. "Now, if you will excuse me, I shall take my wife home and allow you all some peace."

Lady Fairbrass rose gracefully from her chair and took his hand. "And I shall certainly come, but only because I am quite ready."

Lady Westcliffe leant forward and dropped a light kiss on her husband's cheek.

"I had quite given up hope of you arriving today, but I am very happy to see you."

He cleared his throat and patted her hand. "And I am happy that you look so well."

"We would have been here a little sooner," Edward said. "But I wished to see how the repairs of Rose Cottage were coming along." He sighed. "Not that there is any rush, for the enquiries I made in London came to naught."

"Oh," Anne said. "Were you looking for a tenant?"

Edward shook his head. "I had not had time to tell you, but I found the deed to the cottage. It is not mine after all; the person named is Susanna Croft, who appears to have disappeared off the face of the earth. I had only one clue, but it led nowhere. Westcliffe has offered to help me."

Lady Westcliffe gave a little laugh. "That will not be necessary. I think I may have the answer to your riddle. How fortuitous."

Edward looked perplexed. "Whilst that would be wonderful, I do not quite see how you might possibly do so."

Lord Westcliffe smiled fondly at his wife. "Never underestimate my lady, Turner. She is a force to be reckoned with."

"Thank you, my love." She held up the note. "Anne found this in a reticule a friend from Ashwick Hall had given her. Her name is Susanna Croft. It addresses a lady named Sukey and is from her sister, Lizzie. I happen to know that my Sukey had a sister she was estranged from."

"That is promising," Edward allowed. "Did this lady perhaps work at one time in a mantua makers in Bruton Street?"

"She did indeed."

"Oh, but there is more," Anne said. "The portrait in your bedroom!" She blushed as Lord Westcliffe raised an eyebrow. "I saw it quite by accident and Edward was not there, I assure you."

Lady Westcliffe rose to her feet. "Let us see this portrait."

They trooped upstairs and gathered in front of it.

"There is a clear resemblance," Lady Westcliffe said.

Anne nodded. "It was my immediate thought, but I had been prey to so many odd fancies that when I looked closer, I doubted myself."

"Well, this is splendid." The countess smiled at her husband and took his hand. "Come, my love, I have some other splendid news that I think will please you."

Anne and Edward were left alone in his chamber, and she felt suddenly shy.

"How well did it go at the admiralty? Were you perhaps tempted to… to…."

He grasped her hands. "Anne, you goose. Did you really think I would leave you or the children?"

She raised her eyes and blushed as she saw the gleam in his. "I had hoped you would not, but it was all you ever wanted."

He smiled lazily. "It was once, but it is no longer. I have everything that I could ever want or dream of here."

He kissed her then. Long and tenderly and when he lifted his head she felt as if the world were spinning.

"Anne, my brave, sensible, wonderful darling, will you be my wife and guide me through the squalls of country living?"

Tears blurred her eyes. "Yes, Edward, I will."

ALSO BY JENNY HAMBLY

Thank you for your support! I do hope you enjoyed For Duty, Love & Honour. If you would consider leaving a short review on Amazon, I would be very grateful. I love to hear from my readers and can be contacted at:
jenny@jennyhambly.com

Other books by Jenny Hambly

Belle – Bachelor Brides 0

Rosalind – Bachelor Brides 1

Sophie – Bachelor Brides 2

Katherine – Bachelor Brides 3

Bachelor Brides Collection

Marianne - Miss Wolfraston's Ladies Book 1

Miss Hayes - Miss Wolfraston's Ladies Book 2

Georgianna - Miss Wolfraston's Ladies Book 3

Miss Wolfraston's Ladies Collection

Allerdale - Confirmed Bachelors Book 1

Bassington - Confirmed Bachelors Book 2

Carteret - Confirmed Bachelors Book 3

Confirmed Bachelors Books 1-3

Ormsley - Confirmed Bachelors Book 4

Derriford - Confirmed Bachelors Book 5

Eagleton - Confirmed Bachelors Book 6

Confirmed Bachelors Books 4-6

What's in a Name? - Residents of Ashwick Hall Book 1

True Companions - Residents of Ashwick Hall Book 2

ABOUT THE AUTHOR

I love history and the Regency period in particular. I grew up on a diet of Jane Austen and Georgette Heyer.

I like to think my characters though flawed, are likeable, strong and true to the period.

I live by the sea in Plymouth, England, with my partner, Dave. I like reading, sailing, wine, getting up early to watch the sunrise in summer, and long quiet evenings by the wood burner in our cabin on the cliffs in Cornwall in winter.

Printed in Dunstable, United Kingdom